SLIGHTLY *Abridged*

ALSO BY Ellen Pall

Corpse de Ballet

Among the Ginzburgs

Back East

SLIGHTLY *Abridged*

A Nine Muses Mystery:

Erato

E L L E N   P A L L

ST. MARTIN'S MINOTAUR
NEW YORK

 For information, address St. Martin's Press, 175 Fifth Avenue, New York, N.Y. 10010.

www.minotaurbooks.com

Library of Congress Cataloging-in-Publication Data

Pall, Ellen, 1952–.
Slightly abridged : a nine muses mystery : Erato / Ellen Pall.—1st ed.
p. cm.
ISBN 0-312-28185-4
1. Women novelists—Fiction. 2. Aged women—Crimes against—Fiction. 3. New York (N.Y.)—Fiction. 4. Manuscripts—Fiction. I. Title.

PS3566.A463 S57 2003
813'.54—dc21

2002031886

First Edition: April 2003

10 9 8 7 6 5 4 3 2 1

For Maury and Debbie Sankey

Fire and Ice

Some say the world will end in fire,
Some say in ice.
From what I've tasted of desire
I hold with those who favor fire.
But if it had to perish twice,
I think I know enough of hate
To say that for destruction ice
Is also great
And would suffice.

—Robert Frost

CONTENTS

SLIGHTLY
Abridged

chapter ONE

Tea

It is never too late to die violently.

Past a certain age, we may be sure we will not die young. Farther along, we may wish that we had. But yearn for it or dread it, sudden death is always near: across the intersection, in the baseball whizzing toward the stands, curled into a spring in our neighbor's temperamental gas stove. So that, on any day, the full and shapely life we contemplate for ourselves may turn out to be, after all, slightly abridged.

Ada Case Caffrey, the remarkable old lady whose abrupt exit from the world was to teach Juliet Bodine this melancholy lesson, arrived in New York City on a frigid January afternoon.

It was a Monday, the first one after New Year's, and Juliet had spent the entire day in her office, grimly not writing the novel she owed her publisher on April 1. A small, thirty-oddish woman with a soft face, a fringe of wispy blonde hair, and a distinctly worried expression, she had been sitting for the last hour almost immobile at her desk. It was a large, highly polished, very orderly desk. (She had spent forty-five of her not-writing minutes clearing it off.) A wooden standing lamp carved and painted to resemble a lemon tree lit it from before her, a large window overlooking the Hudson River from behind. Near the swiveling oak chair where Juliet sat failing to create anything stood a tall bookcase containing numerous reference works on the English Regency, the historical period in which all her novels were set. The shelves also displayed a dozen brightly bound romance novels by Angelica Kestrel-Haven, the pen name under which Juliet wrote.

When she wrote.

In a wicker tray on the desk, an ominously thin sheaf of paper represented all there was so far of "A Christian Gentleman," the next book with which Juliet hoped to delight Angelica Kestrel-Haven's fans. She gave this a despairing glance, then stood and went to the window. She could, she told herself, always sell her apartment, a large and extremely comfortable one on Manhattan's Upper West Side. She might even find a job teaching English literature, probably at some small college with a sense of humor. It would be embarrassing to have to admit to her editor, Portia Klein, that she had been unable to write "A Christian Gentleman," which currently consisted of two and a half chapters of exposition, a handful of conversations, and next to nothing in the way of plot. She would have to return the money that Excelsior Books had advanced her. She would have to let go of her diligent, treasured assistant, Ames. And it would be a disappointment to Angelica Kestrel-Haven fans to learn that A K-H had thrown in the tea towel.

But Juliet was only human—surely, they would all have to see that. Her friends would understand. And, on the bright side, her failure would be sure to please certain others—some of her former teaching colleagues at Barnard, for example, and her ex-husband, Rob. Juliet often thought this was an overlooked up side of failure: One might feel bitterly humiliated oneself, but it did bring so much pleasure to those who had always resented one's success.

Leaning her forehead against the thick, cold glass of the window, she found temporary distraction in the sight, sixteen stories below, of a middle-aged woman in a red beret dragging a woebegone fir toward a small mountain of defunct Christmas trees just inside the entrance to Riverside Park. The woman went into the park, stopped, crouched, hefted her burden, and tossed it to the top of the mountain. It rolled down, landing with a soft bounce on the dirty pathway, then revolved gently till it stopped against an iron fence two or three yards away. The woman, her breath densely visible in the bone-chilling cold, retrieved it, lugged it back to the heap, and heaved it up again.

It rolled back down.

The woman looked around. North, south, east, west: In the frigid afternoon, she was all but alone. Furtively, she kicked the tree toward the edge of the path and walked out of the park. In due course, her tree and the little mountain it had almost joined would be turned into mulch by a thrifty, resourceful New York City Parks Department.

Watching, Juliet sighed. If only she, too, could kick and walk away from her problem. As a writer of Regencies, she considered it her job to manufacture light entertainment—to churn the attraction between an imaginary young Englishman and an imaginary young Englishwoman of two hundred years ago into a froth of such density and dazzle that a reader could plunge into page one and lose all track of time, all memory of personal cares, until she or he resurfaced, refreshed and relaxed, at "The End."

But froth was not always easily to be had. The trick was to invent a couple whose particular push-me-pull-you had just enough air, yet just enough substance also, to whip readily into foam. Last summer, when she had conceived the idea of a book with a determinedly chaste hero, the notion had seemed richly suggestive, irresistibly appealing—true to the genre, yet new. In the decade or so since she had invented Angelica Kestrel-Haven, thus beginning the writing career that had freed her from academe, Juliet had dealt exclusively in heroes on the make. Elegantly on the make, of course. Stylishly so, surreptitiously so at times, but definitely on the make.

Sir James Aptley Clendinning, however, would be a suitor of a different sort. A restrained suitor, a superlatively subtle one, who held himself in check not only to spare the feelings of his chosen lady but because he himself deeply embraced the teachings of his church, believed in the union of souls before the union of flesh. Sir James was to be a gentleman-farmer, an enthusiast of the new agricultural techniques that would shortly transform the English landscape forever. Here would be no rake, no gadabout. Here, in fact, would be more of a Goody Two-shoes. But still a fine challenge for the perceptive woman who wanted him and—surely?—a delightful springboard for a romp of a romance.

Or not. Teeth clenched, forehead pressed to the cold glass as she looked beyond her wintry terrace to survey the now empty sidewalk below, Juliet assured herself that, considered purely as a character, Sir James Clendinning was a magnificent invention. She would go to her grave swearing that.

But as a narrative springboard, as a spur to action, the man had proved to have all the driving force of a Teletubby. Poor Selena Walkingshaw, the honorable lady whose quixotic desire it was to wed him, had run out of ideas for attracting his attention before Chapter Two was done. So had Juliet. If Regency romance characters could think such things (which they emphatically could not; Regency characters might go as far as a kiss; but for reasons that had more to do with the twenty-first century than the nineteenth, real sexuality was unknown to them, except by implication), Selena Walkingshaw might well be forgiven for imagining Sir James was gay. What did he mean by ignoring every hint and lure she cast out? How could she know if he liked her at all? And why should she care? Juliet herself was starting to loathe him.

And yet . . .

Juliet sighed deeply, her breath forming an amoeba-shaped cloud of mist on the chilly glass. And yet, Murray Landis, the NYPD detective whose marked chasteness (toward Juliet, anyhow) had suggested to her the idea of Sir James in the first place, had generated plenty of plots in her own mind last summer, when events had thrown them together to solve a murder at the Jansch Ballet Repertory Troupe. The trouble was, those private story lines had come to nothing. She had seen Murray only a few times during the strange, terrible fall that had followed—the fall of 2001, when New Yorkers woke daily to wonder if the collapsing towers had been a horrible dream, then slowly understood that the years before had been the dream, and they sleepwalkers in a world of danger. Once, he had asked her to help him puzzle through a killing at a think tank on West End Avenue. Once, they had met at a court hearing with regard to the death at the Jansch. And they had run into each other at an art gallery.

That was all.

Unlike the teenaged Selena Walkingshaw, Juliet was no longer capable of a sustained crush in a vacuum. So she had forgotten the flavor of Murray's, and therefore Sir James's, attractiveness. Moreover, since November, she had been the object of the direct, unmistakable, openly admiring attention of a very different kind of man. Stylish, articulate, polymathic, almost too romantic, Dennis Daignault had wiped out all but the mere memory of the memory of the delicate frissons Landis's tense diffidence had inspired in Juliet the preceding summer. No wonder Sir James showed so little sign of life.

Although perhaps the fault lay in the other direction, with Selena Walkingshaw? Perhaps Selena should lie supine on a path before Sir James, hoping he would get the hint? If not, Juliet might have to kill off Sir James and start "A Christian Gentleman" all over again. Maybe "A Pagan Gentleman"?

The house phone, buzzing to announce Mrs. Caffrey's arrival, interrupted this train of thought. Juliet went to the door of her office to listen. From the floor below came Ames's resolutely uninflected voice telling the doorman to send Dr. Bodine's visitor up. (In deference to her employer's vestigial academic credentials, Ames always insisted on calling her Dr. Bodine.) Juliet slipped into the bathroom and gave herself a look in the mirror. Round blue eyes, rather unintelligent-looking face, fair complexion made wan today by discontent. Altogether unimpressive. She tried smiling, saw it improved things, went back to discontented, shut off the light, and headed quietly down the wooden stairs.

On the landing she paused and stooped, almost furtively, to get a glimpse of her visitor before she herself could be seen. By the door in her front hall, there now sat a large suitcase of antique design. Next to this stood a large sealskin coat of about the same vintage. Inside the coat, its back turned to Ames as she helped to remove it, a very small lady could just be detected. Such were Juliet's first impressions of Ada Case Caffrey.

Gripped by a sudden desire to get a better look, Juliet hurried down the remaining stairs and into the front hall. As Mrs. Caffrey turned to greet her, a scent of gardenias rose from her person like a flock of pigeons to Juliet's hypersensitive nose.

"Dr. Bodine, please meet Ada Case Caffrey," said Ames, her large, pale face a stolid blank, as usual. "Mrs. Caffrey, this is Dr. Juliet Bodine."

As often happened with people she got to know because they read her books, until now Juliet had had the pleasure of Mrs. Caffrey's acquaintance solely through the mail. Some three or four years ago, Ames had opened a fan letter from an Ada Case Caffrey. She'd answered it, as she routinely answered almost all the letters Juliet received: besides fan mail, requests for her to speak at various luncheons, inquiries as to whether she was the Angelica Kestrel-Haven with whom the letter writer had gone to summer camp in 1947 (no, she was not yet born; and could there ever really have been someone named Angelica Kestrel-Haven?), invitations to contredanses and the occasional offer of marriage from Anglophilic gentlemen who assumed Angelica Kestrel-Haven must be a genteel spinster, offers of honorary degrees from spurious academic institutions, gleeful corrections from fanatical readers ("I'm afraid your Lord Hattersley could not have been in the House of Lords on August 22, 1816, since, in fact, Parliament had been prorogued until the twenty-forth of that month"), offers from antique dealers of bits of Regency arcana Juliet might care to add to her small collection, and the like.

Mrs. Caffrey confided in her letter that she had just read Miss Kestrel-Haven's *Duke's Delight* and had found it delightful indeed. Could Miss Kestrel-Haven spare a moment to tell her how she had come up with the notion of a locket containing a portrait of a tabby cat? And so on. Ames sent a reply.

In her next letter, written after reading *Marianne: or The Actor's Stratagem,* Mrs. Caffrey explained that she had been a lifelong amateur thespian; though now well past eighty, she was still active in the AdirondActors, the community theater group she had helped to found more than sixty years before. Her own mother had been a diseuse, a recitalist, entertaining turn-of-the-century audiences by declaiming the poetry of Wordsworth and Longfellow, and she had brought up her daughters to regard elocution as next to godliness. Ada herself could still recite Tennyson's *Maud* in her sleep, and so how interesting it had been for her to read of Marianne, who etc., etc., etc.

This time Ames showed the letter to Juliet. Always wary of starting a new correspondence—they were so seductive, such a good way to kill time one really ought to spend trying to write books—Juliet found herself too intrigued not to respond. She dashed off a friendly note, and Mrs. Caffrey, of course, dashed one back. From then on, the two had exchanged letters every three or four months, Juliet's printed out from her computer, Mrs. Caffrey's painstakingly handwritten in her spiky, vigorous script. Juliet knew now that Mrs. Caffrey lived alone on the apple farm, long since defunct, where she had grown up, in Espyville, a hamlet on the southern border of the Adirondack Park; that she had taught diction and public speaking at a private girl's academy in Gloversville, the nearest town; that she spent a great deal of her time working on her poetry; that she had two cats, Zsa-Zsa and Marilyn; that she had read and loved all of Angelica Kestrel-Haven's books; and that she strongly believed they would be better if Juliet would ginger them up with some explicit sex.

Then, three or four weeks ago, Mrs. Caffrey had written in great excitement. She had just come across "a short manuscript circa 1825, concerning an English lord," she said, which she wished very much to show to Juliet. She did not want to consult anyone up near Espyville, or even say a word about it until Juliet had seen it. If Juliet would suggest a reasonably priced hotel she might stay in, she would come down to New York City and bring it in person.

In vain did Juliet suggest her elderly friend make a photocopy and mail it. In vain did she point out that 1825 was a bit late for her (the English Regency ended in 1820, with the death of mad King George III and the coronation of the former Prince Regent) and that, in any case, she wasn't an expert on manuscripts. Mrs. Caffrey had never been to New York, and it was high time. Juliet saw she would not be put off. She suggested Ada wait till the weather warmed up, then come with a companion who could help her negotiate the city. Since she had asked, Juliet could, in fact, recommend a very modestly priced bed-and-breakfast run by her friend Suzy Eisenman in a charming building just across the street from her.

Ada replied that she would be there next week, alone, would stay at Ms. Eisenman's bed-and-breakfast, but would come straight from the bus to Juliet, if she might. Bowing to the inevitable, Juliet had FedExed a note inviting her to tea. And now it was next week, and here was Mrs. Caffrey before her.

The face she lifted to Juliet's was the face of an ancient flapper: small, heart-shaped, and crisscrossed with a hundred wrinkles. Still, she looked younger than her real age—Juliet would have guessed she was closer to seventy-four than eighty-four—and her petite figure was, however improbably, still curvy. Cute, in fact. Her wide-set green eyes, bright with cold, were shadowed in teal blue and ringed with kohl. Red lipstick covered her lips, as well as a shaky margin of skin beyond them, forming a largish, bee-stung mouth. Her nose and chin were heavily powdered, her cheeks lavishly rouged. The sealskin coat had come away to reveal a venerable turquoise dress cut well above the knees and garnished with looping strings of beads in jet, turquoise, and white. A matching turquoise toque, which she declined to surrender, sheathed a diminutive head ringed with short hair colored shoe-polish black. As she came forward, Juliet noticed rhinestone buckles clipped to the laces of her orthopedic shoes.

"God grant me moxie when I am old," Juliet prayed silently, while Mrs. Caffrey reached out to her, saying in vibrant tones, "My dear, you are so perfectly sweet to invite me to tea." She took both of Juliet's hands in hers.

Improbably for such a diminutive person, her voice was deep, with a crush of pebbles at the bottom. Her pitch swooped and dipped dramatically through her words. Though Juliet was only five foot four, she towered over her guest. Mrs. Caffrey's hands were encased in elderly but rather nice pink leather gloves, with pearl buttons at the wrists. She wrung her hostess's hand with a vigor that was entirely unexpected, then stepped back a little, tilting her head and smiling as if Juliet had just said something particularly amusing. Juliet felt as if the ghost of Myrna Loy had come into her house.

"It's a pleasure."

From the name Ada and from, perhaps, her spiky handwriting, Juliet had unconsciously formed a mental image of Mrs. Caffrey as tall, gray, depressed, dowdy, like a character in a George Price cartoon. Now, as so often happens when we make someone's acquaintance from a distance, the elderly little flapper before her appeared to be wrong, perhaps even an impostor. She struggled to reconcile the two impressions.

"Is it a pleasure, my dear?" Ada said, removing her gloves at last to reveal nails that were grooved by time and thickly lacquered by Maybelline. "I know you're only being polite. But it is a pleasure for me. And I do believe you will find what I've brought to show you quite interesting."

She handed her gloves to Ames without even looking at her, as if laying them on a table.

"May I use your powder room?"

Watching as Ames ushered her in the right direction, Juliet saw with astonishment a distinct wiggle in the old lady's slow, careful walk. A very large purse (or small piece of luggage) of a kind Juliet believed was called a carpetbag hung from her arm by two stiffly arched leather straps.

Ames returned. Anyone else would have offered at least a raised eyebrow in acknowledgment of the old lady's singular appearance. But this was not Ames's way. "Tea is in the library," was all she said. "Is there anything else you need today? No—?"

She paused suggestively, leaving the noun unspoken.

"No," Juliet answered.

It was not necessary between them to say more. Juliet had written nothing, therefore her assistant had nothing to type into the computer. (Juliet always wrote by hand.) Calmly—and yet, was there a hint of blame in her manner? Or even, for whatever Amesian reason, guilt?—Ames fetched her coat from the closet, said good night, and left.

A few moments later, Mrs. Caffrey emerged from the guest bathroom, mouth redrawn, cheeks redder than ever, a fresh cloud of gardenia invisible around her. She tapped the carpetbag meaningfully as she followed Juliet out of the front hall. "It's in here," she said. "You'll soon see—Oh, my dear!"

Interrupting herself, Mrs. Caffrey had stopped at the entrance to Juliet's library. She clapped her hands.

"Oh, it's just like the set of a Noel Coward play! You are a lucky girl. What fun you must have here! Or I hope you do, anyhow," she amended, catching the uncertain look on her hostess's face. She added, almost sternly, "You ought."

Juliet's library was a snug room lined with books. Heavy red curtains hung beside the windows, a deep red-and-dark blue Persian carpet covered the floor, and a couple of wide leather armchairs sat on either side of a bricked-in fireplace. On a leather-covered coffee table made to look like a pile of gigantic books, Ames had left a little feast drawn from Juliet's teenage imaginings of what "tea" should be: heaps of crustless sandwiches cut into triangles, plates of tiny fruit tarts and petits fours, pots of jam, pats of butter in the shape of stars, a basket of hot scones, and, of course, in a fat pot on its own little brazier, tea.

"Please sit down," she said, wondering at the same time why it was that she did not, in fact, have marvelous fun here day after day. No doubt Mrs. Caffrey was right; she ought. But somehow, life wasn't like that. Not her life, anyway. "Or shall I—?"

Guessing Ada would prefer a seat that was hard (and easy to rise from) to one that was soft and deep, she fetched from a corner a straight-backed wooden chair, its modestly cushioned seat upholstered in velveteen, and placed it by the table. Mrs. Caffrey took it gratefully as Juliet sat herself down in an armchair.

For a few minutes, the air was full of the clink of china and offers of milk and sugar. Mrs. Caffrey told Juliet how much pleasure Angelica Kestrel-Haven's books had brought her. This, in turn, pleased Juliet, who liked to think of her books as helping to pass the too-heavy time of just such people as she conceived Ada Caffrey to be: elderly shut-ins, invalids, night nurses, patients awaiting surgery, acrophobes boarding flights, all those whose sufferings could be palliated with literary anesthesia.

However, when Mrs. Caffrey asked what she was working on now, Juliet dodged the question and turned the subject to her guest's bus journey down. How had she managed, alone with that heavy bag?

Ada (Mrs. Caffrey implored Juliet to call her Ada) smiled. The journey had been a snap; she only wished she'd done it sooner. The bag was nothing. Tom Giddy—the Giddys were her nearest neighbors—had kindly driven her to the bus depot in Gloversville. In Albany, the driver had helped her transfer it to the New York bus. And here, at the Port Authority, a "foreign gentleman" across the aisle from her was good enough to put her and her bag into a cab on Eighth Avenue.

"And your handsome doorman did the rest, of course," she explained.

Juliet smiled a little distractedly. Could there be a couple named Giddy in "A Christian Gentleman," she wondered? It was a very suggestive name. Neighbors of the Walkingshaws, perhaps. Friendly, solid, middle-aged . . . She frowned slightly. Maddening that these characters should stir to life just now, now, when she couldn't do anything about them.

"So tall and slim," Mrs. Caffrey was going on dreamily. "I like a slim, elegant man, don't you? Tom is handsome; but those husky wrestler types don't wear well, do they? They go to seed so early," she went on a moment later, after a pause for a sip of Formosa Oolong. "I'm afraid Cindy Giddy has come to see that. No, tall, slim men are more distinguished, and they last so much longer. Even if they lose their hair," she added meditatively.

Mrs. Caffrey leaned forward, her eyes kindled by some inner spark. Juliet took a couple of inches off her fictional Tom Giddy, thickened his shoulders, expanded his paunch, moved his hairline back, and made Mrs. Giddy a cook. At the same time, she noticed that her guest's lipstick had left a crimson, somehow alarming, stain on her Spode teacup.

"And that reminds me to raise again that business of sex in your books," Mrs. Caffrey continued. "They are so charming, really so delightful, but my dear—people want a bit of meat on their plates! You say your publisher wouldn't like it, but I wonder if you've ever tried. If you lack for material, by the way, I'd be happy to"—she hesitated slyly while, to her extreme irritation, Juliet felt her own cheeks start to flush—"to share some thoughts with you."

"Tell me about Espyville," said Juliet abruptly, unable to think of any better rejoinder. She didn't "lack for material," as it happened. What with one thing and another, she had accumulated a fair amount of material of her own. Moreover, she was finding this earthy, juicy, voluptuous octogenarian disconcerting. Part of her wanted to laugh, part of her reproached herself for being ageist, and yet another part was genuinely shocked. Yet why shouldn't Ada still relish sex—the idea of it, if not the act? Why shouldn't a person of either gender retain a healthy appreciation of sex as long as he or she lived?

Her ideas in confusion, it was a moment before she realized she had inadvertently asked a good question. Mrs. Caffrey was telling her quite interesting things about her home. The hamlet of Espyville, where her family's orchard lay, was adjacent to and largely dependent on the town of Gloversville. Before and after the turn of the twentieth century, that town had enjoyed a long golden age during which it was the national center of glove making. Thanks to the wealth the industry created, and to the skilled European workers drawn there by its specialized needs, by the time Ada was born, the town had its own daily newspaper, an opera house, a legitimate theater, a vaudeville theater, and a Carnegie library, among other cultural amenities. Ada's mother had been Boston-bred, but she had thrived in Gloversville, and had brought her girls up to enjoy all the lively arts.

"Not that the others did," Ada explained between appreciative nibbles at a buttered scone. "My oldest sister, Eugenia, insisted on becoming a missionary in India. She died of typhus, naturally, in Allahabad, within a year of her arrival."

Juliet could not help but feel Ada took a certain satisfaction in this long-gone sister's premature, unhappy end.

"Then there was Florence, the middle child," she was going on. "Not an ounce of drama in her, unless you count self-righteousness. But Mother was a pistol. In a way, it was a blessing she passed away before we lost the glove industry to cheap labor overseas. She didn't live to see her dear home become one of the most impoverished towns in New York State."

Mrs. Caffrey's voice had gone harsh; her face had shrunk to a scowl. Juliet suddenly felt it would not be pleasant to tangle with Ada Caffrey.

"The tannery owners simply dropped everything, took their little bundles of money and ran, leaving Gloversville lethally polluted, riddled with toxic sinkholes, plagued by acid rain. And with too much time on their hands and not enough work, our teenagers are simply shocking. And now this nonsense about Wildernessland. Wilderness indeed," she muttered, indignantly if incomprehensibly.

"Still," she went on a moment later, brightening, "fun is where you make it. I've had some fine times, believe me. I've always performed with the AdirondActors. And you know, men who act, providing they're not pansies, are so . . ."

She produced the pejorative blandly and left the sentence suggestively unfinished as she helped herself to a kiwi tart.

"Apart from which, Father's land is quite, quite beautiful," she resumed. "All the years I've lived there haven't blinded me to that. When I was very young, I thought I would move away—oh, to Boston perhaps, or maybe even here. But I was always Father's favorite, and once he'd left the orchard to me, I simply couldn't sell it. I don't mean that no one would have purchased it. On the contrary, there were several offers. But I wouldn't let it go. Not then, not now," she added, with some fierceness. "Not that I ever worked the orchard myself. No, I went to Saratoga, went to college. Came back, taught, married, was widowed, remarried—In short, life swept me up."

She smiled rather sadly and Juliet suddenly saw her curious clothes for what they were: the hoarded remnants of a happier, more prosperous, more hopeful time.

"Life has a way of doing that, you know. Sweeps one up"—Ada's smile turned grim—"and straps one down. I see it happening to Cindy now. A bit depressing, really . . .

"But you are young, and single, and perhaps you don't know. At any rate, I still have the theater—I'll be the second witch in the AdirondActors's *Macbeth* this spring—and my poetry writing. Lately I've begun attending slams in Albany. Do you like poetry slams?"

"Slams," Juliet noticed, Ada pronounced as Rosalind Russell might have done, setting it off from the words around it by dropping her voice to a resonant, sepulchral purr.

"So much like the recitals dear Mother used to give," she was going on. "I do think they're wonderful."

"I don't believe I've ever been to one," Juliet admitted. "I mean, I haven't."

"Oh, then you must come with me," Ada promptly offered. "I'm going to one on Wednesday night. My friend Matthew McLaurin—he's the person who drives me to the slams in Albany—he looked on the Internet and found there's a very nice slam coming up at a club in Greenwich Village called—Cleopatra's Ashtray, could that be it? I can't say I just love Matt's poems, very long sometimes, and so many of them rather angry. But he is serious about it. And he does get me into Albany. . . . Anyway, I have the address of this Ashtray place and a couple of poems I plan to perform. It's an erotic poetry slam.

"But, oh, speaking of Matthew, it was Matt's little daughter Nina—or is it Gina?—anyway, Nina or Gina, it was his daughter who found the manuscript."

She set her plate down, as if to signal that it was time to get down to business. Juliet snuffed the flame on the brazier.

"Actually, I suppose it's a bit amusing," Ada recommenced in her deep voice, with that theatrical, mid-Atlantic intonation Juliet still found so surprising, "the way I came across the manuscript. I don't think I mentioned it in my letters to you, but Matthew's daughter, a little girl of four, if you can imagine that, found it while scampering about under my bed.

"I should explain that my bed is a quite remarkable one." Mrs. Caffrey lifted an eyebrow and paused for a sip of cold Formosa Oolong. "My second husband, Oliver, bought it at an auction in 1952. Oliver loved auctions. Nothing pleased him better than to drive a couple of hundred miles to look over somebody else's junk."

"Junk," like "slam," Ada segregated from her other words, as if picking it up and holding it at arm's length.

"And as often as not, he came home with something or other. Mind you, Oliver had other qualities that were much more"—she smiled—"much more agreeable. However, this bed. It was made in England, of rosewood, and it is simply gigantic. It has four posts like church spires, a headboard carved with little angels, and a roof on it like a miniature steeple. The legs—"

At this point, the sound of the phone ringing at various extensions throughout the apartment startled her, and she interrupted herself. "Ought you to answer that?"

Annoyed—just when the story was getting good!—Juliet glanced at the caller ID display on the silent phone beside her.

"That's all right; it's my father. The machine will get it. He probably just wants to make a date for dinner. Nothing that can't wait till next Christmas," she added briskly, thus demonstrating, as she later reflected, her complete lack of psychic ability. "You were saying—the legs on your bed?"

"Oh, yes. Well, they're rather thick, puffy, if you see what I mean, and quite tall. It's a high bed. I like a high bed," Ada went on, her voice momentarily dipping toward languor. She paused to smile as if in reminiscence. Juliet wondered what Bacchanalian memories might be flickering in her mind. Something to do with the second husband's "more agreeable" qualities, no doubt.

Then she resumed. "Naturally, I never spent much time under

it, however. So it wasn't until little Gina—no, it is Tina, isn't it? Tina? Or Nina. Well, I can't remember, children never did interest me," she interpolated, an aside Juliet found somewhat surprising from a former schoolteacher. "Whatever her name is, this tiny child somehow discovered a hidden compartment in one of the legs. One of the ones by the headboard. Right under my pillow all these years, can you believe it? It's a cunning little hiding place, and I suppose it must have escaped the notice of the former owner and even the auctioneer, because when the girl opened it—you have to place your hands at the corners of a sort of triangular panel and press your fingers just so, and then it slides *in* rather than *out*—there inside was the manuscript. I don't ordinarily receive visitors in bed, by the way. Not Matthew McLaurin, certainly. Bit of an awkward look to him, not my type at all. He's a clerk at an insurance agency. I was ill, brought low" (her voice thrilled, as if an empire had been "brought low") "by some sort of grippe. Matt was kind enough to stop by on his way home from Gallop Insurance that day with a book for me to read—he lives out in my direction, that's how we met—and he had little Tina with him. In any event—"

At last, Ada leaned over to catch hold of the carpetbag, which she had set on the floor beside her. With a giggle, she heaved it up onto her lap and fumbled at the catch. "I'm really so excited," she burst out, almost girlishly. "Isn't it just like finding buried treasure?" From the bag, rather confusingly, she withdrew a worn paperback copy of Angelica Kestrel-Haven's third book, *Cousin Cecilia.*

"I've been rereading your work," she explained, opening *Cousin Cecilia* and removing from between its pages a small rectangle of folded paper. At the sight of it, a shiver ran down Juliet's spine. "Such fun." Mrs. Caffrey put the book in her turquoise lap and sat clutching her folded rectangle with both hands.

"I haven't told a soul about this," she went on, almost whispering. "Even Matthew only knows Nina found something, some scrap of old paper. 'Loose lips sink ships,' I say. If it is valuable, I don't want the government getting wind of it. They can make you sell your assets, you know, if you're unlucky enough to wind up in a nursing home."

"Are you sure? I wouldn't imagine—"

But her visitor was too excited to listen. "Never mind," she said. "I can trust you, I know. You'll tell me what you think."

And with that she handed the papers across the table. Later, Juliet was surprised to think how much of this first conversation—no more than a polite preliminary, she would have said at the time—she would come to see as a map to Ada's murderer.

chapter

TWO

Buried Treasure

Juliet's heart beat more quickly than Selena Walkingshaw's at the sight of Sir James Clendinning. The rectangle Mrs. Caffrey had given her was composed of three sheets of paper, two small and flimsy, the third, on the outside, heavier and larger. All had been folded together, then curled into a cylinder, somewhat relaxed after their time within the pages of *Cousin Cecilia*.

Juliet carefully unfolded them. The larger sheet was a letter dated March 4, 1825.

no. 111, Rue du Faubourg St. Honoré,
à Paris.

My Lord,

Inclosed are your pages. Treasure or burn them, it is all the same to me.

How near your head came to the chopping block! You ought to be more careful.

Yours,

Harriette Rochfort late Wilson

"Harriette Wilson!" Juliet exclaimed without thinking.

She looked up to find Mrs. Caffrey's wrinkled features suffused with an expression of crafty acquisitiveness mixed with hope. "Was she famous? Is it valuable?"

Juliet looked down again at the papers in her lap. The two small pages were covered with text, the words written in the same large, forward-leaning handwriting as the letter. Eagerly, she scanned them. Harriette Wilson had touched this paper, written these words. The very thought was strangely delicious. She read thirstily: *Fanny, Shakspeare, Cashmere, Byron (Byron!)*

Juliet glanced up again to find Mrs. Caffrey's avid eyes fastened on her, glittering with greed. How much nicer it would be to taste Harriette's words unobserved, savor them slowly, in solitude.

"Would you mind very much leaving this with me overnight?" she heard herself ask primly. "I'd be able to give it my full attention that way, see what I can learn in some of my research books." She nodded at the walls of books around them, though in fact almost all of these were contemporary novels. "It will be perfectly safe, I promise."

Ada looked less than enthusiastic. Still, "If you prefer," she agreed, "but who was Harriette Wilson?"

Juliet smiled. Carefully, she placed the pages on the coffee table between them, well away from the teapot and cups.

"I'll tell you what I know," she said, "but tomorrow, you absolutely must take these to a dealer. Maybe one of the auction houses, Christie's or Sotheby's."

Mrs. Caffrey's features shifted. Juliet saw, or thought she saw, the beginnings of mistrust. "Who was she?" she demanded.

Juliet was embarrassed to feel her cheeks flush. "I don't recognize the name Rochfort," she began, "but Harriette Wilson was the preeminent—well, courtesan is the word she would probably have preferred, of the English Regency period. Her lovers and keepers included the Duke of Wellington, perhaps the Prince of Wales, and dozens of others of the most wealthy and powerful men of her time. I see she mentions Byron here. He wasn't among her lovers, that I remember reading, but I believe she claimed to know him.

"If I remember correctly, after a good long professional run, Harriette decided to write her memoirs. But before she published each installment, she contacted her former lovers. 'I am going to write my memoirs,' she told them, more or less. 'For two hundred pounds, I will leave you out.' It wasn't always two hundred, I think she had a sort of means-based sliding scale. Anyway, my guess is that what you have here is an episode somebody bought in the nick of time. Do you know if your bed was imported from England?"

"Yes, I believe it was. But how much do you imagine my find might be worth? Assuming it's what you think."

"I'm sorry, I just don't know. Would you like me to call Christie's for you?"

The old lady's look of mistrust had returned. "Do you know anyone there?"

"Not personally, no. But they're very reputable."

Ada sniffed. Juliet wondered if she could have read about the price-fixing scandal both auction houses had been involved in not long ago.

"Isn't there someone you know yourself? Someone you've dealt with?" Ada asked. "I don't want to hand it over to a stranger. Where would *you* go?"

Juliet thought. Reluctantly, "Well, as it happens, a friend of mine does deal in rare manuscripts," she said, after a moment. "In fact, he specializes in the English romantic poets, so with the Byron mention . . . But he's a small dealer; he works from his home. I don't know if it's the best idea to . . ."

Her words trailed off. It was not quite accurate to say that Dennis Daignault was her friend. She had met him less than two months ago, shortly before Thanksgiving, when she bought a book from him on the etiquette of dueling. The book had been in a catalogue; but the dealership turned out to be in the dealer's own apartment, just a few blocks up Riverside Drive from her own. She had gone to pick up her purchase in person, and they had seen each other every week or so since.

She found Dennis friendly, attractive, single, and rivetingly well-informed on an astonishing variety of subjects. That first afternoon alone, he had talked knowledgeably about shipwrecks, string theory, the chemistry of cooking, fluctuations in the Japanese yen, and ladies' underclothes of the seventeenth century. But bringing prospective clients to friends was a very tricky business. Sometimes it worked. Sometimes it backfired spectacularly.

In Mrs. Caffrey's old green eyes, she read suspicion—suspicion that her hostess had been holding out on her, keeping the good dealer for herself.

"Of course, I'd be glad to call him for you if you like," Juliet blurted out, eager to prove her innocence. "Rara Avis Books. He's right up Riverside Drive, as it happens."

With a readiness that startled her hostess, Ada Caffrey picked up her carpetbag and sprang to her feet.

"That would be wonderful," she said. "I am certain he will give it his particular attention. And now if you would just write me out a little receipt for the manuscript . . ."

She fell silent and stood looking hard at Juliet, her little head tilted, her green eyes flinty. Juliet felt offended but ordered herself to suppress her indignation. No doubt Mrs. Caffrey was terrified of losing her new-found treasure. From a drawer in an end table across the room, she took a notebook and pen. Quickly she scribbled an informal receipt for three pages apparently in the hand of Harriette Wilson. This satisfied Ada, who asked her to inscribe the copy of *Cousin Cecilia,* then began to thank her prettily for the tea.

"It's been marvelous to meet you," she gushed, the pebbles at the bottom of her rich voice returning. "I think I'd best check in now at that bed-and-breakfast you so kindly recommended. I told your friend I'd be there just about now."

Handing the signed book back to her, Juliet remembered the suitcase by the door. "I'll go with you."

"Oh! If it's not an imposition . . ."

"Not at all," said Juliet, understanding now how the "foreign gentleman" on the bus had gotten drafted into service. Ada Caffrey had ways of getting what she needed.

"Just a minute," Juliet said. After a moment's thought, she took a key from her pocket and unlocked the glass case wherein she kept her little collection of Regencyana. She slipped the manuscript inside and locked it up again.

"For safekeeping" she explained, leading her guest to her coat. A minute later, she, Ada, and the suitcase were in the elevator.

Juliet and Ada ventured through the freezing wind off the river, crossed the street, and rang Suzy Eisenman's bell. A freelance illustrator who had once been married to the art director of a prominent glossy magazine, Suzy was divorced now but retained custody of the apartment she and her husband had bought together, a two-bedroom on the ground floor of a small, redbrick town house on a corner of Riverside Drive. The town house was a sort of late Victorian fantasy, a miniature castle complete with turret and tiny battlements, and embellished with a concrete coat of arms. It was four stories high and had been divided into eight apartments before going co-op in the 1980s.

The artist's face appeared in one of the little leaded windows beside the building's front door. There was a chevron of color under her right eye, the result of a habit of resting the tip of her brush there while she painted. Smiling, she hurried them out of the wind and into the communal vestibule. Suzy was skinny and intense, with short, dark, straight hair parted in the middle to frame a narrow, somehow wistful face. Juliet found her quite lovely, despite her habit of dressing in oversized denim overalls and army boots. The two had met at a block association auction four or five years before, when Suzy donated a watercolor portrait of "the Upper West Side tree of your choice" and Juliet bid on it and won. (Juliet donated "Your name in a published novel," a gift she regretted when the winning bidder had turned out to be Kelsi Ng.) Since then, the women had gotten into the habit of eating dinner together once or twice a month, trading neighborhood gossip, complaints about work, and critiques of recent art shows.

Now, with practiced hospitality, Suzy grabbed Ada's suitcase and ushered her into her apartment. This was entered by way of a small foyer furnished with a coat tree bristling with faux antlers; a tall, very narrow, mesquite-wood bookcase (containing mostly art books but also—Juliet was always touched to see—a complete set of the works of Angelica Kestrel-Haven), and a small, rather threadbare, Navajo rug. There was also a little metal rack of the sort found in hotel lobbies, offering subway maps and brochures about such New York City attractions as Circle Line cruises and Madame Tussaud's Waãx Museum in Times Square. Directly in contravention of her co-op's rules, Suzy routinely rented out her second bedroom for short-term stays. It was the only way she could continue to pay her maintenance, she said; and really, when you thought about it, it was no different from having a series of roommates. Several of the building's shareholders knew what she was up to but kindly kept quiet, especially when the board president was within earshot.

Tempted to race back across the street and read the Wilson manuscript, Juliet instead followed the others in and politely lingered, moseying into the living room-cum-studio to inspect the unfinished work on the drafting table there while Mrs. Caffrey toured her bedroom, the guest bath, and the kitchen. Suzy Eisenman was known for her almost childlike line, her intricate conceptions, and the tiny visual jokes she often hid inside her pictures. She made her scanty living doing illustrations for magazines and newspapers, with an occasional book jacket or advertisement. Today's work was a picture of a toothbrush, shown in surreal close-up. Among the bristles, little elflike creatures seemed to dance. A real toothbrush lay on the farther verge of the desk, under a strong light.

Juliet was startled from contemplation of this curious still life by the sound of Ada Caffrey's voice, slightly raised, as if in annoyance.

"Oh, certainly I must go up there tonight," she was saying. "I had a lovely nap on the bus, and I've promised myself this for years. I won't sleep tonight if I haven't had a view of the city."

"But you—It's going to be very cold there, you know," Suzy answered, as the two came in from the corridor. Suzy glanced a mute appeal to Juliet. "Mrs. Caffrey is planning to visit the Empire State Building tonight," she said. "Do you think it's even open?"

"Oh, it's open," Ada told her serenely. "It's open till midnight every day of the year. Now, you girls go on about your business and don't mind me. Just tell me where you've hidden my coat, Miss Eisenman."

"I—Please, call me Suzy. Your coat is right here, but—"

"How will you get to the Empire State Building?" Juliet interposed. "Wouldn't you like to have some dinner first?"

"Not so soon after all your treats," said Ada, answering the second question first. "I'll just hop on a bus, I suppose. It's a pretty well-known destination. I can't go very far wrong, can I?"

Suzy looked meaningfully out at the wind-howling dark, then desperately back at Juliet. Juliet raised her eyebrows. Meantime, Ada had jousted her way back into the ratty, voluminous coat and was about to pick up her carpetbag.

"I'll go with you," Juliet heard herself say for the second time that day.

Mrs. Caffrey looked at her doubtfully. It occurred to Juliet that her company might not be welcome. "If you don't mind, that is," she added. "I haven't been up to the top of the Empire State Building since—Good God, I think it was a class trip in third grade."

"Then by all means, dear girl," said Mrs. Caffrey. "What about you, Miss Eisenman?"

Suzy declined on the grounds of a looming deadline.

Ada shrugged. *"Tant pis pour vous,"* she said, accepting a set of keys to the building and the apartment, then taking Juliet's arm. "Now, how much does it cost to take the subway? I believe it was a nickel, but that must have been some time ago."

Aside from the fact that a wind like fingers of ice was chasing the tourists around the Empire State Building Observatory, Juliet's visit with Mrs. Caffrey to that monument was a great success. Mrs. Caffrey had had it in mind to dine at Schrafft's afterward, or the Automat, but on learning that both of these were gone, agreed to try the Tavern on the Green instead. They followed this with a drink at the Plaza, where Mrs. Caffrey took a fancy to their distinguished-looking waiter, flirted ferociously, and ended by making a date to meet him at the skating rink at Rockefeller Center the following afternoon.

It was past midnight when Juliet finally left her at Suzy's and went across the street. In the ticking kitchen, her answering machine blinked, and she remembered the call from her father.

"Hi, sweetheart," began the first message, and the breezy, smooth baritone chilled Juliet's blood more swiftly than had the icy wind at the Observatory. "I've been seeing a great gal lately, and I'd love to get the two of you together. How about dinner tomorrow? Let's say seven-thirty at Le Perigord?"

Then came the sound, not of a receiver settling into its cradle, but of a speaker phone toggling obediently off. Ted Bodine was a man born to speak on a speaker phone, born to project his personality, a man who would not have been troubled had his daily life been displayed in real time on an electronic billboard in Times Square. He oozed confidence and charm. Hardened businessmen melted in his presence. Women clung to him like children. Juliet often wondered how he had come to marry her mother, who, from everything she could learn—Juliet was three when she died—had been a quiet, kind, somewhat frightened soul, nothing like the brassy, energetic girlfriends who had succeeded her.

She made a mental note to call Ted (she had long ago begun to speak and think of him as Ted) in the morning and regret that, due to a string of (fictitious) commitments, she couldn't join him and his great gal tomorrow, or the next day, or the next. She would suggest Saturday. Then he'd almost certainly postpone it till a weeknight the following week (he never gave her time during his weekends). And by the following week, maybe he and the great gal would have broken up.

The second message, left just before nine o'clock, was from Dennis.

"I wondered if I could interest you in a glass of port," he had said. His voice was deep, slow, and faintly southern (he had lived in Louisiana until the sixth grade), and Juliet could hear the smile in it as he went on, "Or a glass of port and a bit of sport. Give me a call when you get in. I'll be here."

Juliet smiled, too, but at the same time was aware of a part of herself that was not entirely charmed. In the first weeks of their acquaintance, she had found Dennis's erudition fascinating, and his courtly, enthusiastic admiration flattering, even delicious. But lately she'd found herself starting to resist him. Something about him struck her as—not insincere, but so conscious of himself that it almost added up to insincerity. When she went to his apartment, it seemed to her that he had set up a scene, a stage set that she could not enter without feeling equally conscious of herself. On their first date, he had set bottles of cognac and Chartreuse beside another of bitters and half a lemon; having mixed these into Champs Elysées, he read aloud a paragraph from a history of cocktails describing these as a favorite of the Lost Generation. But he was so interesting, later on—

on the subject of locks and how to pick them, of all things—that she forgot all about it until her next visit. On that occasion she came in to find a warm throw waiting on the sofa and, on the coffee table before it, a bowl of popcorn, the videotape he proposed they watch, *and* a crisp copy of its review in the *Times* downloaded from the Internet. Sometimes Juliet felt she was dating Martha Stewart. Was that a fault in a man? Surely not a dreadful one, but it made her uneasy.

Still, Dennis was single—rare enough all by itself, it seemed lately—kind, heterosexual, and attractive. He worried constantly about his looks, however, largely because he had been born with talipes equinovarus, or clubfoot. When, at age twelve, he had learned Lord Byron, too, had a clubfoot, he began to identify with him strongly. Dennis's own foot had been insufficiently treated in early life and later required surgery; now he had to wear an orthopedic shoe, which he incorrectly imagined everyone noticed.

Apparently, he was also monogamous, a big plus for Juliet, whose troubled marriage had finally sunk under the weight of an affair between her husband and an adoring actress. And Dennis was fun to listen to; they seemed to have so many interests in common. He had set out in life to be a poet—like Byron—an ambition he modified by the time he graduated from City College to being a poet slash English professor. He paid his way through his B.A., his Master's, and almost a Ph.D. by working part time at a secondhand bookshop on Fourth Avenue. He never finished his dissertation (on Byron, of course) since he had discovered by then, he said, that he was neither a very good poet nor a very good teacher. What he was quite good at was selling books, especially rare ones. He started Rara Avis by selling much of the private collection he had slowly built up during his school years. Now, though he still wrote poems for the pleasure of doing it, he never tried to publish them. Juliet had to agree that he wasn't a very good poet, but she liked him for trying. Too bad she got his phone message three hours too late.

On the other hand, those curious pages that might have been

suppressed from Harriette Wilson's famous memoirs had been tantalizing her all evening. She fixed herself a mug of peppermint tea, went into her library, unlocked the cabinet, and sat down to read.

At the top of the page a few words had been crossed out, probably pertaining to the previous victim.

Apropos to finery,

were the first words she could make out,

did you ever know a gentleman who preferred wearing his inamorata's clothes to admiring her in them? Such a one was the Hon. Edward Hertbrooke, later Viscount Quiddenham, of Quiddenham cum Nottington, who used to come to my house near Bedford-Square in order to wear my gowns. When my sister, Fanny, was with me, as often happened, the good gentleman also would borrow her cap or shawl. This embarrassed poor Fanny no small amount; but she was ever too good-natured to refuse him.

Up and down the drawing room this modish beau, or rather belle, would go—he was about nineteen or twenty at the time I write of—quaintly arrayed in a walking dress, cap and ribands, or a thin petticoat with nothing below. He was a well-looking boy, tall and slender, with a countenance beautifully expressive, and a serious, soft and graceful manner. Fanny and I sometimes amiably disputed whose friend he was. He frequented my house, but Fanny generally laced his stays.

As it was this gentleman's wish that we should comport ourselves during his visits exactly as if he wore a coat and breeches, he would often sit quietly by the fire, in his muslin skirt, while I read aloud from Shakspeare, whose command of human nature ever thrilled and delighted me. Or he would trip about the room, Fanny's best Cashmere shawl carefully draped about his arms, a pair of my old slippers groaning under his toes, giving us news from the clubs. After an hour or so of conversation, the future viscount would retire alone upstairs.

It was all he ever asked of us. Poor boy, it made him so happy!

After he succeeded to his title, this lord married a lady very much à la mode, though whether it was the lady or the mode he loved, I cannot say. I hope he had the courtesy to make his tastes known to his bride beforehand. Else, how distressed she might be to learn she must share her wedding-clothes! However, no harm came of his pleasure that I know of, save an occasional ript hem.

Lord Byron once observed of his lordship,

"A lad—or is it lady?—of high virtue!
"He may unseam your gown, but can not
hurt you."

That's all! Vive l'amour!

The boldly written lines had gone right down to the bottom of the paper, and this exclamation was crammed in along the right-hand margin.

Juliet set the page down and returned to the letter, then reread the fragment of manuscript. How could one know if these pages were authentic? If so, were they, in fact, absent from the complete memoirs? Had Byron really "observed" what Harriette reported, and if so, when, where, and to whom? Who was Viscount Quiddenham, and did he once own a bed like a church? There was quite a famous general of the British Raj named Quiddenham, she seemed to recall; could this one have been his father? Juliet was quite sure she had read not long ago of a movement afoot in London to remove a statue of this general from its pedestal near Pall Mall as being an unseemly celebration of British imperialism.

Thoughtfully, she locked the manuscript back into the glass case. She sat up late into the night reading Lesley Blanch's (highly abridged, alas) edition of Harriette's memoirs, scanning a biography of Wilson published in 1936 by Angela Thirkell, rereading Virginia Woolf's brief essay on Harriette as a figure on the "shadow side of the sword" that divided womanhood in two parts, ferreting among various Regency diaries, collections of letters, biographies of Byron, and in other, more abstruse volumes for any information that might shed light on the legitimacy of Mrs. Caffrey's find. All this sufficed to keep her mind well occupied (she even dreamed of a male figure fleeing down a mirrored corridor dressed in a gown of lawn) until the morning, when she paid an earlyish visit to Ada Caffrey at Suzy's apartment.

Suzy came to the door wrapped in a thick burgundy robe. She looked tired and not particularly happy.

"Mrs. C. is very chatty, isn't she?" she whispered, as Juliet followed her in from the vestibule. More loudly, "I'll get you some tea," she added.

Ada was at the breakfast table, bright-eyed and fully made up, arrayed in a vintage, quilted, salmon pink dressing gown, with a broad sash and considerable décolletage. She reeked of gardenia. A matching band of salmon ribbon was tied rakishly around her head.

Suzy, Juliet could see, had made a conscientious effort to transcend her army boot-and-overall instincts and provide the style of morning meal the phrase "bed-and-breakfast" conjured up: baskets of toast and muffins, fruit salad, scrambled eggs, and a set of Blue Willow dishes Juliet had never seen. From the look of Ada's plate, though, she had eaten nothing except a quarter of a blueberry muffin. Her coffee cup was well stained with her crimson mark, however, and the saucer liberally sloshed with drips.

She looked at Juliet sharply. "Well?" she demanded, as Suzy vanished into the kitchen.

"Well, to my eye, the pages are authentic enough. But I don't think my opinion means much." She took the manuscript fragment and letter from a leather portfolio she used to carry her papers when she spoke publicly. "Where shall I put them?"

Ada waved her impatiently to a small sideboard near the door to the kitchen. Juliet set the pages down there, at the same time making a mental note to be sure to get her receipt back before she left.

"How valuable do you think they are?"

"I don't know." She took an empty place beside the old lady. "The memoirs are very, very long, and I only have an abridged copy anyway. You'd need an expert to say whether it's Harriette's handwriting, if she really could have known this Lord Quiddenham, whether these pages appeared in the memoirs or not, I'm really not expert enough—Oh, thank you." She interrupted herself to accept a steaming mug from Suzy. "I'm really not qualified to guess how much someone might pay for them if they are authentic," she went on. Reaching into the pocket of her jeans, she brought forth a folded paper. "But I've written down my friend Dennis Daignault's name and number. I imagine he'd need to keep them for a day or two while he looks them over. Please don't feel you must go to him just because he's a friend of mine. I think the best thing for you to do is give him a call and meet him, see if he seems like the right—"

"I'm sure he's perfect, my dear," Ada interrupted, "but I wonder if you would mind terribly calling him for me?"

Juliet glanced uneasily at Suzy, who had resumed her own seat.

"I'm sending her to Dennis," she explained. "But I'd really feel more comfortable if you spoke with him yourself," she went on, turning again to Ada. "It's just a matter of a phone call—"

"Then I'll let you make it. May I?" Mrs. Caffrey batted her mascaraed eyelashes at Juliet. "And perhaps you would even be kind enough to run the pages up there yourself? These old bones . . ."

She shook her head, smiling wistfully. It was the first hint she had given that she felt her age. After last night's hijinks, Juliet could not help but suspect she was using it as an excuse to get out of a bit of business she considered tedious compared with the fun of visiting architectural landmarks and flirting with the waiters of New York.

But a lifetime of standing up for old ladies on the bus, holding doors for them, and generally deferring to their needs prevented her from arguing further. And maybe Ada really was tired; at the least, New York must be very noisy after the quiet of the country.

"Did you sleep all right?" she asked, glancing apologetically at Suzy. "This is a quiet neighborhood, but it certainly isn't rural. I'm afraid the garbage trucks must have woken you."

"Obviously, my dear," Ada said, smiling brilliantly as she adjusted the bow in her dashing hair ribbon, "you have never heard a snowmobile. I slept like a top."

"Ada's going to the Statue of Liberty this afternoon," Suzy reported.

The old lady smiled again. "That's before my rendezvous with Pierre." Pierre was the distinguished waiter of last night.

Juliet and Suzy conferred silently, by glance.

"Ames might like to go with you," Juliet said. "Would you mind if she did?"

Mrs. Caffrey gave her companions a canny look. "You don't think I'm safe on my own, do you?"

There was a pause. Then, "No," Suzy admitted.

Ada lifted her painted eyebrows. "I'd like to see either of you cope with an Espyville winter in a hundred-year-old house," she said. "Your Ames is perfectly welcome if she wants to come to Liberty Island"—her voice dropped an octave—"but I'm not taking her to meet Pierre."

"I'll let her know," Juliet promised.

"Now, after the Statue of Liberty, but before I meet Pierre, I've got to get to TKTS in Times Square," Ada went on, with that brisk zeal Juliet found both admirable and disconcerting. "I'm hoping for tickets to something on Broadway, or do you think off-Broadway is better these days?"

Juliet lingered through some discussion of New York's theater scene, then stood to go. She moved over to the side table to pick up the manuscript.

"If you're certain Dennis is the dealer you'd prefer," she said, "I'll make sure he gets the pages. I suppose you can just keep that receipt we made out yesterday for now."

"Oh, what a dear you are," Ada said, giving her a distracted smile that let Juliet know that "dears" did not rank very high on her list of important people. Once again, she saw that her new friend had a gift for leaving onerous chores to others while she disported herself as she pleased. Juliet thought about this talent later as she scurried up through the cold that morning to give the letter and manuscript to Dennis. He was delighted by the Byron reference. She made her visit short, merely handing over the pages in return for a receipt (mistrustfulness, she found, was catching), then going home to fail at writing "A Christian Gentleman."

Over the next three days, Juliet and Suzy continued, with varying degrees of willingness, to oblige Mrs. Caffrey. When she announced her wish to see the opera, Juliet sprang for tickets and went along. Ames escorted her to the Bronx Zoo, Suzy to Chinatown, Pierre to the Chelsea art galleries. None of them felt it prudent to let Mrs. Caffrey gad about on her own, and so she succeeded in getting them to arrange these and half a dozen other excursions for her.

By far the most interesting outing for Juliet was Wednesday's visit to the poetry slam at Cleopatra's Ashtray, which turned out to be in the basement of a rock club called Scar, on the Bowery. The thick gloom and clouds of cigarette smoke that met them as they descended the concrete steps fazed Mrs. Caffrey not a bit. Dressed all in silver, her penetrating voice easily making itself heard despite the recorded thump of Eminem, she blithely asked the be-nose-ringed barmaid where the sign-up sheet was and inscribed her name below that of a half-dozen others. A crowd of mismatched chairs was arranged before a low, floodlit wooden platform that would serve as a stage. Mrs. Caffrey took a seat in the front row, inches from the booming speakers, then turned to look over the competition. The oldest of these was her junior by about fifty years; most were in their twenties or early thirties, Juliet guessed. A few scribbled in notebooks or studied typewritten sheets, lips moving silently as they prepared to recite from memory. Mrs. Caffrey needed no such aids, it appeared, but sat supremely confident, sipping an Irish coffee while her orthopedic shoe tapped out the music's throbbing beat.

At last the slam started, conducted by a sort of poet-emcee, a burly blond man named Doug Renny, who chose at random five judges from among the thirty or forty members of the audience. These were furnished with scoring pads of the type used at swim meets.

Then the poets began. At the sound of her name, a young woman leapt to the stage, caressed the microphone, and huskily whispered into it a sonnet describing her lust for the counterman at her local deli, who shaved meats to such a fine transparency that the poetess wished he would coat her own skin in spiced ham and . . . and so on.

Juliet stole a glance at Ada, fearing her idea of what constituted poetry stopped short of Hormel. But there was no revulsion or even surprise on Ada's features, only the focused interest of one artist listening to another. The smitten carnivore recited a second poem, this one a free verse appreciation of autoeroticism, which drew sympathetic whoops from several women in the audience and admiring stamps of encouragement from one or two men. Again, Juliet glanced apprehensively at her elderly companion but saw there only a beatific smile. Juliet was forced to conclude that she was more of a prig than Ada.

As the first poetess left the platform amid enthusiastic applause, the ad hoc judges raised their tablets.

"Nine point four!" Doug Renny read out, regaining the stage. "Nine point five! Nine point one, nine point eight" (the applause intensified), "eight point nine" (a chorus of disappointed "aws"). Renny laughed and adroitly moved the proceedings along. He had the patter of a professor who has studied the great stand-up comedians. He announced a rondeau slam for Friday at a club called Jade and gave a spirited reading of Donne's "Elegy XIX. To His Mistress Going to Bed" ("License my roving hands, and let them go / Before, behind, between, above, below . . .") before calling the next slammer to the stage. This was a man who declared in a deafening voice his devotion to his lover's feet, lingering over the cuticles by his toenails (the beloved also was a man), even the fungal flakes from persistent athlete's foot. Presentation, Juliet saw by now, was key in this particular art. The poets, though they looked scruffy enough, had the self-possession of accomplished actors, and used the microphone with polished effect. As to the quality of the poetry, it was, by and large, written to be spoken aloud; without seeing it on the page, Juliet could not judge it further.

The podophile was followed by a man who dreamily delivered a rap-inspired invitation to his beloved to spend the night with him; in the poet's swift, incantatory murmur, Juliet missed quite a few of the details, but the rhythmic urgency of the piece came through loud and clear, and she found herself whistling in appreciation with the others when he finished.

At length, Renny announced a poet new to him and, perhaps, to the New York slam circuit: Ada Case Caffrey!

There was a flutter of polite applause as Ada's silver gown (composed of some fabric no longer made, it seemed to Juliet) shimmered in the pool of light trained on the microphone. Her flapper's face serenely commanding, she scanned the audience with a long, slow, languid gaze. The hard light painted a slippery streak of white onto her shoe-polish hair.

" 'In Memoriam, Frederick A.,' " she announced, her deep voice spreading over the audience like honey.

"Bereft in the moonlight, I, / Like a well gone dry, / Gather dust in the field, / Where once your lips like wings / Beat mine, where once your flesh / Under the hemlocks stripped me / Of thought, of will . . ."

Juliet listened in astonishment as Ada conjured in her thrilling voice the carnal passion of her vanished lover, Frederick A., who, it seemed, had died of an illness—cancer?—brought on by work in a tanning factory. Terms used erotically in the early part of the poem (lips that beat, flesh that stripped the poet of thought) returned in the middle part referring to tanning (flesh stripped from hide, tannin from the shady hemlocks) and finally, in a third part, to grief ("beaten, I dream of that other / Hemlock, pray for death myself . . .") An uproar greeted the end of this poem, which Ada followed with a much lighter one called "Stagecraft," about a kiss exchanged between actors in a play. To some extent because she was herself such a quaint and curious creature, but in no small part because of the poetry itself—and her skill in delivering it—Ada left the stage to a din of clapping and stamping. No judge gave her a score less than nine point eight and two awarded her a ten.

In the second round of the slam, as the highest-scoring contestant, Ada went first. This time, she had lost the element of surprise, and with it some of the drama that had won her listeners. However, she craftily recited a poem full of sly innuendo, comparing sliding into bed with her lover to sliding her hand into a glove. Each digit's experience was described in detail, and with much humorous use of the idea of fitting, wriggling in, warming up, hard fingernails, and so forth. Charmed all over again, the audience roared its approval. The judges issued a straight row of nine-point-nines.

At the end of the slam, Ada was found to be the winner. Juliet could not help but notice a look of furious dislike on the face of Ada's nearest competitor, Mira Branson, she of the translucent deli meats, as she retook the stage in Ada's wake. Doug Renny gave Ada the copy of *Gathered Rosebuds,* an anthology of "poems of desire," which was the evening's prize. She received it with a vibrant "Thank you" into the microphone, then considerably startled the husky emcee by turning back to him and planting a whopping kiss on his mouth. The gesture provoked a new swell of enthusiasm from the crowd (and a deeper scowl from Ms. Branson). Then, in a flash of silver, Ada skipped from the stage and dropped into the seat beside Juliet.

"Let's scram," she panted into Juliet's ear. Juliet rose obediently, and the two hotfooted it through the crowd to the back of the room. They retrieved their coats from the metal rack there and climbed the stairs to the door of the club as quickly as Ada's spry legs could manage.

Out in the icy quiet of the Bowery, still breathing hard, "You have to know when to make your exit," the poet explained. She handed Juliet the anthology to carry and led her briskly up the block. "This way, when I show up at Friday's slam, I'll still be a lady of mystery."

Juliet got home that night at eleven—late, but still early enough to return a machine message from Dennis, a lifelong night owl.

He picked up the phone, sounding slightly spacey.

"Were you asleep?" she asked, instantly contrite.

"No, just in another world. Research world," he said. "I love this manuscript, Juliet. Forgive me for not calling sooner to thank you. I've just have been having a blast checking it out."

"You think it's valuable?"

"I don't know. I promised Mrs. Caffrey an answer on Friday afternoon. But a whole lot depends on the Byron thing, whether that can be authenticated in any way. I don't think it's from any known poem—I've got a grad student double-checking that. I've certainly never read it. But the way Wilson puts it is so unclear. It could be something he said directly to her, or something someone else told her he said, or something he wrote, or she could just have made the whole thing up. She mentions Byron a lot in the memoirs, and there are certainly letters from her in his papers. But people did drop his name in those days, he was so glamorous. And, conveniently for Wilson, he died a year before she published. She does describe a meeting with him, but I'm not at all sure it ever took place. On the other hand, he seems to have sent her money. So she might not have mentioned—"

"And the value—?" Juliet prompted. For Ada's sake, she hoped it was high.

"Oh, yeah. Well, as I say, it very largely depends if the couplet can be traced. Then there's the question of who I can sell it to and how. By the way, are you interested?"

"It did cross my mind. But no, I'd rather just sit this one out. My little collection doesn't really run to manuscripts. Do you think you'll have trouble finding a buyer?"

"Oh, no. In fact, I've already talked to a couple of people. But that's hardly the point. How much money it brings in doesn't matter much—at least, not to me. The point is, this is fun. This is the goods, the kind of thing you hope will come your way. So thank you. That Harriette Wilson was a pip."

"I can't wait to hear what you've learned."

"Well, for the moment, I guess I shouldn't say any more. Professional discretion. Habit of a lifetime," he added apologetically. "You're not a prospective client, and the manuscript still belongs to Mrs. Caffrey. But I'm going to call her tomorrow morning and see if we can come to terms. Once I buy it from her, I promise I'll tell you everything I know."

"Sounds fun."

"It will be fun." There was a pause. Then Dennis went on, "Do I sound crazy?"

"Not at all."

"You don't think glee is a babyish emotion in a man?"

"Quite the contrary," said Juliet, though she realized even as she said it that he did strike her as just a little childish at the moment. How awful! Did she believe men should repress their exuberance, act cool, pretend to be above emotion?

"Then you're in favor of more glee in men?"

Yes, evidently she did believe they should. "Why not?" she said weakly.

"Why not indeed?"

chapter THREE

Snow

*"It is the starved imagination," E. M. Forster wrote, "not the well-*nourished, that is afraid."

Whether Juliet had been nourished by what she had soaked up in the yeasty creative vat of the poetry slam the night before, or simply because her characters were at long last starting to behave, she found herself sitting down at her desk on Thursday morning with no apprehensiveness and worked easily through the day. Sir James Clendinning had traveled up to town to refurbish his sober wardrobe, an errand he undertook annually in a spirit of godly respect for the temple of his soul. He happened to overhear, in the smoking room of his club (Sir James's god said nothing against smoking), an interchange suggesting to him that a penniless young puppy named Charles Vizor, an army captain, was head over ears in love with Selena Walkingshaw. Sir James had not meant to eavesdrop, and he naturally removed himself from his chance listening post as soon as discretion would allow, but the incident set him thinking as he strolled out into—Strolled out into—

It was July in "A Christian Gentleman," and Juliet stopped dead. What would a gentleman up in London stroll out into in July of 1813? She put her pen down, swiveled her chair around, and gazed absently out the window. The difficulty of imagining one kind of weather while enduring another never failed to surprise her. Outside her office, the sky over Riverside Park, so blue only yesterday, was leaden. A storm system over the Great Lakes was moving toward the city; on WNYC that morning, the forecast had been for snow—light snow starting tonight and falling heavily by tomorrow.

Juliet sighed and turned back to her desk. Whatever the temperature, Sir James would certainly have strolled out into a miasma of ghastly odors, the warmth of the season evoking the maximum possible stench from the open sewers flowing everywhere through the metropolis. Wondering how to put this delicately, she picked up her pen.

Some hours later, as she crossed the street to fetch Ada and take her to *The Phantom of the Opera,* Juliet doubtfully checked the sky. Listening to the news while she had been dressing, she had heard the word "blizzard" being excitedly tossed about. Yet the snow had stopped, and a crescent moon shone dully behind a thin veil of cloud.

Still, she would make a point of mentioning the forecast to her elderly date, who planned, Juliet knew, to attend another poetry slam tomorrow.

"Blizzard! Pff!" said the lady airily, when Juliet had delivered her warning. She flung one end of a gold lamé stole around her shoulders, picked up a matching gold clutch, and shoved it under her arm. "I could tell them about blizzards!"

And off they went on another long and somewhat exhausting expedition. By the time they got home (having taken in the show, supper at Sardi's, and a slightly queasy-making nightcap in the revolving cocktail lounge at the top of the Marriott), the sky was thickly overcast and snow was falling fast. Juliet was still worried about "A Christian Gentleman"—very worried—and yet she once again went to bed in a pretty contented frame of mind. *Phantom* had not been to her taste, but Ada Caffrey rather was. The woman was indefatigable. She seemed to have no idea she was eighty-four. Which was, in some respects, distressing—there had been a painful interlude this evening when she attempted to pick up a fiftyish theater usher—but in most ways delightful. From her poems and the stories she told, Juliet had concluded that Ada Caffrey, like Ulysses, had drunk life to the lees. The fact that she had done most of her drinking in and around Espyville, New York, and not—as would have seemed more proportionate to her interests and appetites—Manhattan, Paris, or Hollywood, hardly seemed to matter. She had been married three times to three very different men and had "carried on" (her term) with dozens of others.

At first, Juliet had taken "carrying on" to mean some sort of gentle flirtation; but the poems, coupled with some remarks the old lady made apropos of a nude male torso in the Metropolitan Museum's Greek Gallery, had changed her interpretation. From a few references she made to funerals, Juliet gathered that Ada's circle of friends had contracted very much of late. But she did not seem to allow that circumstance to sap her joie de vivre. In fact, the thought seemed never to have crossed her mind.

If old age could be like this, Juliet thought, she would relish it. She listened again to the radio as she undressed. The current snowfall, according to the forecast, would thicken by the hour; it was indeed a blizzard. School closings were already being announced, and Juliet went to bed contemplating not only the cheerful prospect of a rollicking senescence but the much more immediate one of a lovely day or two with the city crystallized and quiet. Tomorrow, cross-country skiers would glide through Riverside Park, traffic lights would change meaninglessly on empty, snow-bedded side streets, and snuggling in with a good book would become not just socially permissible but practically de rigueur. Ada Caffrey, she knew, had an appointment at Rara Avis to talk with Dennis about the value of the manuscript. But that could be postponed. Even Ada would have to stop running around for a bit (surely!), take a nap, and give her new friends some rest.

When Juliet stumbled downstairs to make tea on Friday morning, thick, lush whorls of small, cold snowflakes were falling swiftly past her windows. In the kitchen, both radio and television fairly rang with delighted, dire warnings. The storm upon the city now was the worst since the Blizzard of '96, since the "Storm of the Century" in '93, since snow was invented. Listeners must stay tuned to (fill in your choice of call letters) Radio (or TV), which would struggle to stay on the air and advise them no matter the obstacles. Juliet experienced a weird sensation of relief. After the World Trade Center disaster, it was a pleasure, almost a luxury, to have a merely natural emergency to cope with.

She had hoped Ames would have the sense to stay at home; but when she called to tell her not to come, there was no answer. She switched off the radio, went upstairs, and sat herself down at her desk, as was (she reminded herself) her bounden duty. Having invented the puppy Vizor, she had decided during breakfast to give Selena Walkingshaw a wealthy uncle, Lord Spafford, who would invite Selena and her younger sister, Catherine, to his country estate. She had a vague idea it might turn out later that Lord Spafford was not wealthy at all but secretly in grave financial difficulties; and she was pretty sure Sir James Clendinning would turn up eventually, large banknotes in hand. But for the morning she considered it enough to describe Spafford, relate the unexpected advent of his invitation, and detail the journey of the girls to his place in Hampshire. She was writing Spafford's letter when Ames showed up; Juliet sent her straight back to Queens again, lest she get stranded in Manhattan. At lunchtime, just as his lordship's nieces were sitting down to their supper at Spafford House, Angelica Kestrel-Haven had a bite of tuna fish.

She returned to her desk around two o'clock, by which time more than a foot of snow had fallen. The day having warmed a little, the flakes were larger, and more was tumbling down all the time. The pile of Christmas trees across the street from Juliet's office window was cloaked in white, as were the branches of the living trees around them. Sitting down again to her manuscript, Juliet was pleasantly surprised to find Selena and Catherine Walkingshaw falling easily into a long bedtime conversation about what constituted a happy life. The phone rang now and then, but she ignored it. It was a pleasure to have something before her worth ignoring the phone about. As for the demanding Ada Caffrey, if Juliet gave her a thought, it was only to feel grateful for her temporary silence. She did think of calling to offer help to Suzy, a captive audience if ever there was one and no doubt condemned to spend today listening to racy stories from Ada Caffrey's past. But, cravenly, even callously, Juliet decided to let her friend endure this penance on her own. If Suzy wanted to run a bed-and-breakfast, she must put up with her guests; surely that was part of the price of doing business.

As for Juliet, she would bask in the silence. This was a sort of day she adored. All over the city, people were forced to abandon their plans. Meetings were canceled, dates postponed (among them, Juliet's own dinner with her father and the Great Gal—they left it that they would get together in a week or two when Ted got back from a business trip to Dallas). Parents, forced to play hooky from work, took their children sledding. Householders slogged to the grocery store and, loaded with food, went home to their apartments as if to rural cabins that might be cut off for weeks. Small dogs peered from lobbies and refused to go outside. Large dogs, freed of their leashes, bounded deliriously through snowdrifts in the parks, chased snowballs, wriggled luxuriously into the huge, cold, white carpet.

Alternate-side-of-the-street parkers, that hardy band who scoff at New York City garage prices and house their cars on the streets, rejoiced in the knowledge that street-sweeping operations would be suspended and their cars, therefore, allowed to remain wherever they were despite the posted no-parking hours, perhaps for days and days. Restaurant deliverymen cried on their bikes, the teardrops freezing in their lashes. Supers counted their staff and cranked up the heat.

Juliet worked easily late into the evening, pausing only to eat some soup in the kitchen and, now and then, to glance out and enjoy the spectacle of the hushed and darkened city under its purifying cloak of white. Back at her desk, while the Walkingshaw girls lay in their beds debating what made for happiness, Lord Spafford's steward, Tom Giddy was taking shape on the page. He was a bluff, burly, practical man famous in the village for his feats of strength as well as his unusual generosity. (On their way home last night, apropos of the sight of circling snowplows, Ada had mentioned with satisfaction that her neighbor, the real Tom Giddy, always plowed her driveway for free. This Tom, she also noted, had once been captain of his high school wrestling team.) Today, he was sternly confronting his employer with a respectful but forthright accounting of his lordship's failing finances. Lord Spafford's finances were of the greater concern to the conscientious steward because his own life's helpmeet, stout, cheerful, comfortable Mrs. Giddy, was his lordship's cook. Juliet went to bed feeling pure and virtuous, a weary but satisfied spinner of fifteen pages of first-rate froth.

The next morning Suzy called to report that Ada had gone out the day before and had never come home.

chapter FOUR

Mrs. Caffrey Gone

Juliet's first thought was of Pierre. If Ada were missing, mightn't his bed be one place to look?

Suzy agreed. "I wouldn't put it past her."

Juliet rubbed her eyes. After her late work last night, she had allowed herself to sleep in. The phone had rung just as she was sitting down at the kitchen table with her first cup of tea. She wasn't at her most alert. Still, there was something—

"Oh, but the storm," she blurted out. "How can Ada be lost in the middle of a blizzard?"

Suzy ignored the apparent idiocy of the question. "I know, but she went out anyway."

"Yesterday?"

Juliet stood and looked out at the white, glaring world to the west. A good eighteen inches of snow must have fallen on Manhattan since the storm began. The cars parked along Riverside Drive were mere swells, soft billows under a sea of white. Even now, a plow hooked up to a garbage truck was shoving more snow against them, marooning them further behind a tall, compacted bank. The pile of Christmas trees had grown to a sugar mountain. On the playground at Eighty-third Street, snowmen and snowdogs made yesterday peered out from under new veils. A few cars moved sedately along the West Side Highway. From the titanium sky, a flurry of flakes still tumbled past the window.

"Where did she go?"

Suzy's voice rose to a worried wail. "I don't know. She was planning to go to some kind of rondeau slam in the East Village last night. She didn't want me to tell you because apparently she had her eye on someone she expected to see there, and she thought you would 'cramp her style.' That's a quote," Suzy noted. "I tried to talk her into staying home, but it was a waste of breath. The only thing I know for sure is that in the afternoon she had an appointment with your friend Dennis. I made her lunch, she took a nap, I walked her up to Rara Avis, and that's the last I saw of her."

"They kept that appointment?" Juliet asked. "Why didn't Dennis come down to her? It was already snowing so hard."

"I don't know. She just said she was going. She was due there at three-thirty."

"Did she come home after that at all?"

"I have no idea. I had to go out myself."

"Yesterday?"

"Well, magazines have to get published on time whether the weather is good or not," Suzy pointed out. "An editor at *Menu* suddenly decided to kill a piece on polenta. They called me up around three, desperate for artwork on silverware. I took Ada up to Dennis's, saw her go into the building, took a bus down Broadway, and spent from four-something till almost eight drawing forks in the art editor's office."

Juliet resisted the temptation to inquire into the nature of the fork article in *Menu,* an upscale book for New York foodies, and focused instead on the matter at hand.

"So the last time you saw her—?"

"Was just before three-thirty."

"And when you got home, you couldn't tell if she had come in and gone out again?"

"No. She has her own keys, of course, and she always wears

that same bear coat, seal, whatever it is, so—I really didn't think about it. Wait a minute."

Juliet heard Suzy walking, heard the old-fashioned click of her aged refrigerator door. A moment later, "No, I bet she never came in," she reported. "I left her some homemade soup for dinner, and she never touched it at all. Although, of course, she could have decided to eat out."

"At her own expense?"

"Yeah, maybe not," Suzy agreed. "Well, whatever, by the time I got home myself, I realized that wherever she was, she'd have a hard time returning. It took me an age to get up Sixth Avenue. The buses were barely running. Anyway, I had no way to find her, so I just figured eventually she'd turn up. And then I got totally distracted. The phone rang, and it was Parker—"

"Parker, huh?"

Parker Scutt was an artist who created detailed suburban dollhouses in which small waxen figures did strange and scary things to each other. Suzy had met him several months before. They had been seeing each other once a week or so.

"Yeah. He said he had his snowshoes on, and he wanted to come by and visit me. So he did."

"And?"

"We went for a walk in the park, which was pretty gorgeous, and then we went back to my place and then—he stayed over."

"Suzy, you slept with Parker Scutt?" Juliet yelped. Parker Scutt was married, although he claimed to be separated.

"Don't yell at me! It was fabulous, and he swears he's not living with Diana anymore—"

"Then why doesn't he ever let you come to his place?"

"Juliet, the point is, I was in bed with him; I didn't come out of the room till I woke up this morning; and when I finally did, Parker was gone and Mrs. Caffrey still hadn't come home. I mean, I didn't realize that first thing. When we got in from the park and I didn't see her coat anywhere, I guessed she was still out. This morning—well, she'd left her room door shut; and when I saw it that way, I figured she'd finally worn herself out and was sleeping. It wasn't until five minutes ago that I thought to look in the closet. Her coat's not there. So then I opened her door, of course, and Juliet, she never came in. Her bed is untouched."

"You don't think she could have come home, slept, got up, made the bed, and gone out again this morning?"

There was a momentary pause. Then, "It's pretty clear you never had Ada Caffrey for a houseguest," Suzy said. "I'm worried about her, of course, but what a pig. Believe me, if she'd been here, I'd know it." There was a pause. "You don't think she could really have gotten lucky at the slam?"

Juliet thought of the youthful faces of the other poets at the Ashtray slam, of the embarrassment of the usher Ada had hit on at *Phantom*. Who could she have expected to flirt with at the slam? She hadn't even talked to anyone, except—

Oh. The image of Ada bussing Doug Renny at the Ashtray returned to her. But wasn't he just the very "husky wrestler type" Ada had deprecated as not "wearing" well? On the other hand, she was eighty-four. Even she must realize she probably wouldn't be around to see him dwindle. Could she really have imagined—?

No doubt she could. Juliet recalled Renny's surprised, rather dismayed look after she'd kissed him.

"No," she said aloud. "But I think I know who she had in mind."

"Do you think I should have offered to pick her up at Dennis's after her appointment?" Suzy asked.

"No, of course not. It's only three blocks, for Pete's sake. And if it seemed so treacherous outside, he could have walked her back himself."

"Maybe he did."

There was silence on the line. It lasted a long moment. Both women were weighing the likelihood of Ada's having the consideration to call if she had stayed out overnight with a man (highly unlikely, they thought). Both were trying to figure out how long a very grown-up woman could be missing from a bed-and-breakfast before the police, for example, would consider her missing. Both wondered if Ada could somehow, suddenly, for some reason, have gone home to Espyville unannounced.

"Her suitcase—?" Juliet asked finally.

"It's here. I mean, I only glanced in her room, but all her things seem to be here. Except—you know, her coat and stuff."

"Do we know how to reach Pierre?"

"Call the Plaza?"

"I'll try Dennis; you try them."

Five minutes later, Juliet's phone rang again.

"Neither snow nor rain nor whatever it is stops the Plaza," Suzy reported. "Pierre's at work. I spoke to him myself. He hasn't seen her."

"Dennis said she left his place about four."

"He didn't go with her?"

"No. He tried to phone you guys to offer to come down to your place, by the way, spare her the walk. But you must have already left. He didn't realize till he looked outside just before the appointment how heavily it was snowing. He also offered to bring her home, but she didn't want him to. He says when she left, she was majorly pissed at him. She took the Wilson pages back. Apparently, their meeting didn't go well. She didn't leave alone, though. Someone else happened to be there, too—a collector Dennis had contacted about the manuscript—and Ada went into the elevator with him, talking a mile a minute."

Like most artists Juliet knew, Suzy was extremely practical. "I'm going to call her number in Espyville," she said briskly. "You see if Dennis will give you the name of the collector she left with; he might know something. Or—there isn't a doorman at his building, is there?" she added hopefully.

"No."

"No, that would be too easy. Okay, let's see . . . It's ten after ten. Let's figure if we learn nothing, and if we don't hear from her by noon, I'll look in her room, see if she was here, see if I can find the manuscript. She definitely had it with her when she left?"

"Yes, Dennis gave it to her."

There was a fractional pause.

Then, "Could she have taken it somewhere else?" Suzy asked. "One of the auction houses?"

"Maybe. But let's try to figure out if she ever came home at all. Check her clothes. Do you remember what she was wearing when you left her?"

"Of course. Who could forget Ada's clothes? A dark purple dress with flounces at the hem and one of those high-necked, drapy collars. Circa 1940, I would say. She had a matching purple purse—a cloth one, fairly large, bunched at the clasp, with a thin silver chain—lavender leather gloves, and a purple felt hat with a little veil."

"So see if those are in her closet. I don't think she's the kind of person who would go out for the evening in her day clothes, do you? Especially if she was angling for a date."

"Good point."

They hung up. Ten minutes later, they were on the phone, comparing notes again.

"Dennis can't reach the collector guy," Juliet reported. "He's not at home, not at the office."

"No one answers her number in Espyville. I don't see the purple dress or the hat and purse."

This, more than anything else, struck fear into both their hearts.

"And the manuscript?"

"I'm still looking."

They hung up. At twelve-fifteen, Suzy called again. She had searched Mrs. Caffrey's things. Of course, the manuscript could be hidden somewhere Suzy hadn't thought of. But she knew that room pretty well; she used to sleep in it when things were really bad with Jack, her ex-husband. The manuscript was missing. So was Mrs. Caffrey.

Juliet hung up and called Murray.

Murray Landis and Juliet Bodine first met when they were nineteen years old. Murray, studying art at Harvard, had then been dating Juliet's Radcliffe roommate, Mona. Their affair, like all of Mona's, had been torrid; but not so torrid that Murray hadn't noticed Juliet, and vice versa.

Nothing had ever been said or done between them. On the contrary, diligent restraint was practiced on both sides, and after Mona and Murray broke up, Juliet lost track of him. Then one morning last summer, he'd turned up at her door, a police detective investigating a death among a group of dancers at the Jansch troupe, where Juliet had been helping a friend restructure the narrative of a ballet based on *Great Expectations*. Murray was still an artist in his off hours, a serious artist. But rather than starve as a sculptor, he had decided to go into the family business: after growing up in Brooklyn, the son of a cop of a son of a cop, he'd joined the NYPD. He had been assigned to Juliet's precinct for some years before the Jansch death brought them together.

Juliet was lucky; he answered his own phone at the station house.

"Jule! I'm sitting here catching up on paperwork, bored out of my skull. How the hell ya doin'?" he shouted, in the broad Brooklynese he could turn on and off at will.

She explained.

"So it's really Suzy who should be calling," he suggested, when the bare bones had been outlined.

"Well, we just weren't sure anyone would care if we called out of the blue. Don't you have to wait twenty-four hours or something?"

"Nah, that's one of those urban folklore things," Murray said, "like alligators in the sewers. Especially after the weather we've had, we'll get on it right away. But it's really not a detective matter. I'll send you a couple of uniforms."

"You don't think you"—Juliet broke off, then finished rather wistfully—"you couldn't come yourself?"

"Oh hell, sure, if it makes you feel better. If she doesn't turn up right away, a detective would be assigned anyhow. But she probably just got lost or something, don'tcha think? I mean, you said she's what, eighty-four?"

"But she's sharp as a tack."

"Yeah, okay . . ."

Landis was quiet a moment, weighing the possibilities. A person finds her way around for eighty-four years, all of a sudden she can't, that is a little screwy. He wouldn't be surprised if she'd had a heart attack or been hit by a car and was in the hospital—or worse. But he didn't want to alarm Juliet.

"Anyway, I'll get myself over to your friend's B and B with a couple of the guys," he said aloud. "Say half an hour?"

Juliet went across the street to wait for him with Suzy. The "uniforms" got there first: a very young, very thin man named Glowacki and a thicker, more senior officer called Lopez. Landis arrived a few minutes later, in an unmarked car.

The last time Juliet had seen Murray was in late November, when she had gone to the opening of a show of sound art at Pierogi in Williamsburg. The artist was an acquaintance—someone she'd met through Suzy, in fact. Murray did a double take when he saw her, as if he could not believe that she, Juliet Bodine, had found her way across the river to Brooklyn. Despite his having spent four years at Harvard, it was always like that with him, this undercurrent of, "You're fancy, I'm regular; you're Manhattan, I'm Sheepshead Bay; you're class, I'm street." It bothered Juliet very much. She felt he would like her to wipe her nose with the back of her arm, or mangle her English, to show she was just folks. It seemed disingenuous on his part; she considered him a reverse snob and, as such, no better than the usual kind.

On the other hand, there was a lot to like about him. His mind was quick and original. She had visited his studio once and found his work extremely interesting. Soon afterward, he had asked her to brainstorm with him on the think-tank case. She admired him for reaching out to her that way. She admired him for choosing to do police work, which he clearly thought of as a way to help people. Moreover, she still found him good-looking, quintessentially male in a dark, lean, nervous way. Last summer, when their college attraction to each other had briefly, very quietly, made itself felt again, she had thought for a while that they might make the jump from casual friendship to romance, sex. Instead, Murray had choked on her, folding his arms when he ought to have reached for her, failing to call when he said he would. He had let it fizzle out—or maybe they both had. Maybe she had been equally timid, equally to blame for not giving the little spark the tinder, the oxygen it needed. Though Rob's lovely young actress had precipitated the final crisis, Juliet believed her marriage had collapsed in large part because her career had outstripped that of her husband. The experience had left her wary of men whose savings accounts were smaller than hers. And Murray, no doubt, had reasons of his own for keeping his distance from her. All the same, she liked him, respected him. Murray had substance. As her oldest friend, Molly, would put it, he was a person.

They kissed hello. She was surprised to feel her blood quicken with pleasure.

"Good to see you; thanks for coming," she murmured.

Murray said nothing, but his eyes held hers a moment longer than she would have expected. An instant longer, a split second.

Didn't they?

They all sat down in Suzy's living room. The toothbrush picture was done, Juliet noticed, and had been replaced by a sketch of a space-sauceresque CD. Murray's eyes wandered approvingly over the walls, where various examples of Suzy's past work hung, while Officer Lopez began a long series of questions, occasionally glancing at Landis as if he expected the detective to correct him. How old was the missing woman? What was her full name? Where did she live? Was she ill; was she on medication? When was the last time she had been seen, where, by whom, where was she planning to go after that? What was she wearing then? What did she look like? Did Suzy have a picture of her?

Suzy had no picture but went to her drawing board and, in a few pencil strokes, produced an extremely good likeness.

The questions resumed. Did she have credit cards? Suzy and Juliet rather thought not. She had not paid for her lodging yet, so they couldn't be sure. Did she own a car? It seemed very doubtful.

When the policemen had finished their questions, Officer Lopez explained what they would do. They would broadcast Mrs. Caffrey's name and description over the police radio, notify the MTA officers, the Port Authority, the airports. They'd run her name, description, and where she was last seen through the NCIC, a national data base listing people the police were looking for, send a description in if they didn't find her there already. They'd see if they could pick up a credit card charge—maybe she'd charged a theater ticket last night. They'd talk to the police in Espyville, get the names of some neighbors and relatives. And of course—Lopez gave another glance at Landis—they would check the New York hospitals. And the morgue.

If Suzy would kindly call her phone company now and get a

list of outgoing calls since Mrs. Caffrey arrived, that might help, too. It was a lot quicker for Suzy to ask for this than for the police to get it, they explained. They would also search her building from top to bottom, beginning with the old lady's room, if Suzy didn't mind.

At this, Suzy's hands, already tightly clasped together, began to writhe. Could they please just tell anyone they spoke to that a friend of hers had vanished, not a paying guest? A furtive awareness that she had never paid the tax due to the city for the room she rented out told her to keep her mouth shut, but the vision of cops knocking on her neighbors' doors, referring to "Ms. Eisenman's bed-and-breakfast" trumped this. Lopez and Glowacki had no objection.

As Suzy picked up the phone to call MCI, they went into Ada's room. Landis also stood up to go. He winked at Juliet.

"I'll get back to the house now and get ahold of my partner. We'll call your friend Dennis, start from that end, retrace her steps. Don't worry," he added, smiling into Juliet's anxious face. "We're gonna find her. She's gotta be somewhere, right?"

He meant it for comfort. But both women immediately pictured Ada dead.

chapter FIVE

Mrs. Caffrey Back Again

On the following Tuesday, the day when Ada Caffrey indeed proved to be "somewhere," Juliet was busy making Selena Walkingshaw discourse with her younger sister on the always interesting (Juliet hoped) topic of love.

The two girls were seated in a gazebo at their uncle's estate waiting for a summer shower to pass. Catherine was arguing that love between man and woman was a thing apart from other kinds of affection. Romantic love, she said, "comes suddenly and gives the heart no more notice than a springing tiger."

But Selena (thinking secretly of Sir James, of course—she was unaware of Captain Vizor's infatuation with her) insisted that, like friendship, romantic attachment could grow "quietly, by degrees, from affinity through affection and so on to—"

Here Selena blushed, to the puzzlement of her sister, who was evidently too much of a dork to realize her sister was in love with Sir James. Neither lady mentioned that they were having this conversation only because the author responsible for them was vamping until she could come up with the next piece of plot, though that would have been truer and more to the point than their various observations.

Instead, Selena was attempting to divert her sister's attention from her own scarlet cheeks by pointing out a cardinal perched on a nearby branch (were there cardinals in England in 1813? Did they turn up in the spring? Were they rare enough that it would be worth a person's breath to point one out?) when the phone rang in Ames's office. A few moments later, there was a reluctant tap on Juliet's door.

"I'm so sorry, Dr. Bodine—"

"That's okay," Juliet called. "What is it?"

"Detective Landis is on the phone."

Ames opened the door, and at the sight of her large, plain face, Juliet felt a jolt of fear. For once, blankness had eluded her assistant: Ames was upset, and Juliet thought she knew why. Four days had passed since Ada's disappearance, but the police had found nothing.

It wasn't for lack of trying. On the contrary, they had been extremely thorough. Glowacki and Lopez had turned Mrs. Caffrey's room upside down, checked Suzy's building from rooftop to basement for any trace of the missing woman, asked all the neighbors whether they'd seen her come in that Friday, canvassed Riverside from there to Rara Avis—and past it—for people who might have noticed her on the street. They went door to door on the side streets, first with Suzy's sketch, later with a photograph FedExed down by Cindy Giddy, the neighbor who sometimes helped Mrs. Caffrey with errands and who was now looking after her cats. (A call made Wednesday evening to Tom and Cindy Giddy's number had turned up on the print-out from Suzy's phone company; indeed, Suzy remembered overhearing the call. Her guest had asked how "Zsa Zsa and Marilyn" were and had mentioned she would not be home before Saturday, since she had an "important appointment" Friday afternoon.) The photograph, taken from a local newspaper account of an AdirondActors's production of *Arsenic and Old Lace* some twenty years before, was somewhat misleading—it made Mrs. Caffrey look like a sweet old lady, as Juliet pointed out. But Mrs. Giddy said it was the best she could find, and along with Suzy's sketch, it gave a pretty good idea of the missing woman's appearance.

With all of this, no trace of Mrs. Caffrey or her purse had shown up. Nor was the manuscript found. It wasn't among the old lady's things in Suzy's spare room. Dennis didn't have it—though he didn't have a receipt showing he'd given it back to its owner, either. John Fitzjohn, the collector who had also been at Rara Avis that Friday afternoon, said he had not noticed where it was when he left the dealer's.

With his partner, Lizzie McKenna, Murray himself conducted the interviews with Dennis, with his elusive client Fitzjohn, with Pierre the waiter, even with Parker Scutt. Together, they reinterviewed the only person who did remember seeing Ada Caffrey on Friday afternoon: Ernesto Guerro, the doorman on duty that day at Juliet's building. He remembered Mrs. Caffrey from the day he'd first announced her, the day she and her antique suitcase had first arrived in New York. He had noticed her going out in the blizzard with Ms. Bodine's friend Suzy around three or so on Friday; it stuck in his mind because the veiled purple hat looked so funny in all that snow. And yeah, he did think he saw her go back in—maybe an hour or so later, with a big guy in a dark hat and a dark jacket. Was that any help?

Daignault confirmed that Mrs. Caffrey arrived at his place at three-thirty and left perhaps half an hour later, going into the elevator with Fitzjohn, a collector of erotica who had come to look at the manuscript. She had been angry at Dennis when she left because she thought he was undervaluing the manuscript, trying to take advantage of an old lady. He'd offered her five thousand dollars for it; she wanted many times that. All in all, it had been an unfortunate interaction.

During her visit, Mr. Fitzjohn had been examining the manuscript. Before handing it back to Mrs. Caffrey, Dennis had placed it inside an archival glassine envelope. He was quite sure she had taken it. She also had in her hands a purple purse and a paperback romance novel with a picture of a girl in a long dress on the cover.

Was the book Angelica Kestrel-Haven's *Cousin Cecilia*? Ms. Bodine had told them Ada was carrying the Wilson manuscript inside a copy of *Cousin Cecilia* when they first met.

It might have been, Daignault thought. But it might not; he hadn't really noticed. Not to be rude, and please don't tell Juliet, but all romance novels looked kind of alike to him. Even Juliet's titles tended to run together in his head.

Landis gave him a disparaging look verging on frank dislike. Juliet had said just enough about Daignault to let Landis guess the two had been dating. However, Ada's signed copy of *Cousin Cecilia* had already been sought out and found in her bedroom at Suzy's, along with three other Angelica Kestrel-Haven books.

Landis and McKenna caught up with John Fitzjohn, an investment analyst, at his office in a glass monolith near Grand Central Station. Fortyish, six feet tall, blond, trim as a Navy SEAL, Fitzjohn received them with ostentatious signs that he was a busy man, too busy for such an interview. He had looked at the manuscript while Daignault and the owner argued about it, he said. It was a nice property, but he wasn't interested in buying. Yes, he remembered using the bathroom shortly before he left the dealer's. He then went downstairs with Mrs. Caffrey, talked to her briefly, shook her hand on the sidewalk outside the building, then walked away east on Eighty-eighth Street while she went south on Riverside.

What was he wearing? McKenna asked. Did he remember?

"God, I don't know. What does it matter?" Fitzjohn had said. "Probably jeans and a flannel shirt. It was casual Friday. Doc Martens."

And his outerwear?

Fitzjohn nodded to a coatrack in a corner of his impressive office. On it hung a navy blue down jacket and a black knit cap with a design of white skiers knitted in.

And where had he gone when he left Mrs. Caffrey? Back to work?

No, it was after four, and the office was practically shut down on account of the blizzard. He'd gone—he'd gone for a walk through Central Park. Walked all the way home, in fact. He liked the snow.

McKenna and Landis had both felt the lie in his answer, but you can't arrest a man for wearing a hat and a jacket.

On the chance that Ada had gone to the East Village slam, not realizing it had been canceled, they checked with bus drivers and token clerks who might have seen her heading downtown.

Nada.

The club, called Jade, had itself been locked and shuttered, the manager home in Queens. Doug Renny, who emceed the slam at the Ashtray and was slated to do the same that Friday night at Jade, lived around the corner on Avenue A. He remembered Ada Caffrey—who could fail to?—and admitted he had gone to Jade around 9:00 P.M. to put up a notice saying the rondeau slam would be rescheduled. But he had seen neither Ada nor anyone else he recognized there, he said, and had gone straight back home, where he had stayed until the following morning. No, he could not produce a witness to verify that claim. Since when was it against the law to stay at home reading Wisława Szymborska during a blizzard?

Pierre Goujon, waiter *élégant et extraordinaire,* had spent Friday afternoon at the dentist's office, where he had endured an extremely painful emergency extraction, followed by a codeine-aided fourteen-hour sleep.

Parker Scutt did know Suzy had a boarder when he stayed at her place Friday night, but he never saw her or any trace of her. To be honest, he had forgotten all about her in the heat of—you know, the moment. He'd woken up at six, scribbled a note for Suzy, and left without seeing anyone.

Calls to Espyville and Gloversville were equally fruitless. Claudia Lunceford, whom police in Gloversville identified as Mrs. Caffrey's closest relation—she was a niece—had neither heard from her Aunt Ada nor, her tone added, cared. No local cab had picked Ada up at the fitfully manned train station, where no one had seen her arrive, nor at the bus depot. The friend Ada had mentioned to Juliet, Matt McLaurin, the one who took the old lady to slams in Albany, said he had last heard from Ada the day before she left for Manhattan.

In New York no hospital or shelter had a match. Nor had the morgue. A description of the manuscript had been posted on the NCIC, but so far, no dealer had reported having seen it. Landis and McKenna worked the case on and off all weekend. By Sunday, they had three candidates for the big man Ernesto Guerro thought he had seen: Fitzjohn, Daignault—he was maybe five ten, not tall, but husky—and Doug Renny. Guerro had seen Mr. Daignault at least once, when he came to visit Ms. Bodine. At first, he believed this might have been the man he saw with Mrs. Caffrey on Friday.

But when Landis and McKenna came back to talk to him on Sunday afternoon, Guerro was having second thoughts. He was not so sure Mrs. Caffrey had really been with the guy he'd noticed anyway. It might have been just some guy going by on the sidewalk behind her. Come to think of it, maybe he hadn't seen Mrs. Caffrey twice. He wasn't really thinking about her at the time, you know, he was busy shoveling snow from the sidewalk; and hundreds of people passed his building on any given shift; and he had worked two shifts that day on account of the night man couldn't get in on account of the snow.

It was, inarguably, a thorough investigation, and by Monday, when Landis had phoned to fill Juliet in on the weekend's progress, she could hear in his voice that he thought the worst. And so, as Catherine Walkingshaw might have said, on Tuesday morning, when Ames came in to say Landis was on the phone, the conviction that he was calling to tell her Ada was dead sprang upon Juliet like a tiger.

"Jule," came Murray's voice over the phone, not shouting today but quiet, almost gentle, "listen, I hate to say it, but I just heard a body turned up in the precinct this morning that I think has to be your friend. She had on the sealskin coat you described and even the purple gloves and hat, and a purple purse with a Social Security card belonging to Ada Caffrey was . . . ah, was with the body. No manuscript, though. Eventually we're going to need a family member to make a positive ID. But as a matter of practicality, you think you'd wanna come down to the morgue and take a look?"

Juliet resisted the temptation to say no, hang up, and forget she had ever heard of Ada Case Caffrey.

"If it would help," she said, her voice small and tight.

"I could ask Suzy Eisenman—"

"No, it's okay. Where was the"—there was a pause as she forced herself to say the word—"the body?"

"Inside a plastic garbage bag, shoved under the back end of a Nissan Xterra parked on Riverside. Right near you. Whoever it was did a neat job—shoved her in, tossed the purse in too, and knotted up the top nice and tight. Nobody knew she was there till this morning, when the owner of the vehicle finally went out with a shovel to dig it out of the snow. They've still got him down here now, but it doesn't look like he did it. Guy's almost seventy himself, Puerto Rican, owns a dry-cleaning shop up in Harlem. It's hard to see a connection."

"Where do I need to go?"

"I'll get a car and pick you up," Murray offered. "How's fifteen minutes?"

Juliet gave her pages to Ames and dressed to go out in a sort of trance. Downstairs, she slid into the passenger seat of an unmarked car and kissed Murray's cheek. It was scratchy, like Daddy's in the *Pat the Bunny.*

"I'm sorry about this," he said, squeezing her arm.

Though it was the first time they'd been alone together in months, they drove across the city mostly in silence. Juliet asked how Murray's New Year's had been ("Quiet") and whether he was finding time to sculpt ("Some"). If he was curious about her New Year's, her work, he contained himself. It crossed her mind to ask him why he hadn't come to the New Year's Day open house she'd invited him to—he hadn't even RSVP'd—but she decided not to bring it up.

Instead, "How did she die, can they tell?" she asked, her voice even smaller than usual.

"Well, it's nothing official yet, but it looks to the guys like someone strangled her. She's got what they call petechial hemorrhages, which you get if the jugular vein is obstructed, on her face. And there are marks on her neck consistent with manual strangulation. Also, the way she was lying—"

"No, no. That's okay," Juliet interrupted faintly. She tried to smile. "Sorry I asked."

The rest of the way, they drove in silence. At the morgue, Murray parked and came around to her side of the car to lead her in. She checked on the doorstep, then forced herself forward. Juliet suffered from hyperosmia, an abnormally keen sense of smell; for her, the world was a constant barrage of odors she could not ignore. Murray, for example, smelled of Mennen deodorant, Ivory soap, and the coffee he had had that morning; the car he came in held the lingering scent of someone else's sweat and a pork sandwich that had probably spent part of the night in the glove compartment. She had been dreading the odors of the morgue.

But only the faintest chemical scent, if that, reached this administrative floor. Murray ushered her into a drab little room off the lobby. Still, as she filled out a form testifying to her own identity, Juliet braced herself for a visit to a nauseating room full of oversized file drawers, from one of which Ada's corpse would be rolled out.

But that was in olden times, Murray informed her.

"We found some people had problems with trauma after a thing like that, so nowadays we just show you a Polaroid. Which I'll go and get."

He was gone a few minutes, then returned with a square, very recent snapshot (Juliet imagined she could smell the developing solution on its surface) of an old woman's very dead but only slightly distorted face. Ada Caffrey's sojourn under the snow on Riverside Drive had preserved the little flapper nicely. Juliet recognized her at a glance.

Her stomach gave an alarming lurch, and she felt the color drain from her face. Tactfully, Murray took the picture away.

"It's Ada," Juliet said. "Poor woman. Poor woman."

Juliet asked for the ladies' room, stumbled down a corridor, and washed her face with cold water again and again. The chemical undertone in the morgue's air, whether real or imagined, seemed to bang at her head like a little hammer.

"Poor old lady," she said, when she rejoined Landis in the office. "Imagine living eighty-four peaceful years out in the middle of the country, only to come to New York and finish up a victim of random violence." And she shuddered with shame that the city, her city, could do this to a guest.

"Oh, I don't think this was random, Jule," Landis said. He eyed her strangely. "Her purse was with her, with cash in it, but that manuscript wasn't. Anyway, street thugs don't generally stuff their victims into bags for neat disposal. And the ME says she was strangled. That's up close and personal. Unless it's a maniac, like a serial murderer or something, I believe we'll find Mrs. Caffrey was killed by somebody she knew."

chapter

SIX

Dennis Makes Dinner

Dennis Daignault was poaching raspberries in a sauce of chicken stock, crème fraîche, and crushed tomatoes. He had insisted on cooking dinner for Suzy and Juliet, despite the kind of day all three of them had had.

"Cooking makes me feel better," he had said. "When I cook, I am king. Vegetables accede to my slightest whim."

"If they do, who am I to quibble?" said Juliet, who rarely felt so out of place as when in front of an oven.

An hour later she and Suzy arrived at his place to find a silver cocktail shaker on the coffee table, ready with gin and dry vermouth, next to it tiny bowls of olives and translucent cocktail onions. The candlelit dinner table that sat at one end of his long kitchen was set with rose-and-white Wedgwood china. Real roses, pale pink and peach, had been strewn over the starched white tablecloth.

Juliet and Suzy exchanged a glance. Juliet had complained to Suzy about Dennis's habit of setting the scene, and Suzy had accused her of trying to think of reasons not to let him get close to her. But Suzy had never been to Dennis's house, nor even spent more than a few minutes talking to him. Now Juliet could see her mind changing. Dennis's apartment *was* stagy. It was weird, the result of insecurity on his part about being himself, probably, but hard to relax around even so. Of course Juliet, too, could put on a show—the tea with scones she had served to Ada Caffrey, for example—but that really was a show, the Angelica Kestrel-Haven Show, trotted out for visiting fans and journalists on a regular basis.

Dennis gave them cocktails and sat them down at the dinner table. Until dinner was finished, he forbade any discussion of criminal matters. Suzy and Juliet watched him roll the berries in the simmering sauce, then gently drizzle the concoction over the waiting chicken breasts. With a proud flourish, his cheeks flushed from the kitchen's heat, he set the resulting platter down in front of them.

"Suprêmes de volaille aux framboises," he announced. "A soupçon of summer in the dark of winter."

He removed his denim apron and sat down, pushing a few damp strands of his fair hair back from his forehead. Dennis Daignault was blond and thickset, with the pink complexion of a Gainsborough subject and sharp blue eyes. He was not, in fact, athletic—perhaps his clubfoot was to blame—but he looked as if he ought to be. Like Byron, he worried a lot about his weight, dieting often. Juliet recognized that he was an attractive man, although, unfortunately, she herself was finding him less and less so.

"Bon appetit," he said.

The women thanked him and plied their flatware with a will. They spoke of the weather, of the snow turning to slush, of the economy likewise, of the war on terrorism and the legacy it might have for civil rights. Dennis entertained them with a long, intricate story concerning a nineteenth-century translation of the Bible, then another about a new means of detecting seismic activity. Only when the last bite had been consumed, the last fork set down, did he agree to let the others raise what was on all their minds. All three had been questioned by the police that afternoon, the women relatively briefly, Dennis for more than three hours.

"That Skelton guy," he said, while water for coffee boiled in an electric kettle. "Wow, I thought I was going to pop him one. 'Go over your movements again, sir,' he kept saying—you know that sneering 'sir' the police use, that means 'you piece of human scum.' 'Would you just take us through your movements last Friday one more time, sir.' 'I'm going to give you a paper and pen, sir. Would you write down your movements, please, for me and Detective Crowder?' "

For reasons Juliet didn't yet understand, Murray was no longer in charge of investigating what had happened to Ada. Instead, a Det. Jeffrey Skelton and his partner, Det. LaTonya Crowder, were on it. Skelton was in his middle thirties, a bear of a man with reddish hair and green eyes that glowered fiercely from his long, jowly face. Crowder was younger by a decade or so but almost as tall, with flawless, dark chocolate skin and fine, elongated features.

"Oh, Detective Crowder," Suzy put in, "that's the one I didn't like. She kept trying to butter me up, you know, play the female solidarity card. Smarmy."

"No one tried to butter me up," said Dennis bitterly. " 'Detective Crowder and I are not conversant with the fine points of rare manuscript dealing, sir.' Sarcastic bastard. 'Would you enlighten us as to the nature of your work, please? Could you explain again, please, why you obtained no receipt from Mrs. Caffrey when you returned the manuscript to her? Sir, could you describe to us what you made of the missing document? Sir, when you—' "

"Why didn't you get a receipt?" Juliet broke in. She knew Dennis wanted sympathetic indignation, but curiosity got the better of her.

"I tried, believe me," he said, immediately exasperated. "But she started to make such a fuss. I didn't want to throw fuel on the fire, especially with Fitzjohn standing there. Well, not standing there, actually," he corrected himself, "he was in the bathroom. But I knew he'd be out any minute. So I figured since she didn't have a receipt from me anyway—the receipt I gave you said I was receiving a manuscript belonging to her *from you,* not her, remember?—like an idiot, I figured we were friends, you knew me, you'd just tear it up. Then when everything went so haywire with Mrs. Caffrey missing and all, I really forgot about it."

"Oh."

Juliet was quiet a moment as she thought this over. She had been obliged to tell the police that she did, indeed, still have a receipt verifying that Dennis Daignault had received from Juliet Bodine three pages, apparently written by Harriette Wilson, belonging to Ada Caffrey. She had stuffed it into her jeans pocket after Dennis had signed it, then left it on her dresser, where all such bits of paper from her pockets spent a month or two before being noticed and discarded. She probably would have forgotten all about it if Ada had not disappeared. She saw now that it rather left Dennis holding the bag, but did not see how he could blame her. She felt uncomfortably, though, as if he might.

"And—And what did you make of the manuscript?" she asked.

"Ah, the manuscript." Dennis sighed deeply. "I guess we can safely throw professional discretion out the window now. Wait a minute."

Pushing his chair back, he stood and vanished into the living room. Soon he returned, holding three photocopied pages.

"Have you seen these?" he asked Suzy.

Suzy shook her head, and Dennis handed them to her. She bent her head and read avidly while he went into the kitchen to grind coffee beans. When Suzy looked up from her reading, he sat down again and resumed his explanation.

"Here's what I figure," he began. "Those pages were certainly written by Harriette Wilson. I found the place in the published memoirs where they were initially meant to appear—you can tell by the words "a dozen annuities" crossed out at the top. The phrase occurs in a passage about attending the opera while Harriette's protector, Lord Worcester, went off to war with the Duke of Wellington. The passage that was to follow, about Quiddenham, would have been a digression, quite out of chronological order. But that was typical of Harriette. In any case, it didn't appear.

"If it had, it certainly would have embarrassed the intended victim, Edward Hertbrooke, the future fourth Viscount Quiddenham. Edward was born in 1784, so he would have been quite young when he was—well, cross-dressing over at Harriette's place, and just over forty when she tried to blackmail him. He came from a solid family, not wildly rich, but well-to-do, and he married a woman with a substantial settlement. When his father died, he came into quite a bit of money."

The kettle boiled and Dennis went into the kitchen again to make the coffee, still talking.

"But young Edward was a gambler," he said. "There's a reference to his addiction to faro in Greville's diary. It was a lifelong problem for him, and I imagine that when Harriette made her demand for payment, he was at a low point and not able to come up with it. By the time she'd written his section, though, he must have won or borrowed enough to pay her off. He sent the money to her where she was living in Paris, and she sent back the pages concerning him. She was as good as her word—there's no reference to Quiddenham at all in the memoirs. But instead of doing the sensible thing and burning the pages Harriette had written, Edward hid them. Who knows, maybe reading them still gave him a charge."

He came back to the table, bringing with him a tray of mugs. His tone, his whole demeanor, had become professional now. Juliet saw again what had initially attracted her about him. He was completely focused, absorbed. Even after all that had happened today, his face was lit with enthusiasm for the snippet of history that had been in his hands.

"I spoke to a furniture dealer about Mrs. Caffrey's rosewood bed," he was going on, "and we tracked it down to a catalog of items auctioned off in 1851, after Lord Quiddenham died in considerable debt. Obviously, his survivors were unaware of the hidden compartment in it, not to mention its contents. Such compartments—meant for hiding jewels and papers—were often built into desks of that period. It's less common to find one in a bed, though the dealer did know of at least one other, at a Louisiana plantation mansion called Nottoway; legend has it that important documents were hidden there during the Civil War. Anyway, Mrs. Caffrey's bed was purchased by a traveling American, a prosperous Connecticut shipbuilder who was spending a year in England with his wife and oldest daughter. He must have had it brought over here, because it was sold about thirty years later to someone in Woodstock, New York. That's who Mrs. Caffrey's husband bought it from in 1952. It's all quite legitimate."

"And the handwriting matches Harriette Wilson's?" asked Juliet.

"Oh, definitely. That was the easiest thing to check. In 1975, an English scholar named Kenneth Bourne published a book called *The Blackmailing of the Chancellor,* which details the correspondence between Harriette and one of her many lovers, Henry Brougham. Besides being a literary man—as it happens, he was the Scots critic who lambasted Byron's first published book of poems in the *Edinburgh Review,* prompting Byron to retaliate with the satirical *English Bards and Scotch Reviewers*—Brougham was an extraordinarily able lawyer. In 1820, when George IV tried to divorce Queen Caroline, Brougham successfully defended her. He was an influential member of Parliament and, years after his liaison with Harriette, Lord Chancellor of England. According to Bourne, he kept on Harriette's good side by acting, however unwillingly, as her de facto legal adviser during the hysteria the memoirs set off. There are—"

"Hysteria?" Suzy interrupted.

"Oh. Well, the main part of the memoirs, the first four volumes, were published in installments, you see, twelve installments between January and April of 1825. At the end of each, there were hints about who was going to be exposed next. People lined up in the streets to get the first glimpse of each new section—such big crowds that traffic was brought to a halt. The publisher had to put up barricades in front of his store on the days new installments appeared—you know the kind of madness. Like at Madison Square Garden when a Springsteen concert is announced. They were translated into French and German; they appeared in dozens of pirated editions; the newspapers were full of outraged and amused accounts of them—they were even mentioned in Parliament. If you think of what happened when the transcripts of Monica Lewinsky's testimony on Clinton appeared in the *Times,* you'll get a pretty fair idea of the stir Harriette's memoirs caused. And hers went on appearing for months. Harriette and her publisher, John Joseph Stockdale, made a huge amount of money—about ten thousand pounds. That's hard to convert into current U.S. dollars, figure maybe a couple of mill. But there were also lawsuits and disagreements between author and publisher, and that's where having Henry Brougham in your pocket came in so handy, you see.

"Anyway, in his book about Harriette and Brougham, Bourne includes transcriptions of some of her letters—one written from the very same address as Mrs. Caffrey's letter—as well as a couple of photostats. It's certainly Harriette's writing."

"And the Byron—?"

"Ah, the Byron."

Dennis leaned forward, his hands cupped around the red-and-white mug before him. Everything in Dennis's apartment was color-coordinated, and the mugs matched not only the dishes but the curtains, the throw pillows on the couch, and a couple of lampshades.

"Well, there are existing letters from Wilson to Byron. But we have only her word for it that he wrote back. As to the couplet, I've been in touch with a Byron scholar, a former professor of my own, in fact," he went on. "The word 'unseam' does appear in Byron's *Childe Harold.* And in the first canto of *Don Juan,* he rhymes 'virtue' with 'hurt you.' But did he ever say what Harriette reports him as saying, or was she or someone around her clever enough to invent a plausible couplet? That is the question—and unless some hitherto unknown letter or diary or suchlike comes to light, it isn't likely anyone will ever be able to answer it."

"Too bad," said Juliet.

"Yes," agreed Dennis. "Too bad. It was my explanation of just that very regrettable fact that made Ada Caffrey so angry with me. Once I assured her the manuscript was almost surely legit, she insisted the couplet had to be Byron, a fragment of unpublished Byron. And that should make the manuscript very valuable indeed, she thought. Which it would, if it could be proven. I suppose the manuscript might go for as much as a hundred thousand, if the Byron link proved authentic.

"But there seems to be no way to authenticate it. So it remains a curiosity. According to Bourne, the last anyone heard of the rest of Wilson's manuscript of the memoirs was late in the 1840s, when Stockdale's widow wrote to Brougham to say she had it. The crossed-out passages were still legible, she kindly informed him, and though she'd hate to have to publish them, she did need money badly. She also had Harriette's letters to her late husband, she said, detailing who had bought out and should be excised, and who had not. Bourne speculates that Brougham purchased the whole thing from her and burnt it. Quiddenham's pages may be the only ones that survived.

"Now, Harriette Wilson was not Byron. She wasn't Thomas Moore, either, or Leigh Hunt, or even John Hunt. The manuscript is short and of limited scholarly interest. I offered Mrs. Caffrey five thousand, an entirely appropriate amount considering that the Byron can never be authenticated—if anything, it was a little generous, I'd say. When she questioned me, I admitted that I hoped to sell it for more than that—maybe twice that, which again is a perfectly ordinary proportion, ask any dealer.

"Well, Mrs. Caffrey saw red. Why should I get twice what she got? And why should it only be worth ten thousand anyway, why not a hundred thousand, a thousand thousand? Byron wasn't writing more poems now, she knew that!

"I explained my profit was recompense for my expertise, for knowing what it was, how to research it, what to do with it, how to sell it—and for selling it. I offered to take it on consignment. I told her if she could wait a bit, let me build up some interest, I'd be willing to keep just 15 percent of whatever it fetched. But by then she was in a fury. I was chiseling her, I was bilking her, I was holding out. It wasn't a very nice scene, our little visit."

He said this with his eyes on Juliet, who immediately began to apologize for having brought him into the business in the first place. Dennis had already told her some of this part of the story when Mrs. Caffrey had first gone missing. She had apologized to him then, as well.

"Oh, well, don't apologize!" he said. He put a large hand over hers. "You couldn't have had any idea. What was unfortunate was that, at that very moment, John Fitzjohn dropped in for a visit. He's a client I've had for a long time," he explained to Suzy, "who collects nineteenth-century erotica. I called him the same day Juliet brought me the manuscript because I thought that, at age eighty-four, Mrs. Caffrey might like a nice, quick sale. Fitzjohn said he'd stop by in the next day or two and take a look. It was just pure bad luck that he happened to do it right in time to hear Mrs. Caffrey throwing a fit in my living room."

Dennis shook his head at the recollection of that fraught, uncomfortable moment. "God, how I wish you'd still been in when I called to say I'd come down to you," he told Suzy.

Suzy looked uneasy. "Did you—did you leave a message?" she said tentatively. "Maybe my answering machine—

"No, I didn't leave a message." Dennis gave her a controlled glare, fully aware she was questioning his word. The police had raised this matter, too. "What would have been the point?"

He took a sip of coffee, trying to compose himself.

"Fitzjohn phoned me a couple of hours ago, by the way," he went on presently, "completely enraged. The police questioned him today, too. They didn't even tell him Mrs. Caffrey was dead till they'd been at him for an hour. He thought she was missing, bent over backward to give them all the details, never thought of calling a lawyer . . . Well, he's called a lawyer now."

"Jesus, how many people did they talk to today?" asked Suzy.

Dennis shrugged. "It's because he left here with Mrs. Caffrey—much against my wishes, I may add, but she insisted on getting into the elevator with him. He was the last to see her. Now he's calling other dealers to complain about the zoo I run. Oh, he's a lovely man."

"Maybe he did it," Juliet said.

"Fitzjohn? Killed her?"

She nodded.

Dennis closed his eyes and cocked his head, thinking. Or rather, Juliet couldn't help noticing, looking like somebody who was thinking. Like a caricature of thought. She couldn't see what required so much cogitation: To her mind, Fitzjohn seemed an ideal suspect. Right place, right time, good motive—the manuscript—nasty sort. In a few words, she said as much.

"I suppose it's possible," Dennis finally conceded.

"But why?" This from Suzy. "Couldn't he have bought the manuscript if he'd wanted it? You said he was rich."

"Yes, he is. And, as a matter of fact, he told me that when they went downstairs together, Mrs. Caffrey offered to sell it to him directly."

"See? How much did she want?" Suzy asked curiously.

"Twenty thousand dollars." Dennis shook his head again and gave a gloomy laugh. "I guess she really did think I was trying to cheat her. But Fitzjohn had taken a look at the pages even while she was berating me, and he wasn't very intrigued. That's not so surprising; collectors of erotica generally want something with pictures, something a little less genteel than what Mrs. Caffrey had to offer. I only thought of him because he is big on the nineteenth century. And he spends pretty freely when he sees something he wants. It's more likely a university would buy it, for a women's studies collection, say. But probably not so quickly, and not for as much money as Fitzjohn would pay.

"Not that it will sell to anyone now," he added darkly, "considering that it's missing."

"You don't think the police will track it down?"

"If someone tries to sell it to a reputable dealer, yeah, they'll probably nab it. I gave them a copy of my photocopy. They've put it out through their art theft unit on the NCIC, and the Antiquarian Booksellers Association will alert their members. But that only works if whoever has it tries to sell it. The police seem to think the thief will keep it. In fact, they wanted to come over here and look around. See if she left it here by accident, is what they said. But my lawyer said no way should I let them."

"You called a lawyer?"

"Didn't you guys?"

Suzy shook her head.

"Me, neither," Juliet said.

"Why not? Didn't they question you?"

"Oh, God, yes," Juliet replied. "How did I meet Ada, when did she arrive, what did we do together, how long was the manuscript in my hands, why did I suggest she take it to you, why did I still have the receipt, where was I on Friday—I already said in the missing persons investigation that I never left my house that day; you would think they could look it up—who did she mention when we were talking, who did I think might want to kill her, where was I on Friday, where was I on Friday, where was I on—well, you get the picture."

"And you never thought to call a lawyer?"

"Well, you know, I thought of it, of course—but they were perfectly polite. And they said if I had nothing to hide, why would I need a lawyer? And I don't have anything to hide, so . . ."

As she heard her own answer, Juliet began to wonder if she had, after all, been very foolish indeed.

More defensively, she added, "It was just an interview. I was there of my own free will. And I couldn't help feeling that as long as I didn't call a lawyer, I was merely a friendly source of information. But once I did, I'd be a suspect."

"You already are a suspect," Dennis said. "We all are."

"You think?" asked Suzy.

"Are you kidding?" Dennis's normally pink cheeks went a little pinker, and he stood up abruptly from the table. "Of course we are. What did they ask you?"

"Oh, pretty much what they asked Juliet, I guess," Suzy said, her small, pale face looking rather dazed. "Except I did go out on Friday, of course. They asked me about Parker, too. I guess they'll talk to him."

"Parker's the man who Suzy—" Juliet began to explain for Dennis's benefit.

But he cut her off. "Yes, you told me. Listen, both of you should talk to lawyers," he said, with what seemed to Juliet unusual decisiveness for him. "It's naive not to. If you want, I'll give you my guy's name."

Suzy, who didn't particularly have the money to consult a lawyer, said nothing. Juliet, wondering what business it was of Dennis's whether she hired one or not, murmured that she'd think about it. Privately, she decided to ask Murray what he recommended.

Then, to change the subject, "Did you ever find out if Viscount Quiddenham was related to General Quiddenham?" she asked.

"Oh, yes," Dennis answered, calming down almost instantly. He drew out his chair and sat again. "And yes, the general was our viscount's son. As it happens, his great-great-grandson—I think that's the right number of greats—" He paused and counted on his fingers. "Well, anyway, a descendant, recently published a biography of the general. And yes, you were right, there is a group of people in favor of removing his statue from Pall Mall. I found a news story from a couple of years ago on the Web. It's something Ken Livingstone, the mayor of London, was advocating: sending a whole bunch of Great Marble Men of British imperialism from London to the provinces—or the guillotine."

"I don't imagine his family are very happy about that," Juliet said.

"You bet your saber they're not. Oddly enough, there's a Quiddenham descendant living in New York City right now. Son of the general's biographer. I talked to him. Michael Hertbrooke."

"The gossip columnist?" Suzy exclaimed. Suzy, as Juliet knew, was a loyal reader of the tabloids.

"That's the one. He's mentioned on the jacket flap of his father's book. I called him to see if he'd be interested in buying the manuscript."

"Was he?" Suzy asked.

"Yes, he was. Interested enough to come and take a look, anyway. He was here Friday morning."

"The Friday Ada disappeared? You never told me that," Juliet said, looking at him hard.

"Have I ever told you about *any* of my clients? Except for Fitzjohn, I mean. I don't talk about clients. That's the way this business is; you don't go around telling everybody everything. It's that question of professional discretion again. That's why I never filled you in on my research until now. Until I got the okay from Mrs. Caffrey, I only spoke to a select few potential buyers. I'm particularly careful about keeping my mouth shut and my profile low; I'm known for it. And that," he added darkly, "is why it's so crappy that John Fitzjohn is phoning around to dump on my good name."

"Oh."

There was a moment of silence while all three contemplated the prospect of Rara Avis in commercial ruins. Juliet had never been quite sure how successful Dennis was. He seemed to do pretty well—witness the silver cocktail shaker and the ready supply of raspberries—but he had recently let her know he also took on insurance appraisals and odd bits of cataloging for auction houses now and then. That was not the sort of work people did for the love of it. She wondered if Rara Avis was less prosperous than she had thought. She also wondered if Dennis's ideas of professional discretion weren't a bit exaggerated.

Of course, exaggeration of a certain kind seemed to be his stock-in-trade.

Finally, "But what made you call Michael Hertbrooke?" she asked.

"Just routine. Sooner or later, I call everybody I can think of who might have an interest in a property."

"And did he want to buy it?" Suzy prompted.

"I'm not sure. He asked me the price," Dennis answered. "I told him I'd have to run it by the owner when she came in later, but I thought about ten thousand. He just laughed. He said I must think gossip columnists are a lot better paid than they are."

"Did he seem upset?" Juliet asked.

"Upset?"

"Like he thought you were threatening him, holding his feet to the fire?"

"No, he just said—Holding his feet to the fire?"

"Well, yes," said Juliet. "I mean, he must have thought you were trying to blackmail him."

"Blackmail?"

"Sure. Especially with his ancestor's statue in jeopardy, don't you think he'd read your call that way?"

"I never thought of it," Dennis replied slowly. "I mean, I realized it was sort of funny to call him because he is a gossip columnist. But I always look for descendants if something comes in with a name on it like that. If Harriette Wilson had had descendants I could trace, I'd have called them, too."

"But, Dennis, didn't it strike you that his family wouldn't want this manuscript published?"

"A little snippet about a great-great-great-whatever-grandfather having been a cross-dresser two centuries ago?" He shook his head, smiling a confused smile. "Who would care? And anyway, who said anything about it being published?"

He paused briefly, looking from one to the other of his guests. Both were looking back at him as if urging him to think, think. "Although I did—" he resumed, then stopped.

"You did what?" Juliet prodded.

Dennis's cheeks had gone pinker again. "I may have mentioned to Hertbrooke that I'd thought of contacting a friend at the *Times*. Sometimes if you can get a little ink about an item—the Louisa May Alcott manuscript found in a trunkful of dress patterns in an attic, the Melville diary used for half a century to prop up an uneven table leg—you know the kind of thing, well, sometimes you can jack the price up quite a bit. So I mentioned I might call this culture reporter I know at the *Times*. But I only said it because it occurred to me that, as a journalist, Hertbrooke might know her. I didn't mean to threaten him!"

There was another silence. Then Juliet said quietly, "Speaking of naive."

"Did you tell the police about this?" Suzy asked, as yet another uncomfortable silence grew.

"Of course. I told them everything, everyone I talked to about the manuscript. I told them what I had for breakfast this morning, for chrissake. Whatever they asked me, I told them." He dropped his head into his hands and ran his fingers through his pale hair, then looked up and shrugged. "Anyway, it doesn't matter now what Michael Hertbrooke thought. The manuscript's gone."

"So it is. But I wouldn't say it doesn't matter what Hertbrooke thought," Juliet said. "Mrs. Caffrey is dead."

"Yes. But—sorry, how does that relate to Michael Hertbrooke exactly?" Dennis looked at her blankly.

"Well, you called him, Dennis. And then somebody killed her," Juliet explained. "Cause, effect. Couldn't it be?"

chapter SEVEN

Murray Makes Dinner

Juliet spent the following day at a ruined abbey some miles from Spafford House, in company with Selena and Catherine Walkingshaw.

As his author expected he might, Sir James Clendinning had indeed turned up here, having come to view a model farm in the vicinity. Sir James was a great enthusiast of the new system of large farms; he had already visited with both John Ellman and Charles Colling to learn their systems of breeding sheep and cattle, and was now determined to profit by the experience of Lord Spafford's neighbor, the Hon. Francis Browne, a celebrated breeder of bulls. Sir James had spent a morning in the company of Sir Francis who, having known the Misses Walkingshaw from girls, happened to mention to his visitor that they were even now in the neighborhood.

Having learned this much, Sir James promptly went to Spafford House to pay his respects. Rather depressingly, though, on learning of their intention to have a pique-nique on the grounds of the erstwhile abbey, the virtuous Sir James chose to question whether such a meal might not be disrespectful to the holy brotherhood who had lived and worshiped there three hundred years before. Nevertheless, in the end, he had agreed to accompany the sisters, giving Selena another shot at jolting him out of his maddening catatonia.

At four-thirty, with a considerable sense of satisfaction, Juliet handed Ames seven handwritten pages and went back into her office to phone Murray. This whole business of whether she ought to call a lawyer had her perplexed. If she called one, whoever she called would no doubt say that she should. If she didn't, she left herself without legal advice.

To her surprise, she again reached Landis at his desk at the station house on the first try. His tone was businesslike. But the content was quite otherwise.

"This is not a good time for me to talk," he said, as soon as she started hemming and hawing about asking his advice. "Could you come over to my place late tonight, say around eleven-thirty? I don't get off till eleven."

Murray Landis had never before invited Juliet to his apartment. Indeed, it had taken many weeks for her to get him to show her the work in his studio. After the death at the Jansch had been resolved, when he had called to ask for her help with the think-tank killing, Juliet had briefly foreseen an ongoing crime-solving alliance of some sort between them. In fact, she had thought of trying to get a PI's license. As a writer, Juliet had a habit of getting—not *blocked,* she did not like to use that harsh, alarming term—but of taking, one might say, the scenic route to getting a manuscript finished. Midway through a book (or earlier than midway, truth to tell) she often . . . refreshed her mind by enrolling in courses on various disciplines, Introduction to American Sign Language, for example, or Modern Pottery. These seemed to replenish her imagination, and certainly had the welcome effect of getting her temporarily out of a frustrating manuscript's clutches. Alas, however, she had learned that in New York State, becoming a private investigator was not merely a question of course work. Before taking the licensing exam, it was necessary to spend three years as a police detective, a federal agent, a state investigator, or an apprentice in the office of a licensed PI. Juliet's scenic routes were roundabout, but not as roundabout as that.

Still, she had gone to the Learning Annex and taken a short class on elementary detection. And she had looked into enrolling in the next available class of the Citizen's Police Academy, a miniversion of real police academy training intended to help civilians understand the law-enforcement officer's point of view. But then Murray had disappeared, and her thoughts had turned to batik. Now, although the proud owner of a unique and colorful set of handprinted dinner napkins, she wistfully recalled that missed opportunity to learn the secrets of New York's Finest.

Aloud, she said she would gladly be at his apartment at eleven-thirty if he would tell her where it was. This information, too, was something Murray had somehow never volunteered.

And so it happened that at 11:45 that night (she didn't want to appear too eager), Juliet pushed a button in the dim, cramped cubicle between two glass doors that led into a six-story walk-up at 229 West 107th Street, then stood and waited. A minute later she heard feet pounding down the concrete-and-metal stairs. A flash of boot and black denim appeared through the smudged glass door, followed by a shin, another, denimed thighs, crotch, red sweater, black turtleneck, Murray's sharp chin, his bony, olive-skinned face, smiling, his curling salt-and-pepper hair—Murray, whole, his arm extended to the handle to let her in. Drawing her into the warmth, the hard light, he bent and kissed her cold cheek.

"Sorry about this stupid door. You're supposed to be able to release the lock with the buzzer upstairs, but of course it hasn't worked in years," he said. "Come up. You want dinner?"

Juliet tried not to breathe audibly as she followed her host up the steep stairs. Detective Landis was lean, hard, all muscle and bone. Juliet Bodine, softly rounded, had an on-again-off-again relationship with the treadmill in her dressing room; any other exercise she got was pretty much accidental.

The door to 4R rested on its latch. Murray ushered her into a small entrance hall (at the moment deeply infused with the fragrance of teriyaki sauce); took her hat, gloves, scarf, coat; then gestured her into his living room. It was a good-sized room, with two large windows looking into a courtyard and over a few low roofs to 108th Street. The furniture was simple and spare—two small oatmeal-colored sofas facing one another across an uncluttered coffee table. But her general impression of the place was of sensory overload. Almost every inch of wall was covered with drawings and paintings, the small ones hung above and below one another three or four in a row, as in a Victorian picture gallery, the topmost just a few inches from the ceiling. Most were the work of so-called emerging artists, artists represented by small, struggling galleries in fringe neighborhoods, artists with perhaps one New York solo show or a few out of town on their résumés.

Drawn in, Juliet slowly began to circle the room. She saw only one of Murray's sculptures, a twisted marble archway perhaps eighteen inches high, the stone deliberately pitted along one side and pierced on the other by a smooth, tunnel-like hole. Shades of Henry Moore. It must have been quite old, she thought, since it was nothing like the work he had shown her in his studio last fall. That was all about—and largely fashioned of—light and shadow. Substance and illusion, Murray had said of these materials; good and evil, Juliet had thought. Still, his treatment of the traditional medium was interesting. She inspected it closely, dared to stroke it gently with an index finger, then wandered slowly from picture to picture, examining them with thoughtful pleasure. There was a small Ricci Albenda word picture, a bird by Cindy Kane; there was a biggish, early Christian Schumann, a Kenny Schachter computer-manipulated photo, a charged Jill Nathanson grid. Juliet could feel Murray standing behind her, watching her. He was, she felt, content for her to look.

Finally she turned, smiling, and said, "Very nice. You have some wonderful pieces."

He shrugged. "Friends, mostly." He roused himself. "I'm just making some stir-fry, do you want some?"

Juliet trailed him around the side of the L-shaped living room to a small kitchen adjoining the dining area. Like his living room, Murray's kitchen was sparsely furnished and immaculately kept. A set of thick, blue mugs hung below the white wooden cabinets, a couple of copper-bottomed pots were suspended over the stove, a white dish rack sat beside the sink, a white microwave oven was tucked into a corner. On the range sat a large wok filled with sauteed broccoli, carrots, onions, and cabbage, and a small, covered pot that her nose told her contained jasmine rice. Other than these objects, nothing showed. There was not a fork out of place, not a broccoli leaf on the small, bright Formica counter. Juliet wondered if Murray had tidied especially for her or if he always lived like this. She suspected the latter.

"Thanks, I've eaten."

"Want a drink?" he offered. "Wine? Scotch? Vodka?"

Juliet accepted a small scotch and water. With, apparently, none of the self-consciousness she would have felt in his position, Murray finished cooking, fixed himself a heaping plate of rice and vegetables, and sat her down at a small oak table in the dining area.

"So tell me what's on your mind," he said, dousing his food with soy sauce.

Somewhat hesitantly, Juliet described her interview with Detectives Skelton and Crowder, then her discussion last night with Dennis and Suzy.

"Do you know Detective Skelton?" she asked rather plaintively. "Why did they give *him* the case?"

To her surprise, Landis's face suddenly darkened. He poked his laden chopsticks into his mouth, chewed and swallowed deliberately. "Skelton just happened to catch it," he finally answered. "You know, there's a rotation for murders. I get one, you get one, he gets one. I get one, you get one, he gets one."

"But you already knew so much about Ada. You investigated her—"

"Yeah, I pointed that out to my lieutenant," Murray interrupted. "Lieutenant Weber thought a fresh pair of eyes would be an advantage."

In point of fact, Landis had bitterly argued that Caffrey's murder should be reassigned to him. Aware of his friendship with Juliet Bodine, however, Weber had declined.

Forcing the anger out of his voice, Landis asked, "So who do you think killed her?"

"You know about Michael Hertbrooke, right?"

Murray did. He had talked to him during the missing person investigation.

"Well, that's who I'd guess," Juliet said. "Not that I've ever met him."

"You don't think it was Fitzjohn?"

"I did at first. But Fitzjohn had nothing to gain. Why would he?"

"Why, schmy." Murray shrugged. "He was there, he was the last person to see her, and if there's a type, he's it. Arrogant, selfish, quick to anger; he's my personal favorite so far."

Fitzjohn worked out daily at a gym in the basement of his building. A guy like that could have pulled Caffrey into the courtyard behind Daignault's building, wrung her neck, and popped her into a garbage bag in no time flat. The bag was standard for New York apartment buildings from Inwood to Red Hook: fifty-five gallons, thirty-eight by sixty inches, flat-bottomed, extra heavy duty. It came from an industrial supplier in New Jersey. You could find a dozen of them in cans on Murray's block this very second.

"Of course, there's also your friend Dennis," Murray said.

"Why would Dennis do it?"

"Again, why? So what, why?" Murray answered. "Why is not the first question I worry about. But since you ask, how about to keep the manuscript?"

"But he couldn't sell it."

"Not openly." Murray nabbed another fat pinch of rice and vegetables in his chopsticks. "And maybe he didn't want to sell it. Jule, how well do you know him?"

There was something about the way he asked this question that made Juliet look sharply up from her scotch. Landis had stopped eating and was looking at her with hard, bright, fixed intensity.

Juliet thought about the answer. How well did anyone know anyone? "Pretty well. I know he's not crazy. Not homicidal."

"You think you know."

"He's a friend of mine. He writes poetry. He's a rare book dealer, a bibliophile, for crying out loud."

Landis recommenced eating. "Thomas James Wise was a bibliophile," he said. "He had friends. In fact, he was one of the most widely respected bookmen of his day—president of the Bibliographical Society. He was also a superb forger. Mark Hofmann was a rare book dealer, an expert on Joseph Smith. He forged a series of documents—real beauties—relating to the Mormons and sold them to the church. Come to think of it, he was a poet, too: He forged a new Emily Dickinson poem. Too bad he killed a couple of people. I'm pretty sure he was somebody's friend, though. Maybe he even scratched out some verse of his own. My point being, anyone can be a killer given the right circumstances, Jule."

Juliet felt her lips tighten. "If anyone can be a killer, why are you talking to me?" she asked.

Murray looked momentarily puzzled, then burst into laughter so violent he had to set down his chopsticks. "You think I couldn't tell if you'd committed a murder last week, Jule? You'd be on the floor, you'd be so nuts. You'd be trembling just to be in the same room with me."

He laughed again, raucously, shook his head, actually used his napkin to wipe a tear from the corner of his eye, so hilarious, apparently, was the idea that Juliet Bodine could elude his keen detective skills.

Juliet waited him out. Then, "Don't underestimate me," she said, thoroughly annoyed.

Murray calmed down enough to take up his chopsticks again. "I didn't say you could never kill anyone," he pointed out. "I just said you haven't lately. Or are you telling me you have?"

"Of course I haven't," she snapped irritably. "I liked Ada. She was a pain in the ass in some ways, but I liked her quite a bit. I'm sad she died. But now that you've reminded me—"

In a few words, she sketched out her concern about whether she should hire a lawyer.

"Of course you should have a lawyer, Juliet," Murray told her. "Are you crazy?"

"But if the police are talking to me as just a friendly witness—"

Murray looked at her as if in disbelief. "You mean the if-you-have-nothing-to-hide-why-would-you-need-a-lawyer thing? You bought that? Jule, that's just standard police bullshit. I wouldn't say this to just any suspect, mind you—officially, we don't like lawyers down at the station. In fact, we sort of hate 'em. But hell yes, you should talk to one. Don't kid yourself. Jeff Skelton doesn't fuck around."

"You never answered me about whether you know him."

"Yes, I know him."

Except for his own partner, in fact, Skelton was probably the cop Landis knew best at the precinct. They spent a lot of time together after hours, drinking beer at the Irish Harp, sometimes taking in a ball game. Skelton was smart, persistent, methodical, and he'd made detective a couple of years younger than Landis. Much as he admired the guy, that was something Landis held against him. He'd been pissed as hell when Jeff caught the Caffrey case. He tried to get him to hand it back. No dice. Not with Weber, and not with Skelton, either.

"And—Does he consider me a suspect, do you know?"

Murray shrugged. As it happened, Skelton was nursing a

theory that Juliet and Daignault had conspired to kill Caffrey. Juliet set the victim up with Daignault, he figured, and Daignault did the actual strangling. Daignault had been lying, that was sure. He had said he never left his place that Friday afternoon. But yesterday, Ernesto Guerro, the doorman at Juliet's building, had reversed himself again, shaking his doubts to identify Daignault positively as the man he'd seen with the victim late Friday afternoon in front of Suzy's place. And a neighbor from the seventh floor of Daignault's building remembered seeing him coming up in the elevator "around five" (granted, the neighbor didn't remember a hat or jacket, but he could have ditched those). Confronted, Daignault said Guerro must be mistaken. But he did "remember" he'd gone down to get his mail.

That wasn't all he was lying about. Michael Hertbrooke had said that Daignault had tried to blackmail him into buying the manuscript. Daignault claimed no such thing as blackmail had come into his mind.

Didn't play that way to Skelton.

And the bag Caffrey had been found in was the kind used by Daignault's super. The super said he'd lined half a dozen garbage cans in the building areaway with fresh bags that Friday morning, hauling the old stuff out and tying it up (the garbage hadn't been picked up that day on account of the snow, of course, but he'd needed to make room in the cans). The cans were kept by the side of the building, behind a narrow, cast-iron gate, but anyone could stick their hand between the bars and pull a bag out easy. And, yeah, he had seen one was missing when he checked on Saturday afternoon.

As for physical evidence, forensics had found no prints of value on the garbage bag or the victim's neck—though the strangling had been manual, that was certain. But they had turned up a couple of blond hairs, two to three inches in length, in the palm of the victim's right hand. Daignault was blond. Naturally, he swore he'd never seen Caffrey after she left his apartment with Fitzjohn. He had no idea how his hair could have gotten where it had, he said—if it was his. He'd been questioned again today. When he'd resisted surrendering a DNA sample—hair or a saliva swab—a judge had provided a warrant. On visual analysis, the hair looked like a pretty good match. A DNA test had been ordered and expedited, but the lab was jammed as usual and it would still be a couple of weeks before the results were back.

Of course, Landis wasn't going to tell Juliet any of this.

"Look, any murder, any detective is going to have maybe four or five theories right out of the gate," he said instead. "In descending order of likelihood, let's say, in this case, we have the last guy with her, that's Fitzjohn. We have Daignault; it was his premises where she was last seen. We have Suzy Eisenman; she reported her missing. Maybe we have you, I don't know; you knew her longest of all."

"Even if I wanted to kill her, I never went out on Friday—"

"Or it could be something we don't know about yet," Murray went on, over her objection. "She's a gunrunner for the mob; she was scoring cocaine and the buy went bad. Or it could be, it always could be, a random crime. The serial killer just starting out the series." Murray set down his chopsticks, finished. "And that's what we have," he said.

"What about Michael Hertbrooke? At least he had a motive. Which is more than you can say about anyone else you've mentioned."

Landis shrugged. "I'm not sure how great of a motive suppressing a two-hundred-year-old indiscretion is, but don't worry, they'll look into him," he said. "They'll run with the hottest theory for the first couple of days, but they'll get to him eventually. For what it's worth, during the missing person investigation, Hertbrooke told me he was in his office in Chelsea at the paper on Friday from noon until about eleven o'clock at night. Which about thirty or forty people can confirm."

"Why does that let him out when my being in my apartment all day doesn't?"

He shrugged again. "I know motive and alibi get a lot of play in Agatha Christie novels," he said. "But around here, they're more for lawyers to blow about than for police to worry over—at least, not in the early stages. Motive is all very logical, but lots of times things just go wrong. It's not in a person's interest to kill someone, but they lose it and kill them anyway. Legally, there's no requirement to prove a motive when you prove a murder. As for alibi, people can hire a killer. If a guy tells me 'I was in Europe,' if I have enough evidence that he was involved, I'm going to charge him anyway. He wants to prove he was somewhere else, he can do it at trial.

"Now on a dump job, the rule of thumb is, you draw a circle with a one-mile radius around where you found the body, the killer is in there. People who kill usually like to stick around; they like to know what's going on. And they're usually just dying to talk about it. Most people who kill, it's their first time. They're walking around with this big secret; they can hardly shut themselves up. If you give them a little window, suggest an out—'I know it was an accident, you didn't mean for him to die'; or, 'That guy you killed, I hear he threatened you'—more times than not, 'Yeah, that's right,' they'll say, 'that's how it was; I just meant to scare him.' They want to tell you. They want that release.

"As it happens," he added, standing up to take his plate into the kitchen, "Michael Hertbrooke spent the weekend in D.C. attending a series of parties. He took a train there early Saturday morning and didn't come back till Monday. Can I make you some coffee?"

Juliet shook her head. "What's a dump job?" she asked sullenly.

"Oh, sorry. That's where a body is found someplace away from the crime scene, where the killer dumped it. It's one of the hardest kinds of cases to solve. A lot of times you don't know who the victim even is for quite a while. Of course, we were lucky here."

"Oh, very lucky," Juliet echoed. She could not understand why Murray was thinking about this crime so differently from the way she would. His view seemed to be all about rules of thumb, all about how "people" behave, rather than individuals. She felt disappointed in him; she'd thought he would have a subtler grasp of character, a more compelling sense of narrative than that. Accidents, blurted confessions; this was not her idea of the proper, logical approach to solving a crime. Solving a crime was a matter of noticing details, judging character, applying logic, constructing a story, sorting out puzzle pieces—and, in her opinion, there were probably a few pieces missing here. No, Landis had been wrong about the killing at the Jansch, and he was wrong now.

Deep inside her, Juliet felt that stubborn part of herself that secretly considered her own brain superior to the brain of anyone else come alive. She could practically hear the lid of the coffin in which she had tried to bury it last time creaking open, the swish of robes as the Undead within sat up and looked hungrily around. Intellectual arrogance was one of Juliet's oldest and most persistent failings, one she'd tried to kill off many times. Apart from her own disapproval of the trait, she couldn't help letting others see it—and it was, she had found, the opposite of endearing.

But it was also darned handy when a difficult problem came along.

"Who are Ada's heirs?" she asked Landis now, peremptoriness audible in her voice despite her best efforts. "Did Skelton look into that?"

There was a pause, during which, she presumed, Murray decided how much he should say.

Then, "Yeah, they're checking," he replied. "Mrs. Giddy, the cat sitter–neighbor lady, she couldn't find a will, and unfortunately, Mrs. Caffrey's lawyer happens to be in the hospital with pneumonia. He's on a respirator, matter of fact."

"Jeeze. Do they think he'll be okay?"

"They don't know. Apparently he's an old friend of Mrs. Caffrey's. I mean really old, like eighty-nine or ninety. He doesn't have a secretary, either. Works from his home, when he works at all, and evidently keeps his papers there. So no one knows how to put their hand on any will. But the next of kin, the presumable heir, that's Claudia Lunceford. I talked to her on the missing, remember?"

Juliet nodded.

"Skelton sent a picture of the stiff—excuse me, of Mrs. Caffrey—up to Mrs. Lunceford in Gloversville, so she could ID it. It's only a matter of looking at a Polaroid, of course, but you need a family member for the ID to be official. I think we talked about that. He asked her to come down and do it in person—we like the opportunity for a little face time with someone closely connected to the victim—but she wasn't interested. In fact, she's not interested in shipping the body up there for burial, either. If no one claims your Mrs. Caffrey, she'll be buried in Potter's Field, on Hart Island.

"But Skelton will wait awhile, see if Lunceford changes her mind. They can't release the body anyhow until the paperwork is done, and that can take awhile."

"Well, isn't that suspicious?" Juliet asked. "Her own niece doesn't even want to claim her body?"

Murray came to the doorway of the kitchen, where he had been bumping around, brewing coffee and washing the dinner things.

"I can think of three or four relatives of my own I wouldn't pay to ship home," he said. "Dead or alive."

Juliet frowned, but she had to admit he might have a point. Ada had been a pistol, as she had said of her own mother, but she could also be mighty exasperating.

Still, not to bury even your most annoying relative, that was extreme.

"FYI, as a general thing, it's pretty unusual for an heir to kill,"

Murray added. "You see it, but you don't see it very often."

There it was again. The odds, the rule of thumb. Juliet suppressed her irritation.

"Where does Fitzjohn say he went on Friday afternoon?" she asked.

Murray resumed his seat across from her, setting down a mug of coffee for each of them. "Well, now, that's why I like Fitzjohn so much," he said, one eyebrow lifting. "He says he went for a walk in the snow. Walked home to Turtle Bay, all the way through Central Park. That's a heck of a walk in a blizzard, and my thought is, a guy like John Fitzjohn, he wants to see snow, he flies to Aspen."

Juliet looked at him hopefully. This was more like it; this was observing character. As her eyes rested briefly on his dark face, she couldn't help noticing how much more attractive than Dennis he was to her. Murray was tense. He had a chip on his shoulder a lot of the time. But he never posed. His insecurities might make him guarded, but they could not make him obsequious. She supposed Dennis was to be admired for his gentle wish to be loved, the soft throat he willingly turned up to a woman. But admiration was not, alas, desire. She hated to admit it, but an hour alone with Landis had her thinking about sex—about love, even—with a greed that two months of dating Dennis Daignault had never provoked.

Aloud, "There were other people who knew about the Wilson manuscript, too," she reminded Landis now. "The man whose daughter found it, Matthew McLaurin, isn't that his name?"

"Yeah, don't worry. I take it you saw the newspapers this morning," he said, with a grim smile.

Juliet had. The *Daily News* had run the single-word headline "BAGGED!" in three-inch-high type on its front page, and reported beneath it the discovery of an eighty-four-year-old lady tourist inside an industrial-strength trash-can liner. The *Post,* having gotten hold of the newspaper photograph of Ada in *Arsenic and Old Lace,* had featured a large reproduction captioned, "VIOLENCE AND OLD

LACE." Even the *Times* had covered Ada's death at length, in an above-the-fold story on the first page of the Metro section.

"Your friend got herself brutally murdered in a good neighborhood in Manhattan. Believe me, the department is going to be on this case six ways to sundown," Murray said, with zestful pride. "Jeff Skelton drives me nuts sometimes, but he's a thorough son of a bitch. He's going to work this sucker till it's done."

He seemed to have forgotten that, as a suspect herself, Juliet might find his colleague's determination more ominous than reassuring.

chapter

EIGHT

Dennis Under the Microscope

The letter in the Times *the next day ran as follows:*

> *To the Editor:*
>
> *Your story of Jan. 16 regarding my ancestor, the fourth Viscount Quiddenham, makes the assertion that, as a youth, he engaged in a certain harmless, if mildly eccentric, sexual practice. May I point out that the alleged source of this information is a fragment of manuscript attributed to one of the most notorious women of her day? I would further observe that Dennis Daignault, the single person cited in your article as testifying to having seen this purported manuscript (now mysteriously missing), is a maverick dealer in rare manuscripts who is, as we say on this side of the pond, currently "helping the police" in their inquiries.*
>
> *Viscount Quiddenham*
>
> *London.*

Juliet, who had not read the editorial page until Dennis handed her his copy that evening in his living room, looked up to find him slumped in his armchair, arms dangling limply, heavy legs inert, eyes bleakly fixed on nothingness—a picture of the Death of Hope.

"Apparently Michael Hertbrooke called his father after he met with you," she said, tactfully omitting the observation that the son must have thought he smelled a whiff of extortion in the air. With more conviction than she felt, she added, "Obviously, you must write a letter back."

"I did," Dennis said, not bothering to turn his eyes on her. "They'll never run it, of course."

"They may," said Juliet, though she knew they would not. A second letter would look like a private argument between two readers. Letters to the Editor were letters *to* the editor.

"Why do you suppose he called me a 'maverick' dealer?" Dennis asked, without moving.

"I'd read it to mean that you're some sort of renegade or contrarian within the business." Juliet hesitated, then dared to add, "Are you?"

"Not that I'm aware of." Finally, he turned his blue eyes on her, though without moving any other part of his body. "I take him to mean that I'm a one-person operation, as opposed to a thriving, centuries-old English firm or something. I take it he was trying to come up with a pejorative vague enough not to be actionable but precise enough to cast doubt on my word."

There was a silence. Then Juliet said, "Did pretty well, didn't he?"

"Yes, didn't he?"

It was nine-thirty. Dennis still smelled faintly of the canned clam chowder he had, most uncharacteristically, eaten for dinner. His clothes—dark corduroy pants, a flannel shirt, and a red sweater-vest—were rumpled and slightly unclean. Following the shock of this morning's letter in the *Times*, he had had a fresh request from Detectives Skelton and Crowder for another hour of his time. Today, they had come to chat with him in his own living room, a pleasure (now that he had an attorney in the matter and could not legally be interviewed without his presence) that cost him two hundred dollars.

Today they had chosen to focus on the estimated value he'd set on Ada's manuscript. Evidently, Skelton had dug up some dealer Dennis never heard of to testify that, if the Byron proved genuine, the pages could be worth up to twice as much as the $100,000 maximum Dennis had named. How the Byron could ever be proved genuine, this previously unrecognized genius of the antiquarian world hadn't explained, Dennis bitterly observed. Nor did it mean anything that Dennis had acknowledged expertise as an appraiser. All that seemed to matter to Skelton was that Dennis had told the police the fragment was worth a lot less than someone else thought it might be worth. Despite the detective's elaborate politeness ("I'm still struggling to get a grip on this appraisal thing," he had apologized, with Columboesque humility, "You gotta forgive me"), it was obvious he thought Dennis had been trying to minimize its importance and, by extension, to downplay the likelihood anyone would kill for it.

Dennis said next to nothing because his lawyer told him to say next to nothing. Instead, he sat and listened while his reputation, motives, and integrity were gently examined and, tacitly, trashed. Now, though he had invited Juliet to come over and talk this evening, it was perhaps inevitable that the press of events—and maybe the matter of the receipt she had retained—was taking a toll on his affection for her. Tonight when she apologized (yet again) for having involved him with Mrs. Caffrey, he did not say (as before), Oh, don't be silly, you couldn't have known. He was silent.

Juliet's own day had not been without incident. Somehow an enterprising reporter from a local television news show had learned it was she who initially identified Ada Caffrey's body. A simple Internet search had no doubt turned up her pen name and, after that, the idea of a story that included the dead old lady, a missing naughty manuscript, *and* a successful New York writer of romance novels was too much for the news show to resist. This reporter, whose name was Leslie Flent, had worked the publishing and literary networks until she tracked Juliet down. When Juliet advised her, via Ames, that her phone calls would not be returned, Flent came to the building. She and a camera crew spent the entire afternoon on the sidewalk making nuisances of themselves. After trying unsuccessfully to send them away through the doorman's intercom, Juliet dispatched Ames to get rid of them in person.

Instead, they taped the messenger. Ames had returned unprecedentedly flustered, bearing with her a note from the president of Juliet's co-op board begging her to bear in mind that it was very unpleasant for her neighbors to have the media camped out on their doorstep.

As a result, Juliet had spent the day trapped indoors. Theoretically, this might have meant a considerable chunk of Chapter Seven of "A Christian Gentleman" got written. In fact, she had produced a mere two pages—neither of them, she thought, particularly inspired. When she left for Dennis's, she did so with a scarf wrapped around her face up to her eyes and a stocking cap pulled down to the bridge of her nose. She buzzed down and warned the doorman—it was Francisco tonight—not to acknowledge her as she passed the still-waiting camera, only to run smack into a neighbor from the floor below who immediately exclaimed at the top of her lungs, "Juliet? I hardly recognized you under all that!"

A chase ensued, during which Juliet had just enough presence of mind not to lead her pursuers straight to Rara Avis but rather to the pizza parlor at Eighty-second and Amsterdam, which she remembered conveniently had two doors. She went in the front, came right out the side, and hopped into a providentially passing cab. The only good thing she could say for the whole experience was that it had suggested to her an ending to the excursion to the ruined abbey: Catherine Walkingshaw would accidentally disturb a bull, setting off a chase in which Sir James might come to her rescue. The dispensable Catherine could then be laid up with the painful and disfiguring aftereffects of her scramble across the fields while Selena, picturesquely unblemished, nursed her sister in an attractively Christian fashion.

Dennis shifted in his chair and let out a groan. " 'No worst, there is none,' " he said. " 'Pitched past pitch of grief, / More pangs will, schooled at forepangs, wilder wring.' "

Juliet smiled as sympathetically as she could. She recognized the lines from Gerard Manley Hopkins, but did not think the poem an apposite one. Dennis was losing his grip. Gone was the romantic, gone the polymath, gone even the stylish poseur. Two days ago, fortified, perhaps, by his poached raspberries, he had seemed to be holding up pretty well in the face of his troubles. Now he appeared to be falling to shreds before her eyes.

Or maybe, she told herself in fairness, it was not Dennis himself, but rather whatever hopeful, falsely romantic image of Dennis she had built up in her own mind that was crumbling. ("In her first passion Woman loves her lover," Byron had written. "In all the others all she loves is Love.")

If so, it wasn't only the apparent cooling of his ardor for her that had caused the change. Watching a man go whiny and helpless in the face of difficulties was—well, it was not very seductive, put it that way. If she were a better person—someone Sir James Clendinning might approve of, for example—Juliet had no doubt she would find herself more drawn than ever to Dennis in his plight. Not being so exemplary, however, she found herself wondering how long he expected her to stay tonight.

"I'm sure that in a day or two the police will come up with evidence to identify the real killer," she said consolingly, though she was not in the least sure of anything of the sort. "Maybe Fitzjohn will confess. Don't you think he did it?"

Dennis shrugged. "I'd like to. But I don't really see his motive."

Juliet could not argue. A moment later, she instead said lightly,

" 'If you can trust yourself when all men doubt you, But make allowance for their doubting too, If you can wait and not be tired by waiting, Or—' "

"Are you quoting 'If' to me?"

"Well, technically, yes."

Dennis dropped his head again. "Dear God, you know you're in trouble when your friends start quoting Rudyard Kipling. What's next? 'To thine own self be true?' "

"I was joking. Trying to lighten the mood." Perhaps it was her annoyance with him tonight, perhaps something less immediately identifiable—for whatever reason, it now, for the first time, flashed through Juliet's mind that Dennis really could be guilty of murder. She shook herself mentally. I'll be suspecting myself in a minute, she thought.

Meantime, "Ha, ha," Dennis was saying. He shifted in his chair, drawing his knees up so he was almost curled in a ball. He had taken off his shoes, and the malformation of his right foot was unmistakable.

And suddenly Juliet did want to put her arms around him. It wasn't his fault he was immobilized. Trouble took people in different ways. She was scared herself. It was just that, with her, fear usually galvanized rather than paralyzed. She stood, went around behind his chair, and began to massage his shoulders. If she were the cops' favorite suspect, instead of the poor fourth or fifth she reckoned herself to be, she hoped she would go on the offensive to find the real culprit, maybe hire a private eye to investigate the case on her behalf. But of course, she reminded herself with a humility even Sir James Clendinning would have admired, one could not really know what one would do in another person's place until one had walked a mile in his shoes.

It was an advantage she was to have before long.

chapter

NINE

Juliet Under the Microscope

At nine in the morning of the second Thursday after the discovery of Mrs. Caffrey's body, that lady's lawyer, whose name was Bert Nilsson, was at last discharged from Nathan Littauer Hospital and went home.

Mr. Nilsson seemed to have made an excellent recovery: By eleven, he was in the disused office where he kept the moldering relics of his once busy practice. By noon, he had informed the police that under a will dated November 5 of last year, his late client (after providing for her own cremation and a memorial service) had left her land, house, furnishings, personal effects, and savings to a small, nonprofit environmental advocacy organization called Free Earth, with a request that most of the land be kept intact and used as a sanctuary for animals and "all those who revered Nature." Free Earth was based in the town of Speculator, inside the Adirondack Park; Matthew McLaurin, the coexecutor named by testatrix, was a member. To Mr. McLaurin personally she had bequeathed her cats, with the stipulation that he keep them in the house—the only home they had ever known—for as long as possible.

Mr. Nilsson had already told the police the rough outlines of these arrangements as he remembered them from his hospital bed, but Mrs. Caffrey had been in the habit of remaking her will so often that some of the details had escaped him. Now he was able to add a matter he had forgotten before. Testatrix had left her "books, writings, photographs, letters and papers" to an author who had brought her much pleasure in her late years, despite the lack of "spice" in her novels. Testatrix hoped her legatee would be moved by this bequest to put more sex in. But whether she did or no, the books, writings, etc., were left to the author known to her readers as Angelica Kestrel-Haven, but in private life called Juliet Bodine.

Juliet learned of her inheritance an hour later, Mr. Nilsson having diligently contacted her by phone to convey what he would subsequently document for her more officially by letter. For a moment, she was stupid enough to feel touched. Fans had sent her gifts in the past—afghans, tea sets, ancient etiquette manuals. But no one, fan or otherwise, had ever left her so personal and profoundly trusting a gift as this.

It was only after she hung up the phone that she understood what had happened. Frantically, she called Mr. Nilsson back. Would the very old manuscript and letter Mrs. Caffrey had come to New York to show her—in his opinion, would those be interpreted as belonging to his late client's "books, writings, photographs, letters, and papers"?

Mr. Nilsson was not aware of the particular papers Ms. Bodine had in mind, but yes, if they were papers belonging to Ada Caffrey, they were certainly Juliet's now. Forgive his curiosity, but why did she ask?

Juliet's second interview with the police—conducted this time in the company of Zoe B. Grossbardt, the first criminal attorney Juliet had ever had occasion to hire—took place at their request late that afternoon and lasted into the evening. The suspicions Landis had tactfully refrained from mentioning to her—that in order to gain control of the Harriette Wilson manuscript, she and Dennis Daignault had conspired to do away with Ada Caffrey—were made quite clear to her by the officers' line of questioning, although, thanks to Zoe, they learned very little in return. Had Mrs. Caffrey ever asked her for advice on how to leave her property? Had Mrs. Caffrey ever mentioned her will to her at all? Was Mr. Matthew McLaurin's name known to her? Had she met him? Juliet's answers were terse.

She went back to her apartment in a state in which frustrated fury mingled freely with sheer terror. After Skelton's implications, she did not even care to phone Dennis. Though Zoe insisted it was unlikely in the extreme—the police would need a court order—she had conceded it was just barely possible Dennis's phone might be tapped. His and Juliet's movements might also be watched for at least the next few days.

Anyone watching Juliet's movements that particular evening would have seen her hang up her coat and hat, pour herself a stiff scotch, then sit all but motionless next to the bricked-in fireplace in her little library for the better part of an hour. An impulse to call her father (their planned dinner date had been postponed several times and was now scheduled to take place the following Monday) gave way to another to turn to Murray Landis, then to the idea of calling a friend (Suzy, perhaps, or her old friend Molly, or her college friend Ruth Renswick, or half a dozen others) just for the solace and, perhaps, the clarification of going over the situation aloud. She had once, very briefly, dated a criminal lawyer, and it crossed her mind to put her difficulties before him. She even entertained the idea of phoning Rob, who lived in Toronto to be near the child he had had with the woman—now his second ex-wife—for whom he had left Juliet. Rob, who loathed Toronto and gave every sign of thoroughly regretting the loss of his starting wife, would be delighted to have an occasion to rescue her.

On reflection, however, she did not quite see what help a modestly successful director of regional theater could give her just now. In fact, the more she thought about it, the more convinced she was that thinking—just thinking—was what she must do. How had she come to be in this situation? What links connected her to the murder of an old lady from upstate New York? And how could she sever them now?

Her instinct was to do just that, to pull away, deny knowledge, insist on the marginality of Ada Caffrey to her life. Close the episode; shake herself free of the incubus. But circumstances—the police, notably—would not allow this. Though she might ignore, deny her ties to Ada, they would not.

Reluctantly, she acknowledged that she was no longer in a position where she could simply turn away. She had known Ada Caffrey, helped her, and now Ada had been killed, leaving Juliet caught in the tangled aftermath. It was a Chinese finger puzzle, one of those tubes of braided straw that constrict more tightly around one's fingers the more one pulls away. The only route of escape was to move into the puzzle, deeper into the trap. Like turning into a skid. Or developing a character. She must think about Ada, learn about Ada, immerse herself in Ada, see what she had seen, know what she had known, think as she had thought. " 'To the destructive element submit yourself,' " as Conrad had it. It was in this very room that she had first talked with Ada Caffrey. Closing her eyes, she tried to summon up that conversation. What had Mrs. Caffrey told her of her past, her home, her life in Espyville? What names had she mentioned? What information that might be of use now still hovered half-forgotten in her own memory?

A line came to her from the twelfth-century Persian poet Nizami: "Who can decipher fate's handwriting?" it ran, as she recalled. "However, what at first we are unable to read, we then have to endure later on."

It was true: The course of life, so ambiguous, so mysterious in advance, was often cruelly plain in retrospect. And yet, could Juliet—could anyone—ever have guessed that Ada Caffrey might be murdered? The woman herself, her habits and thoughts and personality, had been displayed before Juliet over the course of four days. She must try to read them. Go back to the beginning. In her mind's eye, she saw the old lady come into the library, remembered her clap at the sight of the childish tea table, heard her thrilling voice invoke Noel Coward, saw herself fetching the hard-backed chair to seat her guest . . .

Juliet had liked Ada personally. But, as often happened with her, she had been distracted at first by Ada's charm, her vivacity, her delightful strangeness. It had taken her a while to see that Ada had been a very stubborn, willful person who saw her convenience, her pleasure, as more important than other people's responsibilities. She enjoyed herself while encouraging others to see to the tiresome administrative work her comfort and entertainment required, to pick up any pieces the gratification of her whims might leave behind. Juliet had introduced her to Dennis Daignault, who spent two full days and three nights working like a dog to determine the value of her manuscript. But when Ada had not liked what he had to say, she had summarily dropped him. Not only dropped him, accused him of dishonesty in front of another client. Had she lived, Juliet was sure she would have offered no apologies for this hard treatment, either to Dennis or to Juliet. On the contrary, Ada had considered herself the injured party.

On a more quotidian level, Suzy had laughed at the idea that Ada might literally clean up after herself. Such a person might make a very entertaining acquaintance but an extremely trying relative. Perhaps it was no wonder Ada's niece would not pay for her burial. Although surely there was something more specific behind Mrs. Caffrey's choosing to leave all her worldly goods to a nonprofit organization (and her sentimental ones to Juliet), ignoring her niece completely. At the very least, Ada must have had family photographs, souvenirs, that Mrs. Lunceford, and no one else, would have valued. Why not leave these to her?

With a sigh, Juliet lifted her glass and drank off the last of the scotch. Why did people kill? Certainly for money. Sometimes for revenge. In anger. Sexual jealousy. To shut someone up. Iago destroyed Othello from frustrated ambition. Of course, Iago was not your typical killer . . . but it was interesting that Othello, close as he was to his brother officer, never mistrusted him.

Once more Juliet's thoughts returned to her suspected co-conspirator. How well, in fact, did she know Dennis Daignault? "A wink, a bow, a hand, an eye," he had written of himself soon after they had first met, in a poem to her titled "Juliet." "No Romeo, no Casanova either," he had continued, conjuring various other romantic heroes and disclaiming any right to be compared to them. He had painted himself as "a shadow, a way of putting it." He was certainly an odd person, Dennis. Secretive. Somehow furtive. But homicidal? Impossible to imagine.

Although . . . With another sigh, Juliet admitted to herself that people did sometimes kill by accident. And, as Murray had suggested, they were probably later dismayed that they had. Probably, too, like most people, they had been at least one other person's friend.

A friend . . . Her thoughts returned to Dennis's poems: so like him, wistful, courtly, inventive, veiled, rueful, and, slightly, feminine. But—but what had Ada said about her friend, Matt McLaurin; what had she said about the poems of her friend? So many of them were—What had she said? So angry.

Angry.

And yet it was Matt who'd driven Ada to Albany, who'd brought her a book to read when she was sick. How angry could such a person be? She tried to remember what else Ada had said about this friend. He did office work in an insurance brokerage in Gloversville—Gallop Insurance, hadn't she said? So far as Juliet could remember, Ada never mentioned Matt's little daughter Nina-Tina-Gina's mother. Was he married? Divorced? A widower? Some intemperate poems were not much to go on, but on the whole, Juliet preferred to think that McLaurin, or Claudia Lunceford, or almost anyone had killed Ada Caffrey rather than Dennis Daignault.

At the end of the hour, she removed a pen and pad of paper from a drawer in the table at her side. Sherlock Holmes or Hercule Poirot, she knew, would by now have reasoned their way to some answers. She, alas, had come up only with questions. Still, she had the habit of doing research. And in research, good answers started with good questions.

Who was Ada Caffrey? she wrote. *World view? Preoccupations?*

Who is Matthew McLaurin? Knew about legacy? When? Recog. ms? Where was he on Fri?

What is Free Earth?

Why no legacy to Lunceford? Knew re: this?? Mr. Lunceford? Where were they Fri?

Giddys. Knew reason for NY trip? Hard up for $? Ask them re: Ada.

Ada Caffrey had made Juliet her legatee. Very well, then, she would go and examine her legacy—surely McLaurin and Mr. Nilsson would have to allow her that—and so see where Ada had lived. Reading her poems, too, might be fruitful. She would find an excuse to visit Claudia Lunceford. And the Giddys; that would be easy, since they lived next door. Setting, character, narrative, these were Juliet's strengths. The police knew rules of thumb, but she knew plot, individuals. If she saw where Ada had lived, met the people around her, picked up the plot threads of her life, what might her novelist's instincts tell her?

Juliet slept like a rock and woke uncommonly early. By nine, when Ames arrived, she had already learned there was no Matthew or M. or McLaurin of any kind listed in the Espyville-Gloversville phone directory, that a J. Lunceford lived on Partridge Lane in Gloversville, and that the Candlewick was the only inn or bed-and-breakfast open at this season in the immediate area (a B and B or an inn seemed a likelier place to pick up gossip than a motel). She had also gone online to check into Free Earth, but found little more than their own Web page. It appeared to be a small, grass-roots group committed to lobbying politicians on environmental issues. Leaving Ames to arrange for a car rental, reserve a room, call Bert Nilsson (or McLaurin, at Gallop Insurance) for permission to enter the house, and learn where in the Espyville area she might donate Ada's books, she went back into her office.

She dialed J. Lunceford's phone number, at the same time flipping idly through the collected *Ladies' Monthly Museum* magazines of 1816. Lately the Walkingshaw girls seemed to have nothing to wear—a circumstance made even more inconvenient by Catherine Walkingshaw's newly conceived infatuation with young Capt. Charles Vizor. Juliet had just picked out an Iris scarf, to be used as a turban, a scarf or a shawl, when her call went through.

The voice at the other end was middle aged, somewhat mannered, but relaxed.

"Mrs. Lunceford? My name is Juliet Bodine. I was a friend of your aunt, Ada Caffrey—"

"Why are you calling, please, Miss Bodine?" Mrs. Lunceford interrupted. Her voice had sharpened. "I have a very busy morning ahead of me."

Juliet paused, her fingers resting on a note about a caped wrapping coat.

"Well, first I wanted to offer my condolences, of course—" she began.

"Offer them to someone else. Was that all?"

Juliet was so surprised that she actually took the receiver from her ear and looked at it. Returning it, she explained, "Well, I'm planning to come up there—"

"That's no business of mine."

Juliet put a bookmark into the *Ladies' Monthly Museum,* closed it, and mustered the small resources of her lamblike voice. It was never easy for her to sound brisk and bullying on the phone.

"You see, in her will," she said, as forcefully as she could, "your aunt left her books and papers to me. I thought there might be family things among them that you or your relatives would like to have, so—"

"There won't be. I really must go now. Thank you for calling." And she hung up.

The phone clattered down loudly enough to cause a hard little jolt inside Juliet's chest. Whatever had happened between Ada Caffrey and her niece must have been pretty spectacular. The phone rang just as she was about to pick up the receiver again herself. She pulled her hand back. No telling who it was. Letting Ames find out, she opened the *Monthly Museum* to her bookmark.

"Spencer *à la Duchesse de Berri,*" she was copying down on a sheet of lined paper, when Ames knocked on her door. "Parisian travelling costume, satin, pearl colored, trimmed with—"

"Yes?"

"Dr. Bodine?" The door opened slightly. "I'm sorry to disturb you, but a Matthew McLaurin is calling."

"Oh!" She picked up.

Matthew McLaurin was speaking. Matthew McLaurin was a friend of Ada Caffrey's, a thin, reedy voice seemed rather to ask than to tell her. The phrase "painfully shy" is a common one. Matt McLaurin's shyness was excruciating.

"I'm calling for two reasons," he went on, his voice almost a whisper. Somewhere near him, Juliet could hear a little girl singing "Born Free" at the top of her lungs. "First of all, I don't know if Mr.

Nilsson mentioned this to you already, but in her will, Ada arranged to have a memorial service held for her?"

"Yes, he mentioned that."

"Oh, good. Because, I don't know why exactly, but she asked me to run it. So I just wondered if you'd want to be there, maybe even say something. I mean, you probably don't have time on such short notice. It's this Sunday. But—"

Juliet hesitated. She would certainly attend the memorial; indeed, it was the perfect opportunity to learn more about Ada. But should she agree to "say something"?

Eulogies had always stumped Juliet. She admired but did not understand the ease with which others could celebrate aloud a life just ended. And yet the chance to contribute to the service was surely an opportunity to move deeper into the puzzle. It would make her known to Ada's friends, perhaps even encourage them to confide in her. She ought to try.

"I'd be delighted to come," she said. "I mean, not delighted, but I'd appreciate a chance to participate in the memorial. What was the other reason you called?"

"Oh. That's a little more awkward. But, um, I understand Ada left you her books and papers," McLaurin went on.

Juliet's heart beat faster. Was he going to raise the question of the Wilson manuscript? Maybe contest its ownership? Say his daughter had found it? Argue that it shouldn't really be considered as belonging to Ada's "papers"?

"I hope you won't think I'm being pushy or anything," he continued. "I mean, she did leave them to you, but—well, are you thinking of doing anything with her poems? Because I'd really like to have copies of them, if that's okay."

Her poems? "Oh, of course," Juliet mumbled, swallowing her disappointment.

"I think she wrote quite a few. I was wondering if she'd want me to try to get them published. Or maybe you were already thinking that?"

"No," Juliet admitted.

"Do you think she wouldn't like it?"

"I don't know. She certainly seemed to enjoy sharing them." Her ideas about Matt McLaurin tumbling confusedly into a new order, Juliet described her evening with Ada at Cleopatra's Ashtray.

"I don't think they are very likely to sell," she went on. "Not that they aren't good, but just from what little I know about publishing poetry. Still, I could show them to my own editor," she heard herself offer, then cringed slightly. Portia Klein probably hadn't read a poem since college. And would Matt then want Juliet to show her his own poems? She'd better dampen any hopes before this became a Pandora's box. "Not that she would ever acquire poetry, but she might know someone."

"That would be great. Though I think it's much more likely a small, local publisher . . ."

He didn't finish the sentence. Juliet felt relieved by his apparent grasp of the realities of publishing verse.

"There probably wouldn't be much in the way of royalties," he added, his voice barely audible. "But of course if there were, they'd belong to you."

"I don't believe distribution of poetry royalties is a problem that comes up too often," Juliet said. "But if there were any, I'd be glad to donate them to Free Earth. By the way, what will they do with Ada's property?" she added, as casually as she could. "Will they use it for a headquarters?"

"Oh, I have no idea. We're all just flabbergasted. We only learned about it this week."

"Is that so?" asked Juliet, her suspicions returning. Usually when she asked, "Is that so?" she meant, "How interesting!" Today she meant, "Is that so?"

"Yes, Ada never said a word. We aren't at all sure we'll be able to keep it. The property tax alone is more than Free Earth raises in a typical year. Plus there's insurance and stuff. Mr. Nilsson is finding someone to help us look into it."

"I see. But did Ada ever mention—I mean, do you have any idea why she chose not to leave it to her family?"

There was a momentary pause. Then, "Pretty much anyone up here in Espyville could tell you that," Matt said uncomfortably. "But I'm not sure it's for me to do."

"Oh."

His muted voice turned anxious, propitiatory. In the background, the little girl started to belt out, "The sun'll come out tomorrow! Bet your bottom dollar that—"

"I don't mean to be rude," said Matt. "It's just—"

"No, of course not."

"I know Ada enjoyed your books very much. I'm glad you can come to the service."

Juliet explained that she had hoped to come up anyhow. "Would that be all right? I was going to ask Mr. Nilsson, but—maybe you'd like to meet me at Ada's house? Would you have any time tomorrow?"

"No. Cindy Giddy can probably let you in. She's looking after the cats. I'm sorry, I'd like to help you, but I'll have to be getting ready for the memorial tomorrow. And I have to take care of my daughter. So . . ."

Again, his sentence trailed off. Juliet had the distinct impression something more than other commitments made him disinclined to meet, that he was trying to evade her. She wondered again who the child's mother was. Couldn't she watch her daughter?

"Would another day be better? Maybe Sunday, after the service?"

"No, I'll . . . I'll need to get Gina home to bed."

Juliet hesitated. "I could stay till Monday. Maybe we could

have lunch? We could talk a little about Ada's poems."

"I'll be working," Matt said, this time with unmistakable curtness. It made a strange mixture, the brusque tone and the whispery voice. Rather sinister.

Thwarted, Juliet gave up. He gave her the name of the funeral home where the service would take place (the Regency, for heaven's sake; why did people name things "Regency" when they wanted them to sound classy?), and the time, and the Giddys' telephone number. She would have to try to grab him at the service, that was all. At the very least, she wanted to mention the Wilson papers to him and see how he reacted. And find out where he had been the Friday Ada was killed. Espyville was not so very far from New York City. Her thoughts churned as she finished her note from the *Monthly Museum.*

"—trimmed with a cordon of pink and white, with a pelerine cape, trimmed with crape."

She set down her pen but left the book open on the same page while she tried the Giddys. The phone rang a long time.

Then Cindy Giddy answered. Her voice was slow and husky, not at all like the cheery voice of the good-hearted, middle-aged Mrs. Giddy in "A Christian Gentleman." Still, it had a kind of dreaminess in it that was somehow (but how?) tantalizingly familiar. "Hello?"

Juliet explained who she was and that she had inherited Ada Caffrey's books and papers. She asked if Mrs. Giddy would be at home tomorrow around lunchtime and could let her into the house.

Mrs. Giddy, for reasons that were unclear, gave a short laugh. "Oh, sure. I'll be around."

Detached, spacey, sleepy—what was that in the husky voice? Oh, of course: Drugged! High, at ten in the morning! Juliet thought of some of the students she used to teach at Barnard, and of a classmate or two at Radcliffe years ago. Yes, there had been those who smoked dope even as they drank their morning coffee.

She felt a fleeting pang of envy. How long ago it had been.

And yet, how vivid her recollections. She could almost smell it over the phone.

"But wait a minute, did you check with the Free Earth people?" Cindy asked.

Was it Juliet's imagination, or had a note of anger or envy crept into the lazy voice? Why should that be? Perhaps they did not relish the idea of Free Earth as neighbors. Or perhaps the Giddys had been hoping to buy Ada's place themselves, combine it with their own. In Manhattan, the death of an apartment owner often set off a frantic race among the late resident's space-starved neighbors, especially those with adjacent walls. Sometimes, tipped off by the doorman, or the comings and goings of nurses, they did not even wait for death.

Aloud, she explained that she had just okayed it with Matt McLaurin.

"He was very nice," she added. "He invited me to the memorial service. Will you be going?"

"Memorial service? Whose?"

Juliet hoped the Giddys didn't have children. Cindy seemed to be barely functional.

"For Ada. At the Regency Funeral Home in Gloversville," she explained. "Sunday at one."

"Oh. I'll see if we can come," the dazed voice replied. There was the sound of an inhalation, then a long, sputtering cough. "Excuse me, I have to go now."

Juliet heard the entire phone drop to the floor, heard Cindy curse, then finally manage to deposit the receiver in its cradle. Juliet was left with the somewhat unsavory impression of a middle-aged pothead.

Ames knocked, then came in, several papers in her hand.

"Dr. Bodine, I've printed out a map and directions from MapQuest," she said. "A Dodge Intrepid will be waiting for you at Hertz on West Ninety-sixth Street till ten o'clock tomorrow morning.

I've spoken to Caroline Walsh, the owner of the Candlewick Inn, and reserved a room for you there starting tomorrow night. I think you'll find Ms. Walsh a good source of information. She's also the proprietor of Walsh Novelties Incorporated, which maintains a storefront in downtown Gloversville. You can stop by there to pick up a key if you should arrive before three o'clock."

"Really?"

"I don't think you'll find the Candlewick overstaffed. Or excessively formal," Ames said, rather ominously.

Juliet thanked her. "Listen, you wouldn't care to put in some overtime this weekend?"

An anguished look replaced her assistant's usual serenity. "I'd like to help you, but my niece is getting married in Queens on Sunday. There's a rehearsal dinner tomorrow night."

"Oh. How nice for her."

"If I can do anything for you during the day tomorrow—"

"No, I'll just . . ."

Juliet subsided in mumbles. Her glance fell on the *Monthly Museum* again, and she turned the page. A book by Alexander Rowland, jun., titled, *An Historical, Philosophical, and Practical Essay on the Human Hair* was reviewed. She was still reading the notice as she picked up the phone once more. Maybe she could guilt trip Suzy into coming.

But it was not to be. The next day, at an unseasonably early hour, Juliet lugged a suitcase full of warm clothes, no-frills toiletries, and books (on the history of sheep farming, the English commons system, and the Enclosure Acts) down the stairs to her front hall. She set them beside Mrs. Caffrey's repacked vintage valise, sealskin coat, and carpetbag. (These belonged to Free Earth now, and Suzy had asked her to take them away. Sitting in her spare room, they were reminders of a painful episode: Apart from the emotional toll, Ada had never paid her, the man who ran the online reservations service where she used to list her B and B had seen her name in the papers and dropped her, and other members of her co-op were looking at her funny.) Then she went into the kitchen to check that the gas was off (it was) and returned to the front hall. She put on her coat and hat, wrapped her scarf around her neck, picked up her own purse, and went into the kitchen to check that the gas was off.

It still was.

She turned away, reassured, and started back to the front hall. The phone rang.

Juliet cursed. She dithered. Could it be Suzy, agreeing at the last minute to come? She had claimed to have work to do all weekend; Juliet suspected she was mainly working on Parker Scutt, but discreetly refrained from pressing the point. But if she had relented . . .

Juliet picked up the phone.

"Just wondered how you were holding up," Murray's voice said easily. "Skelton been leaning on you?"

He sounded unusually relaxed, and there were none of the usual noises of the squad room, or whatever you called it, behind him.

"Not since day before yesterday, thank God. Where are you? Don't you work on weekends?"

"Sometimes. Four days on, two days off, that's the schedule. Today's an RDO for me. Regular day off," he translated.

"Oh. Well, enjoy it. Listen, I appreciate your concern, but I have my coat on. I was just on my way out—"

"Oh yeah? Where are you going so bright and early?"

"As a matter of fact, I'm driving up to Espyville."

There was a brief silence before Murray, no longer relaxed, asked, "What for?"

Juliet explained that she had been named in Ada's will.

"Yeah, I heard about that. That's why I was wondering about Skelton. So what are you telling me, you're going up there to look at her books and papers?"

"Yes."

"Jule, you can't play detective. We've discussed this. It's dangerous, and it's against the law."

"I'm aware of that," said Juliet, as icily as her babyish voice would allow. "Now, if you don't mind—"

"I mean it, Jule. I don't want you up in Espyville running around asking questions. Not that there's anything sinister up there. As a matter of fact, Skelton and Crowder just came back from a trip there yesterday."

"They did? What'd they learn?"

"Nothing. Nothing to learn. Everything's shipshape in Espyville."

"What's Claudia Lunceford's story?"

"Story?"

Juliet felt herself starting to sweat. Reluctantly, she unbuttoned the top three buttons of her coat. "You know what I mean. Why didn't Ada leave the house to her?"

"The question is not why didn't she. The question is, did Mrs. Lunceford know she wouldn't? And the answer is yes. There's been bad blood between them for years. Apparently Ada Caffrey was the type to make a new will every two or three months or so—liked to imagine rewarding her latest friends, Nilsson says, or sometimes cut out someone she'd gone sour on. According to him, Mr. and Mrs. Lunceford were never in any will of Caffrey's that he knew of, and he wrote plenty for her. They had no expectation of inheriting."

"Hmph," said Juliet. "They say."

"They say. Everybody says. Listen, Jeff Skelton's no dope. He says the Luncefords are clean, they're clean."

"Uh huh. And did he meet with Matt McLaurin?"

"Who?"

"The Free Earth guy, the guy who does get—Oh, forget it." On the brink of taking her coat off completely, Juliet hesitated, then changed her mind. "Look, Murray, I have a rental car I said I'd pick up by ten. I really have to be trotting along."

There was a long silence, so long that Juliet wondered if he had quietly hung up. Then, "I'll come with you," he said.

"What?"

"Trot my way. Better yet, I'll meet you at the rental car place, so you can sign me onto the contract. Where is it? I can be out of here in ten minutes."

"You want to come with me?" Juliet tried to think if this was a good or a bad thing. Now it was her turn to ask, rather curtly, "What for?"

She could hear his smile as he answered, "To keep you a little company, as my grandmother used to say. How long are you planning to stay?"

"Overnight."

"So I'll pack a bag. Listen, tell me where to meet you and let me go, or I'll be holding you up."

"I'm staying two days," Juliet warned.

"Perfect. I have two days. Jule, I'm serious, where's the car place? If I'm coming, I gotta get going."

Now Juliet was silent, thinking hard. A child who grows up in Manhattan enjoys many cultural advantages. She may play hide-and-seek among the sarcophagi at the Met. She may learn to know people of every hue, practitioners of a dozen religions, denizens of a hundred nations. If she is drawn to theater or dance or music, she will find some of the greatest exponents of these arts a mere bus ride away. But, unless she is very lucky, she will not learn to drive.

Juliet had not learned to drive until she was twenty-three and in graduate school at Princeton University. Since then, she had seldom had occasion to go more than thirty or forty miles from home on her own. She often didn't drive at all for six months or longer, and she hadn't been behind the wheel of a car since last May. Though she had tried to pooh-pooh her own fears, the prospect of zipping alone along a couple of hundred miles of highway into the frozen north had thoroughly dismayed her. A driving companion was the obvious answer, but Ames had her family wedding, Suzy her urgent work, and Dennis might have misunderstood her to mean she wanted to sleep with him.

Murray, on the other hand, could be counted on to be all business. It was true that he would probably try to hinder her planned investigations. But he must be an excellent driver.

In all three of which suppositions, she would shortly be proven quite wrong.

chapter

TEN

Mrs. Caffrey Under the Microscope

For whatever reason, on the drive up, neither Juliet nor Murray raised the subject of Ada Caffrey, the missing manuscript, or anything at all touching murder. Instead, from the George Washington Bridge to the town of Catskill, they discussed beauty: why it had fallen from favor with artists and art critics (and in which order), why it persisted, its appeal and significance.

Unfashionably, Murray was very much involved with beauty in his sculpture. The oldest profession, he said, was not prostitution but painting—think of the drawings in the caves at Lascaux. For at least that long, man had hungered for imagery to reshape experience, share, preserve, manipulate, and reproduce it in a new way. Juliet did not disagree, but she wondered if beauty was not more a matter of individual association than social consensus.

Their talk meandered on as the miles fell away behind them. What with one thing and another, Juliet had arrived rather late at the rental agency. The Intrepid that Ames had reserved for her was gone; so were all the other ordinary cars of similar size. All that was left were a couple of Dodge vans and a Jaguar S-type. The rental agents were sorry. They would be glad to call another agency for her if she preferred. In fact, they had a branch of their own over on the East Side, down in the thirties. If Juliet wouldn't mind waiting for a few minutes, they could call over there and set her up. She could jump in a cab, be down there in twenty, thirty minutes, and hit the road an hour from now—well, say an hour and a half, tops.

She took the Jag. It was red. It was not unobtrusive, but it certainly drove smoothly. Now, in its plush, leather-smelling front seat, conversation flowed. Was beauty intrinsic in the object or truly "in the eye of the beholder"? Could it be called central to the business of life when a pebble in the shoe could instantly break its spell? Why did one culture and time prize shapes and colors another scorned? How much did the symmetry of the human form account for human ideas of shapeliness and completion? As an evolutionary matter, was it all about sex?

They looked out the windows—the day was cold but the sky blue and the surrounding, snow-covered countryside increasingly pristine—and found examples. Was the appreciation of beauty a kind of happiness? Or only a pleasure? Or was pleasure happiness? Each question suggested another, so that the miles slipped away and Juliet forgot for minutes at a time that she was impelling a large mass of metal at the rate of a mile a minute among hundreds of other such masses, any one of which would, should it happen to hit them or she hit it, shatter at least two lives and probably more. This was the first time she had really thrashed out an abstract subject with Murray, and she could not help but notice that he argued (though she did not care to say so to him) like a girl. He didn't want to score points; he didn't care if he was "right" or "wrong"; he gladly turned his attention from his thought to her emendation if the latter seemed more interesting or suggestive. Their discussion was almost all inquiry and hardly any conclusion. This was in itself a pleasure, and she asked herself if it was also, in some sense at least, happiness.

As they neared Albany, however, she gave in to nature and announced her urgent need to visit a bathroom. They pulled in at the New Baltimore Travel Plaza for a quick, barely digestible bite and a cup of coffee. It was after this brief stop that Juliet learned that being a police officer does not necessarily make a person an exemplary driver. Back in the parking lot, Murray took the wheel, revved the motor, sped past the gas station, rolled down the on-ramp to the highway, and, gunning the engine, inserted the rented Jaguar into a tiny gap between a passing Cherokee Laredo and the pickup truck tailgating it. He did it with surgical precision, she had to admit, but for no reason in the world, since behind the pickup (she saw on looking over her shoulder) there were no cars as far back as the horizon.

"So what about poetry?" he took up, cheerfully zipping across the empty middle lane to enter the busier farthest left.

They had been talking about the appeal of beauty to the senses: music to hearing, painting to vision, and so on. Before Juliet could answer, he had cut back to the middle lane and shot up to eighty to pass a BMW that had been just ahead of him. He slipped back into the left lane, only a foot or two in front of the Beemer, which honked angrily.

"What sense does poetry appeal to?" he asked, with a glance at Juliet that she thought considerably too long for safety.

"Didn't they teach you in policeman school that you're supposed to watch the road?"

He looked at her again—again for much too long, in her opinion. "You worrying about my driving?" He laughed a what-will-you-think-of-next? kind of laugh. "Come on. Poetry. Think."

Juliet closed her eyes—it felt safer that way—and thought about poetry. Of course, good poetry should appeal to the ear—as music had pitch, tone, melody, rhythm, so poetry had rhyme, assonance, alliteration, and rhythm, too, and ought to be read aloud. But the poetry she cherished did not only please her ears but also corresponded to an inner sense of justness or balance. Did those count as senses? She and Murray were still exploring the ramifications of this question some three-quarters of an hour later when a sign directed them off the thruway toward Route 30, the road to Gloversville. Murray took the ramp at fifty miles an hour, then slowed with stomach-wrenching abruptness as they approached the toll booths. They went through (Murray insisted on paying, and she let him) and turned onto 131, the road that would bring them northwest into Espyville.

It had been two weeks since the blizzard in which Mrs. Caffrey had disappeared; in any case, that storm had come into New York City from the west, then blown out to sea, missing Espyville and the surrounding hundred miles or so. Yet there was plenty of snow, piled in tall banks on either side of the road and covering almost every other object in sight. As they passed through a thicket of dark firs, Juliet suddenly remembered Ada's poem in memory of Frederick A. The abundance of hemlock trees, she had learned from Ada, was part of the reason Gloversville had developed into a leather-working center; from hemlocks came tannin, an acid necessary for tanning animal hides. In the poem, Ada linked those hemlocks with the other kind, the poisonous plant. Juliet thought of suicide, then murder. She glanced a little uneasily at Murray's rather flat, bony profile. She hadn't told him anything about her suspicions (if such vague wonderings could be called suspicions) of Matt McLaurin, his "angry" poems, her thought that he might have known about the legacy, might have followed Ada to New York and killed her. Come to think of it, if Ada was in the habit of remaking her will every few months—and if McLaurin knew she was—he had had a fine motive for bumping her off promptly. Stop me before I bequeath again. . . .

But Murray, Juliet feared, would laugh at her. And indeed, compared to a real theory, she supposed her foggy guesswork was risible. Yet since he was here, how could she best make use of him? He was a trained observer; it would be a shame not to profit by that.

As they drove past Amsterdam, Juliet took out her cell phone and called Cindy Giddy. She sounded sober enough today. Maybe she hadn't been smoking dope yesterday, after all, but just a regular cigarette; maybe she had a cold and was groggy on Nyquil or something.

Espyville lay to the north of Gloversville, and Mrs. Caffrey's place was on the northern end of Espyville, just south of the "Blue Line," as the boundary to the Adirondack Park was called. Nominally a hamlet, Espyville was really farm country. Barns, silos, and low outbuildings of snow-covered sheep farms and dairy farms whizzed by on both sides of the road, the people and animals hidden, on this frozen morning, indoors. Juliet noticed a FOR SALE sign at Red Clover Farm, then another on Lazy Acre Stables. In fact, it almost seemed every second property had a broker's sign before it.

A pickup truck carrying a muddy Skidsteer passed them, then another laden with rattling milk containers. The sharp, fragrant cold, so different from that of the city, crept into the car despite the heat from the busy engine. As they turned onto County Road 12, where Mrs. Caffrey had lived, tears came into Juliet's eyes. P.O. Box 10, County Road 12, had been Ada Caffrey's mailing address.

The road curved around a pond, then rose slightly as it approached the mountains. At the first stop sign, they began watching the tenths of a mile on the odometer. The Giddys' mailbox appeared on the right just where Mrs. Giddy had said it would, two-point-two miles along. The driveway was plowed and sanded, and a clear path had been neatly shoveled from it to a small, gray, well-kept ranch house at the near verge of the property, a handsome, considerable place, with a pond visible off to the east and an aluminum-sided barn (shut up, but recently painted) a couple of hundred yards back from the house sitting amid a wide expanse of virgin snow.

"GIDDY-UP FARM" announced a painted board that swung by two chains from the bare branch of a tree in the front yard. Beneath it, a metal FOR SALE sign marked in grease pencil "250 ACRES + HOUSE" was stuck into the snow. She recognized the Giddys' own phone number written on it.

Murray pulled up in front of the wide, closed garage and shut off the engine.

"Sh'I wait for you here?"

She hesitated. When she had imagined getting her first glimpse of Cindy Giddy, she had seen herself on her own. She hoped Cindy would invite her in, chat with her about this and that, the trip up, the weather, and, eventually, Ada. Juliet would like to learn what, if anything, the Giddys had known of the reason for her trip to New York, where they had been on the day of the blizzard, and, more generally, what they knew about their elderly neighbor. Ada had told her that Tom had inherited the farm after his parents died, so he had probably known her for many years. Juliet also hoped to pick up a detail or two to use in portraying the Giddys' fictional namesakes.

But she couldn't sit in their cheerful, roomy kitchen, quaffing hot apple cider and gorging herself on Cindy Giddy's homemade biscuits, while Murray waited in the car.

"No, come," she said. "Just—let me take the lead, okay?"

Murray gave a quick, slightly facetious bow of assent. They left the car and walked up to the red door together. The doorbell chimed a lengthy imitation of Big Ben. Juliet smiled. The bell, the neatness of the house, the well-shoveled walkway, the very name "Giddy-Up Farm" all bespoke a kind of rustic orderliness that accorded well with her own invented characters. It also answered her question about whether the real-life Giddys were hurting for cash; they might not be wealthy, but they were not poor.

The door opened to reveal a tall, lithe blonde somewhere in her late twenties. She wore red hip huggers and, despite the cold, a brief red top that left the gold ring in her navel unconcealed. Her pale hair, perhaps an inch long, made a glowing aureole around a slender, ivory face dominated by large, lazy, almond-shaped, slightly tilted, dark brown eyes. Her nose was straight, her lips full, red, and perfectly curved. Her long, bare feet, the toenails painted scarlet, were thrust into open-toed, three-inch heels. One toe sported a silver ring.

"I'm Juliet Bodine," Juliet heard herself say. She felt confused, off balance. Could this be Tom and Cindy's daughter? "Is Mrs. Giddy—?" she began.

"I'm Mrs. Giddy," the woman said, glancing briefly at her. Then, slowly, she turned her sleepy eyes to Murray. The eyes awoke as she favored him with a long, frankly carnal look. "You can call me Cindy," she announced.

Juliet blinked, confounded. How could Cindy Giddy be in her twenties? Ada had told her she and her husband had inherited the farm from his parents. Naturally, Juliet had assumed they were older. Much older.

"This is my friend, Murray Landis," she said, rallying herself to recover. She had a similar sensation to that which she had had when first meeting Ada—that this person was an impostor, too unlike her imagining to be real.

"Hello, Mr. Landis," purred the real Mrs. Giddy.

Juliet saw a flush darken Murray's olive complexion.

"If I could trouble you for the key to Mrs. Caffrey's house?" Juliet interrupted, wondering if she would even be heard above the roar of Cindy's engines. There would be no homemade biscuits here—at least, not for Juliet. "I'll be sure to bring it back tomorrow."

"Whatever," said Cindy, turning away and so offering her visitors an opportunity to admire the parts of her that had previously been hidden. They were admirable. She sauntered from the door and into the bright kitchen visible at the back of the house, apparently undisturbed by the frigid air the open front door was admitting. Even from the doorstep, Juliet could see that this Mrs. Giddy had never decorated the house. The living room, glimpsed to one side of the front hall, was done up in early Americana and warm plaids. The kitchen, straight ahead, was papered with a pattern of oversized orange kettles. The air was very warm and definitely gave off a scent of dope.

Cindy disappeared briefly into the kitchen, then sauntered back, key in hand. This time Juliet noticed how large her pupils were.

"Let me know if there's anything else I can do to help you," she said, offering the key (and the help) not to Juliet but to Murray. She held it in such a way that he was forced to reach within a few inches of her chin to take it.

Murray took it, handing it to Juliet, his flush subsiding.

"Thank you. I'm sure I'll have questions later," Juliet said. She was trying to keep her voice friendly, but she would have enjoyed giving Cindy Giddy a smack. Part of her annoyance had to do with the woman's simple rudeness. But a second element, she had to admit, was the sense of how far wrong she herself had gone in crafting her Giddys on the pattern of "country neighbors." Stupid, stupid not to realize Espyville was as much a part of the young millennium as Manhattan. Probably Lord Spafford's village, Bywold-on-Tyne, was equally alive to the styles of its day (or would have been, had it existed). Regency romances might not be a high art form, but Juliet did pride herself on resisting the use of stock characters. And here she had fallen right into the trap.

In a private funk, she got back in the car, letting Murray resume the wheel. It was only fifty yards or so down the road to the next mailbox, beyond which Mrs. Caffrey's tall, rambling farmhouse showed through the leafless trees. The driveway was long, plowed but not sanded, and Murray negotiated its slippery length with care. When they got out, they both automatically locked their doors. Then, surveying the landscape around them, they laughed at themselves.

Aside from the house they had come to visit, and the Giddys' place some three hundred yards away through the leafless trees, in every direction there was nothing but empty land: silent road, trees, snow, rolling fields, a series of gnarled orchards on a procession of round, rising hills, groves of pines behind them, and, not so far away now, the dull blue mountains. It was, as Ada had said, quite, quite beautiful.

They walked up the driveway, their booted feet squeaking on the scraped snow. The house before them looked to have been built early in the last century and left to fall apart for at least half the years since. It was white, or had been when it was painted, and was surrounded by a deep wraparound porch whose balusters were coming off in handfuls. Around this, what had doubtless been an orderly planting of hedges and flowering bushes in Ada's father's time had now grown much too high, to become a thick tangle of bramble, laden at this season with clumps of snow. Two tall brick chimneys had crumbled into ruins. The windows were dark and dirty, a few panes cracked, some boarded over. A greenhouse on the side farthest from the Giddys', most of its glass smashed in some distant epoch, was now the home of winter birds, squirrels, raccoons, and, no doubt, more exotic woodland creatures.

Juliet paused at the bottom of the steps to the porch and sighed, sad to think of Ada living alone in this faded wreck. Long ago Ada had mentioned in a letter the size of the apple farm her family had left her; Juliet could not recall the number exactly, but it was over a hundred acres. From what Ada had said of the economy in the Gloversville area, land prices must be extremely depressed. Still, Juliet would have thought she could have sold her place—or some of it, at least—for enough to move into a snug house or condominium and be set for life. The fact that she hadn't Juliet took as an indication of the strength of her attachment to the place, to her long-dead parents, and, perhaps, to the vanished social world in which her family once held a meaningful place.

Sighing again, she walked up the steps and put the key into the lock in the battered door. It stuck, then turned. Mewing and the sensation of warm life surged around her ankles.

"No, kitties, no!" she exclaimed, pulling the door almost shut again for fear the cats would escape. She crept in; Murray slipped in behind her and closed the door.

But it was soon clear that Zsa-Zsa and Marilyn did not have escape in mind. They were merely curious about the visitors. One leapt onto the newel post at the bottom of a set of stairs while the other retreated toward a set of pocket doors on the left of the dank, gloomy front hall. These doors were slightly open; on the opposite side of the hall was another set pulled together and padlocked shut. The stairs, across from the front door, were covered with books, boxes and papers. The flight rose to a large door laid flat over the top of the stairwell, closing off the second floor, no doubt to save on the heating bills. Nevertheless, the hall was very cold.

Tail switching, the cat nearest the open doors glided between them. Juliet nudged one of the heavy doors open wider and followed, Murray behind her. She patted the wall by the door, found an old-fashioned, cylindrical switch, and pressed it. Dim bulbs in a wrought-iron chandelier brought the room to life. It was a sort of parlor, with four tall, narrow windows covered in thick, cheap lace and a stone fireplace, which now contained a couple of cardboard cartons. A well-worn couch upholstered in faded purple occupied one wall; across from it sat a pair of discolored pink-and-white-striped armchairs. Between these lay a dingy Persian rug. On the couch was an untidy stack of magazines, a plate containing a petrified half-sandwich, and an open box of cookies. Juliet saw what Suzy had meant about Ada's housekeeping.

But this pedestrian kind of disorder was nothing beside the parlor's other contents: a weird, dingy jumble of the most unlikely odds and ends. There was a hammock woven of rough grass and filled with antique dolls and moldering teddy bears; there was a huge, weathered ship's anchor, and a fireplace bellows painted with the cheeks of the North Wind. There was a basket the size of a small child filled with Christmas-tree ornaments and colored Easter eggs, a carved lion from a merry-go-round with most of its metal pole intact. Presumably, most of it was loot from the auctions Ada Caffrey's second husband had loved so much.

The other notable feature of the parlor was a floor-to-ceiling bookcase crammed with hardcover books. Some had old-fashioned leather bindings stamped with gold; many were slender, suggesting poetry; but not a few were novels whose familiar, sometimes notorious, titles jumped from their dust jackets: *Tropic of Cancer, Justine, As I Lay Dying* . . . If any of these were first editions, as perhaps one or two of them might be, Juliet's inheritance would have more than sentimental value. Instinctively, she touched them, trailing her fingers along their backs as she read down the shelves: Edna St. Vincent Millay, Nazim Hikmet, Robert Frost, Pablo Neruda, e. e. cummings.

She lingered a moment longer, then, with Murray following, entered the next room. Once a dining room, no doubt, it now contained Ada's famous, gigantic bed, its sheets and covers every which way, of course. The bed was almost the size of a crypt and, with its dark, intricately carved wood, almost as creepy. Juliet did not think she could have slept there, or made love. Against an adjacent wall, a battered art nouveau era vanity table held dozens of pots and tubes of makeup in sensational disarray. A tall dresser and two capacious mirrored wardrobes, both with doors swinging ajar, held Ada's beaded, spangled, draped, and gathered clothes. Spilling out from a set of built-in shelves between the windows was a lifetime of theatrical memorabilia: programs, signed photographs, scripts, prop daggers, swords, costumes, wigs. An unplugged space heater sat on the cold hearth of a second stone fireplace.

One of the cats rubbed herself against Juliet's blue-jeaned leg, and she leaned down to stroke it. Warmer than the parlor, and considerably warmer than the clammy front hall, the room reeked of dust, cosmetics, mildew, and, overwhelmingly, cat. A swinging door into the kitchen stood open, propped with a heavy black raven cast in iron.

The kitchen was unexpectedly small, its walls and linoleum floor both a muddy yellow. Two windows looked onto a tumbled back porch and a broad expanse of snow fringed by spindly rows of leafless fruit trees. There was a freestanding sink and a very old gas range, bare but for a battered kettle; over it, a black Kit Kat clock shifted its eyes and tail in ticking syncopation. Two old crockery bowls sat on the floor beside the sink, one filled with water, the other with dry cat food. Three more doors led off the kitchen: one to a pantry and, thence, a set of stairs into the cellar, another to the out-of-doors, the last to a bathroom. In the old-fashioned tub in this room sat a much-used litter box.

Juliet glanced into the bathroom, then turned back to the kitchen, fumbling in a pocket of her coat. Her heightened sense of smell often delivered insistent volleys of unwanted and useless information. She coped by smoking four or five nose-dulling cigarettes a day.

"Do you mind?" she asked, pausing with cigarette and lighter in her hands.

Murray made a be-my-guest gesture. On his face, Juliet saw a sympathetic reflection of the dismay her own features must be showing. The house was so like her first impressions of Ada herself: eccentric, game, derelict, rich in some ways, poor in others. She tried to imagine the place seventy-five or eighty years ago, when it had been the Case family home, with three girls in calico and pigtails shouting up and down the staircase while Mother adjured them to modulate their voices. Then the big house must have buzzed and clattered with life; now, all but the few rooms they had just passed through were closed off.

Feeling a bit shaky, Juliet took a Melmac saucer from a cupboard to use as an ashtray, then sat abruptly on the vinyl seat of a chair at the kitchen table. Shoved into one corner, this was a small table topped with ancient red Formica and banded in dented aluminum. On it sat a ballpoint pen and a box of the yellowing stationery on which Ada had used to write to her.

Juliet took a deep drag of smoke and closed her eyes. The kitty-cat ticked and tocked. A moment later, she heard the scrape of the other chair as Murray joined her.

"It's horrible to come into the home of a murder victim," he said. "I've always especially hated it."

Juliet nodded, then opened her eyes. Murray was looking at her with more warmth, less amusement than usual. He put his hand on her arm.

"Does it matter that she was very old?" he said. "One thing that wasn't in the newspapers, they found on autopsy that Mrs. Caffrey had a tumor in her brain, quite a big one. Raj Krishnasami, the ME, said it apparently hadn't affected her yet, but it certainly would have set off all kinds of neurological havoc in a month or two. So whoever killed her spared her that."

Juliet took this in. Then she said, "No, I don't think it matters."

"Nah, not for me either."

They sat for a while in the ticking quiet.

"It's funny," Murray said finally. "My line of business, you'd think you'd start to feel sometimes killing is okay. Like when someone takes out a big-time drug dealer, real scum, you'd think, well, glory hallelujah. But somehow, it's not that way. A person should not kill another person. I still believe that. Not even the death penalty." He moved his hand from her arm, put it over her free hand. His hand was warm; his skin tough and dry. "Give me a toke?"

Juliet handed him the cigarette. He took a puff and immediately exploded into coughs.

"God, tobacco is awful."

Juliet laughed, took the cigarette back, and stubbed it out. Murray was still holding her other hand. She looked at him curiously. At the same moment, a muffled roar caught both their ears. It grew rapidly louder, swelling to a frantic scream of pounding metal as they jumped up and rushed to the window. A gleaming streak of red was crossing the snowfield behind the house. It veered, plunged in among the bare trees, and winked over the horizon.

"Jesus." Juliet found she had put her hand to her bosom, the picture of a Regency heroine. "What was that?"

"Snowmobile?"

"Oh, yes, Ada mentioned them. What an awful invention."

The noise of the vehicle gradually vanished. It seemed to have taken with it whatever impulse had warmed them toward each other for those few minutes.

"I take it your friends Skelton and Crowder have already been here?" Juliet asked.

"I'm sure they have."

"Then I'm going to look around a bit myself."

Murray made that be-my-guest gesture again. "I'll see if I can turn up the heat," he offered, and ambled out into the parlor.

In the bedroom, Juliet plugged in the space heater (given the state of the chimneys, it was likely the fireplaces had been unusable for years) and finally took off her coat. Her first wish was to investigate Lord Quiddenham's secret compartment. But, out of an obscure sense of decency, she took a moment beforehand to straighten out the covers on the enormous bedstead. Mrs. Caffrey had slept beneath a couple of peach-colored satin quilts worn down over three or four decades to a fineness suggesting silk. With the sensation of tidying an altar, so grand was the ornate bed, Juliet fluffed the pillows and squared the quilts, then knelt by the crowded night table.

The hiding place in the swollen, polished leg was easy to find. It had been left open—by Jeff Skelton and LaTonya Crowder, probably. It was too dim to see well, but Juliet thrust her fingers inside and groped around. The cavity was small, and perfectly empty. She was tempted to close it up but feared she would be unable to open it again.

"Found the thermostat," Murray announced, coming back in. "By the staircase in the front hall, if you need it later. I turned it up."

Juliet glanced up from the other side of the bed where, in the middle of a worn hooked rug, she had noticed earlier a wooden crate full of photographs. No doubt this was where Cindy Giddy had searched for a recent picture of Ada.

"I'm going to go upstairs, see if anything's up there," Murray said. "Then I'll look through her bills, if I can find them."

Juliet, meantime, seated herself on the rug beside the crate—where both cats immediately joined her—curled and flexed her cold fingers, and began to ferret through the photographs. Nearly all were black and white, and some went back to the 1920s. Dimly registering the sound of Murray's footsteps moving across the floors above, she soon learned to recognize Ada, a darling, black-haired gamine with ivory skin and huge, heart-stopper eyes. There she was in family groups, groups of smiling friends, in wedding photographs (several her own, with her several different husbands). Ada at Niagara Falls, Ada beside a totem pole, Ada in the mouth of a cave, Ada dressed up as Charlie Chaplin. Some were in small albums; one large one was framed.

Carefully, Juliet lifted the latter from the box. The frame, covered in forest-green crushed velvet, enclosed an eight-by-ten studio portrait of the head and shoulders of a very handsome man, circa 1945. He had heavy-lidded dark eyes and thick hair that curled back from his forehead in a gessoed wave; he wore a jacket and tie and a crisp white shirt. Written across his shadowy left shoulder in heavy black script were the words: "To my darling Ada, With all my love forever, Frederick."

Frederick. Frederick A., of the poem Ada had read at Cleopatra's Ashtray.

Juliet looked up, wanting to share this discovery with Murray, then realized she could not hope to explain to him why it struck her as so poignant. But for herself, the image of Ada reading at the mike, her silver dress ashimmer in the spotlight, held her brain with almost paralyzing force; and she sat a moment breathless, head down, tears in her eyes. The poem came back to her, then Ada's vehement reference, over tea and scones at their first meeting, to the tannery owners who made their money and ran, leaving a town "plagued by acid rain" and "riddled with toxic sinkholes." Frederick A. had been her darling. No wonder she wanted Free Earth to keep her own land intact.

She was still leafing through the rest of the photographs when Murray returned to report the upstairs empty (except for dust and mouse droppings). He had also peeked into the padlocked parlor on the opposite side of the front hall. Nada. As he got busy looking for Ada's financial papers, Juliet opened the bottom drawer in the nightstand.

Inside was a thick sheaf of poems, each carefully copied out by hand on lined paper, each dated and identified by a number. There were 412 altogether, the most recent written barely a month ago. Juliet glanced at a few of the earliest ("The Cider Press" was the title of the first, dated August 1932), then set them carefully aside. Were there duplicates anywhere, she wondered? The idea of keeping a single copy of seven decades of writing—no computer backup disk, no photostats—horrified her, but might not have troubled a person of Ada's generation. She had probably known most of them by heart, anyway.

Murray, meantime, had found the drawer he wanted and sat on the bed sorting methodically through a jumble of receipts and letters. Medicare statements, Social Security stubs, documents concerning a pension payable to the widow of Frank Caffrey, utility bills, check registers, bank statements. The most recent of these last were missing, he eventually reported to Juliet, doubtless carried away by Skelton for his investigation (as had been, apparently, any contents of the wastebaskets). But the earlier ones showed savings of a little over $12,000. Other than this, the only correspondence of any interest was a business letter dated some six months before. In it, Kenneth Levenger of Fairground Enterprises asked to meet with Mrs. Caffrey at her convenience. Fairground Enterprises, the crisp letterhead indicated, was a division of the Noble Corporation of Philadelphia; what Noble Corporation might be the letter gave no hint.

Juliet's attention was soon distracted by a bundle of love letters that turned up in another drawer. Tied with a red ribbon, these had been sent to Ada during World War II by a man named Mack. Though they began and ended with predictable, if unusually spicy, endearments, they were filled in the middle with vivid portrayals of the other men in Mack's unit. Mack had a wicked tongue and an easy way with the English language. Juliet was not surprised to gather, from certain references, that before going to war he had been an English teacher at the same academy where Ada taught public speaking—perhaps it was due to him that so many great American novels were represented on Ada's shelves? Soon Juliet was lost in the world his letters conjured.

But the afternoon was hurrying by, with much still to do. With an effort, Juliet set down the letters and turned her attention back to the books. On the shelves, poetry and prose, fiction and nonfiction, were mixed wantonly together, William Carlos Williams beside Robert Benchley, Emily Brontë (in a kitschy early twentieth-century edition) next to Anaïs Nin. Meantime, Murray opened the boxes in the parlor fireplace, discovering hundreds of second-hand paperbacks, including several by Angelica Kestrel-Haven. Carefully, Juliet began to pull the books from the shelves and sort them, checking publication dates and flyleafs. If there was anything of value, she would like to donate it in Ada's name, not leave it to molder unnoticed another fifty years.

At five o'clock, she gave up for the day. The daylight was long gone, she was hungry and tired, and the sadness in the house was seeping into her. She and Murray went out to the car and returned with Ada's valise, carpetbag, and coat. Then they turned down the thermostat, unplugged the space heater, shut off the lights, said good-bye to the cats, and left, taking with them the bundle of love letters and the handwritten poems. The air outside had sharpened; their breath billowed copiously, even inside the car.

Later, they would argue about exactly whose fault the accident was. Murray was driving, but he had asked Juliet to turn around and help him back out. However it happened, one moment the Jaguar was cautiously inching along the driveway, the next its back end was gliding smoothly, elegantly, over a little embankment and down into the snow.

Murray let loose a stream of curses. These had no immediate effect on the car, but they seemed to comfort him a good deal.

When he had finished, Juliet suggested he put the car in drive.

"It won't move," he said.

"You could try."

"The rear wheels are over the edge of the driveway. I'll spin them into a hole."

"You don't want to try?"

"No, I don't."

There was a pause. Juliet had to admit the car was on a distinct slope now, its back end lower than the front.

"But would you?" she asked presently.

"You would like me to try moving forward?"

"Please."

Murray shifted into drive. A brief jolt and a whining sound ensued, but no forward movement.

A cloud, drifting across the dark sky, slowly moved to reveal a sliver of moon.

"What do we do now?"

He shrugged. "You have a cell phone. You want to call Triple A?"

"Are you a member? I'm not."

"Doesn't matter if I am, it's your rental."

"Oh."

"Rental company? Tow truck?"

"You want to sit here and wait?"

"We could go back inside."

At this point in their deliberations they were distracted by a pair of bright lights sweeping over them. A vehicle had swerved from the road into Ada's driveway, its headlamps high off the ground and so bright that only after the driver had stopped and dimmed them could they see it was a pickup truck, not new, but well kept.

"You folks stuck?"

The man's voice, shouting down from the window, was solid, capable, calm, and only a little contemptuous, pretty much the sort of voice you most want to hear when your car won't move.

Murray shouted back. The man left his engine running, climbed out of the pickup, and came over. Murray pulled the parking brake and got out, too. In the dark driveway, they shook hands.

"Murray Landis," Murray Landis yelled.

"Tom Giddy," said the newcomer, then ducked to repeat this to Juliet through the open driver's side door. "I live next door."

She got out of the car. "I know who you are," she said, coming around to him. "Your wife gave us the key to Ada's house this morning. Juliet Bodine."

She put out her hand, looking him over curiously. The real Tom Giddy was tall, ruddy, broad-shouldered, with bluntly handsome features. He was older than his wife by eight or nine years, she would guess. That still made him considerably younger than Lord Spafford's shorter, less attractive steward. But the men had a similar sturdiness. After her wild miscalculation regarding Mrs. Giddy, she experienced a certain relief.

"Thanks so much for stopping," she said.

Giddy shrugged. "Reflex. I'm a pro. I work at Harlan's garage," he explained, to Juliet's puzzled look. "I'm also the one who plowed this driveway. Guess I should have sanded it. Hang on a minute; I'll hitch up a chain." As he moved away, "Nice wheels," he added.

While Juliet suppressed the urge to explain the car was rented—it was cold, it was dark, better just let him go about his business—Giddy reached inside the pickup, put the brights on again, then went around to the back to fetch a chain. Juliet got back in the car and squinted into the glare as the men bent down and worked their mysterious arts. Soon, Tom turned the pickup truck around, got out, and connected the chain to the trailer hitch. A minute later, Murray got back in next to her and shifted into neutral. In seconds, they were up and out. As they headed into the night, Giddy honked good-bye to them on his horn.

chapter ELEVEN

Murray + Juliet

What is an inn?

Is it a snug place of shelter for weary travelers? A center of rest and refreshment for wanderers far from home? A thing of bricks and mortar, of plaster, wood, and nails?

Or is it rather a state of mind, a hospitable impulse, a fond hope, a well-meant wish? Is it, as Caroline Walsh, proprietor of the Candlewick Inn evidently believed, mostly a house with a name and a telephone listing in the business pages?

Juliet and Murray arrived at the address of the Candlewick to discover a hulking wooden wreck on a tumbledown lot. By the plentiful street light and the faint light of the moon, they could see that the homes around it were spacious and elegant, their grounds and fences well kept. In this neighborhood, they later learned, at the start of the last century, had lived prosperous owners of factories, powerful local officials. Now the residents were mostly doctors and executives, almost all of whom commuted to Albany daily.

But here also lived Caroline Walsh, native of Gloversville, who had managed from the proceeds of her wholesale novelty company (joy buzzers, false teeth, inextinguishable birthday candles) to put down just enough to purchase the Cormier Mansion, otherwise doomed to the wrecking ball. Late in the 1800s, the Cormiers had come down from Quebec to make a fortune as purveyors of dyes to the tanneries. The Cormiers had been a canny and philanthropic lot—their interest in color had prompted them to found a local museum dedicated to the artists of the Hudson River School—but not a numerous one, and at the end of the 1980s, the last of their line had died. The house had languished untenanted in the hands of a bank, an escalating eyesore, until Ms. Walsh came to the rescue just five or six years ago.

From the outside, it was perhaps difficult to see the improvements she had made since then. In truth, the roof had been patched in many places, the driveway carved out and cleared from the overgrowth that had covered it, the plumbing to the kitchen and several bathrooms refurbished, the electrical system overhauled. Most of this, Ms. Walsh had accomplished with her own hands. But alas, her admirable industry left untouched the peeling facade, the tumbledown fence surrounding the property, the holes in the front porch. Carefully, cradling Mrs. Caffrey's poems and love letters, Juliet picked her way through the uneven snow to the front door. Murray, who had insisted on carrying both their bags, tromped behind her.

The woman who opened the door was tall and gaunt, with a massy tangle of long, salt-and-pepper hair that descended like a storm cloud over her shoulders and halfway down her back. Her skin was pale, her eyes large and dark, her nose beaky, and her style of dress not dissimilar to that of Suzy Eisenman: denim overalls worn, in her case, over a bulky Irish fisherman's sweater, with a pair of heavy workman's boots. She was about fifty and recognizable at a glance as a child of the 1960s counterculture. It wasn't only her hair or even her style of dress but something in her stance, her gaze—both worldly and naive—and the game way she greeted the arrivals.

She grinned, an enchanting grin that lit up her hooded eyes and instantly comforted Juliet. "Come in."

Ms. Walsh stood back to allow her visitors to walk into what had once been a grand entrance hall and was now the cavelike portal to a vasty ruin. The hall was perhaps twenty feet high, with a floor of marble. Around three sides of it, some ten feet up, a balcony ran—or rather, hobbled, given the state of repair of its once uniform balusters. To this balcony led a double set of curving marble stairs, which debouched on either side of the entrance hall. All of this was illuminated by a crystal chandelier made up of at least a hundred sparkling drops. It ought to have shone down on a gleaming floor and creamy paintwork; instead, the marble was dingy, chipped, badly scuffed, and, mercifully, largely covered by a trapezoid of red broadloom. Paint blistered off the walls and lay in the corners in broken curls.

"Welcome to the Candlewick," said the owner of this humbled pleasure dome. "I'm Caroline." As the others introduced themselves, Caroline came forward to try to wrest the suitcases out of Murray's hands; a brief tussle ensued, which Murray lost. The innkeeper deposited the luggage on the bottom step of the left-hand staircase, then turned her attention to relieving her guests of their coats and hats.

"Wow. I didn't realize there were two of you," she said, returning to them after secreting these somewhere beyond the entrance hall. "Shit, I'm really sorry. The only available room has twin beds. Of course, you could take my room if it's too much of a drag. I have a queen."

She looked from one to the other of her guests, who said nothing.

"Come in, I just started a fire," she said into the silence. "Sit down and warm yourselves."

She turned and led them through an archway in the wall between the two staircases. Juliet and Murray had no time to do more than exchange a glance before they found themselves in a huge, pillared dining hall. At the far left end, flames roared in a fireplace easily six feet high and ten across. A couple of mismatched couches, one of cracked leather, the other upholstered in an ancient brocade, had been drawn up along either side of it. The opposite end of the room contained a dining table perhaps sixteen feet long and three metal folding chairs. This room was paneled in wood. The pillars, also of wood, were ornamented at top and bottom with wreathes of carved oak leaves and acorns.

Caroline grinned again.

"Pretty amazing, huh?"

She beckoned them to the couches by the fire. "What can I get you? Hot chocolate, Irish coffee, maybe a beer? Or do you want to see your room?"

At the repetition of the singular noun, Murray and Juliet again looked at each other. On the way over, they had discussed the possibility that no second room would be available at the Candlewick, that Murray might have to stay at the Johnstown Holiday Inn or the Adirondack Motor Lodge, whose glum premises they had passed on their way into Gloversville. Yet somehow, neither of them corrected Caroline. Instead, they fell into seats across from each other and turned their eyes to the flames.

"A beer would be great," Murray said. "If it's no trouble."

Caroline said it was not, took Juliet's order for hot chocolate and disappeared through a swinging door at the far end of the room.

This would be a good opportunity to discuss sleeping arrangements for the night, said Juliet to herself, while she stared as if hypnotized into the fire. Her body, cold and tense after the sad hours in Ada's house, felt as if it were melting. She had chosen the leather couch, which was terribly worn but also surprisingly soft and accommodating. How long had it been since she'd slept in a twin bed? Maybe not since her dorm room at college.

The recollection of that bed, that room, made her look up again at Murray, who in her sophomore year had often slept with Mona in the twin bed her own was twin to, in that long-ago dorm room. He, too, was gazing mesmerized into the fire. Back in college, Juliet would stay out as late as she could, sometimes even sleep in a friend's room on a bedroll on the floor, to give him and Mona some privacy. Still, she remembered the look of his dark head—his hair was jet black then—on Mona's pillow.

The fire crackled on. She said nothing. He said nothing.

Caroline clomped back in, a tray in her hands. She gave Murray his beer, then sat beside Juliet.

Then, "Oh shit, where'd you guys park?" she asked, almost jumping up.

"Right at the end of your driveway."

"Oh. Phew." Caroline settled back again. "You can't believe how much my neighbors hate me. You're not allowed to park on the streets in this area; and believe me, if they saw a car parked at the curb near my house, they'd call the cops in a minute."

Juliet had caught a swift, speculative look in her direction from Murray. Their eyes had met for a split second before his gaze fled back to the fire. But there had been enough in the glance to make her own cheeks flame up.

"Why should they hate you?" she asked, turning her eyes fully on Caroline and hoping to refocus her own attention on something that didn't make her blush. As for Murray, every time she looked his way, he seemed to be simply listening, gazing steadily into the fire; yet she was sure she felt the flicker of his glance on her every now and then.

Caroline gave them the history of the house and the community it was a part of. Almost all her neighbors had been looking forward to seeing the Cormier Mansion demolished, she said. It was true it had been an eyesore for a long time, and they were sick of it. So they were disappointed when she came in and saved it.

"Not that somebody saved it, I mean," she said, "just that it was me. 'Cause I'm local, I don't have a bankroll. I have to restore the place piecemeal. They wanted someone from maybe New York, like you guys, to come in and dump a million bucks on the place, you know? And then, to raise money, I turned it into an inn. Well, they're just all up in arms about that," Caroline went on, "even though I only have four guest rooms—at this point, one, 'cause two of them aren't redone yet and the third one, I'm replacing the floorboards."

And now, Juliet and Murray did look at each other openly. Both had naturally assumed other guests were occupying the inn's unavailable rooms. It took a moment to rearrange their thoughts. Then Murray smiled. Juliet smiled. Then they looked away from each other again.

"So none of them can believe the zoning allows me to have this little business," Caroline went on, "but it does, and they all just hate that. I would never have guests who were rowdy or raucous. I mean, look, it's my house, you know, I live here. I'm the one who's most concerned to keep things under control, right?"

She paused to take a swallow of the beer she had brought in for herself.

"But they're all freaked. I mean, this is a really beautiful house. They should be glad I saved it. They should support my efforts to make it economically viable. This town, for outsiders, people from Albany or New York or wherever, you can't believe what this town will do to encourage outside business. They have this economic development corporation, you know, and all it does is offer tax advantages, noise variances, zoning waivers, training for workers, God knows what all, all to get companies to agree to move here. I mean, not that they shouldn't. They should. People are hurting for jobs; we need that."

Now Juliet again felt Murray's gaze on her cheek. For a moment, she held still, allowing him to look, obscurely aware of her breath coming a little faster. She turned to him. His eyes were demurely contemplating the fire.

"But do my neighbors give a shit—excuse me—do they care a rat's ass if the Candlewick goes belly-up?" Caroline was going on meantime. "No. They'd be thrilled. There wasn't another soul who would buy the place for anything—it was just rotting here, even though this is the fanciest neighborhood in town. But they don't care." Her light, pleasant voice had become a bit harsh, whiny. "If a guest of mine parks on the street, if I don't mow the lawn, if I put out the garbage a day ahead because I'll be away, whatever, the minute they find an excuse they call the cops on me. And all because one day I might, might, if I'm really lucky, have four strangers staying here and five cars parked in my front driveway."

Distractedly, Juliet shook her head as if in sympathy. She was sure there must be more to the story than Caroline was letting on. But she could well imagine that some homeowners near the inn would like to get rid of it. She herself wondered how the income from an occasional rental could keep such an operation afloat. Then she realized that if the Candlewick was a business, Caroline could claim upkeep and improvements as business expenses on her tax return.

Caroline took another swig of beer and laughed. "Sorry, I get kind of foaming at the mouth about this stuff," she said. Both her auditors felt this too accurate to do more than nod politely. "Tell me what brings you to Gloversville."

Juliet, rousing herself to pay attention to her own words, explained, omitting any mention of the manuscript and hoping that, if it had been described in the local press, Caroline would at least not connect the story with herself. She also left out the fact that Murray was a police detective. In her telling, Mrs. Caffrey was just a fan who became a friend, came to New York to visit, and had, unluckily, been killed. Now Juliet was here with her friend to look over her legacy under the will.

"Yeah, I heard about Ada. I mean, everyone did. This is a small town, so you can imagine." Caroline shook her head. "Not that we haven't had quite a few murders of our own. A few years ago, three teens tied up this girl's ex-boyfriend, beat him, cut him, poured salt in the wounds, then strangled him to death. A few months later, a couple of kids smothered a seventy-seven-year-old man to death in his house, then drove around in his car bragging about it. That made the national papers; you probably read about that. We also had a twenty-year-old take a cab ride that year and shoot the driver. Fuck of a thing to be famous for, huh? Lately the teenagers just pee on the buildings downtown, thank God, try to set them on fire, criminal mischief kind of stuff." She sighed. "A couple have committed suicide. My generation made plenty of noise, but at least we had a point. I remember going down to Washington for a march in 1967—"

"Did you know Ada Caffrey yourself?" Juliet interrupted rudely, before Caroline could go off on another tear. "I'm sorry, I was just curious," she added, trying to soften her words.

"Oh yes, Ada." Apparently unoffended, Caroline drank the last of the beer in her glass. "Yes, I did. I liked Ada. She was bats, but she had a lot of pluck. I knew her from AdirondActors—not that I act, but I get props for them sometimes. It's easy for me on account of my novelty company. My dad knew Ada's folks. When he was a kid, he used to go over to Case's orchard and pick apples every fall. All the kids did. They'd earn like two cents a bushel or something. Of course, that was in the Depression. Ada was young herself, then."

Caroline smiled. "You know about her and her brother-in-law, I guess?" she went on.

Juliet said no.

"Oh, you're a writer; you ought to hear this story. It was a big scandal; you could definitely put it in a book."

From the corner of her eye, Juliet saw Murray straighten, his antennae going up.

"See, Ada's first husband, Mack Someone, he was killed in World War Two. After a while, she got married again to this guy Oliver Lloyd, who used to have a coffee shop in town named Lloyd's. Original, huh?"

Caroline paused to smile and asked whether Juliet wanted more cocoa or Murray another beer.

"Maybe later," Murray answered. "You were saying—?"

"Oh, yeah. So she marries Mr. Lloyd, and they're together five or six years, no kids luckily, when all of a sudden she runs off with Gerry Fowler, her sister Florence's husband. I was like five or six at the time, but I still remember the hoo-ha, because their daughter was in my class. Gerry Fowler was the pastor of Mount Calvary United Methodist Church in Espyville! You can imagine the uproar. Of course, none of the grown-ups told us kids what was going on then, but Ada and Pastor Fowler went to Boston, got on a ship, and sailed to Italy together. They were gone a month or two, maybe. Then they came back and moved into Ada's house—her folks had died by then—and Oliver moved out. They lived there for a few months more, shunned by everyone in town, naturally, and then Ada kicked Pastor Fowler out—well, he wasn't 'Pastor' anyone by then, but Mr. Fowler—and he slunk off to live in Syracuse, I think it was, the rest of his life. Mrs. Fowler became a cafeteria lady to support herself and Claudia. She wouldn't have him back. And she never remarried."

"Claudia was the daughter?" Juliet asked, looking meaningfully at Murray. She could see from his eyes he had already realized perfectly well who Claudia was these days. No wonder there was no love lost between her and her late Aunt Ada. And how like Ada to leave nothing to her niece, even though Claudia had done nothing wrong—indeed, had suffered greatly because of her aunt's perfidy.

"Oh, yeah. Sorry," Caroline was going on. "Claudia Lunceford, she is now. She married Steve Lunceford. He's everybody's orthodontist around here."

Caroline stood up to put another small tree on the fire, then looked at her watch. "Wow, I'd better get dinner going. Hey, you guys want to eat with me? On the house, I mean. I made some vegetable soup yesterday, and I was just going to cook up some macaroni and cheese, so it wouldn't be fancy, but—"

Juliet silently consulted Murray, who made a totally-up-to-you face.

"Sure," she said. What were the odds they would find another such source of gossip in Gloversville tonight? "Thank you."

They trailed Caroline through the swinging door into the kitchen, a roomy, cluttered, cheerful place, but a cold one after the warmth of the fire. Caroline busied herself with the soup and pasta; Juliet grated cheese; and Murray made a salad.

Half an hour later, while the soup simmered and the mac-and-cheese heated up in the oven, Caroline gave them a tour of the rest of her place. On the second floor were a sitting room, a library, and a full-fledged ballroom. She had turned the sitting room into a bedroom for herself, covering the bed with plum-colored velvet and the walls with quilts and woven hangings. But when she opened the doors into the ballroom and the library, they found them still as they had been when she bought the place: unheated and shadowy and, to Juliet's sensitive nose, redolent of wildlife.

A wooden staircase zigzagged up from this floor to the next, where, indeed, only one bedroom proved habitable. It was large and cold and featured its own adjoining bath. Caroline had given in to an impulse to furbish it in frilly chintz, with blue café curtains on the windows and a pile of throw pillows on each narrow white bed.

Even now, nothing had been said by either Juliet or Murray as to where he would stay that night. But to Juliet, the accumulating silence had begun to take on a texture, a weight of meaning, that was both profoundly appealing and a little scary. Like wine laid down in a cool cellar, the attraction she had felt toward Landis years ago in college seemed to have deepened, grown more complex on its own. Of course, she realized later, it was she and Landis who had grown more complex.

"Very pretty."

His voice, close to her ear, startled her. She spun around,

breaking a blank contemplation of the chilly bathroom. The remark, she saw—a compliment about the decor of the bedroom—had been addressed to Caroline.

"Thanks. I know it's kind of girly and cute, but—listen, you two, you're really welcome to my bed—"

Juliet stopped her. "This will be fine."

Murray was now in her peripheral vision, enigmatic and male. She kept her eyes fastened on Caroline. There was always the Holiday Inn.

"That soup will boil over if we don't get back downstairs soon," Juliet said.

The innkeeper led the way back down the stairs, explaining as they went that there was a fourth story taken up with tiny servant's rooms and a large attic she seldom had the courage to go into. "Bats," she confided. "Can't get rid of them. I just keep the whole floor sealed off."

They clattered down, the warmth of the fire and the furnace rising to meet them. Caroline went through the archway, then past the swinging door into the kitchen.

Juliet, aware of Murray behind her, suddenly felt his hand catch at her arm.

She stopped and turned. He was right there, an inch or two from her, his body almost touching hers. She felt his breath warm on her temple. Without speaking, he slid an arm around her back, his fingers skimming her ribs, then briefly touched his lips to the top of her left cheekbone.

Then he slipped by her and went ahead into the kitchen.

Juliet stood still for a moment, trying to understand what had just happened. But the event seemed to fuzz over at once, losing definition. The kiss could have been a gesture of friendly support at the end of a long day. It could have been the result of a sudden impulse. Or, equally, it could have been desire felt and resisted for months. Soon, she was asking herself if it had happened at all.

Rousing herself, she followed him into the kitchen. Caroline was opening the oven, talking about the Giddys.

"I know Cindy three ways," she was saying as, hands encased in oven mitts, she lifted the heavy casserole dish from the oven. "My niece, Brittany, went to school with her. And I know her parents. And Cindy worked for me one summer at Walsh Novelties."

She set the casserole down for a moment on the tiled counter, then hefted it again and brought it through the swinging door to the table. Murray followed her, carrying plates and silverware, and set the table. Juliet, scrutinizing his unreadable back, picked up the salad bowl and trailed behind. The dining room table was washed in heavy, uninviting shadows. She wished they could eat on the couches by the fire.

They sat down. Caroline served, like a mom.

"I hired her because I felt sorry for her," she was going on, as she scooped and doled. "I went to high school with her folks. Joe Lang is a drunk, and I really believe Elaine is certifiably psychotic. If she wasn't when we were kids together, she must be after thirty years with Joe.

"Anyway, they live in a hovel right off Route 81. Six kids, and neither Joe nor Elaine could ever keep a job. Brittany brought Cindy over to my place once or twice, when they were maybe fifteen, and—well, she was so pretty and young, I felt sorry for her. Just a few things she said about life at home, you know, how chaotic it was, and especially about the kids not having enough money for clothes, shoes. Even food, sometimes."

"Poor girl," said Juliet, with a flicker of empathy.

"Well, don't get carried away with pity," Caroline warned. "I learned that lesson the summer I hired her. That girl embezzled from me, can you imagine? As low-level as the job was, she didn't get more than a couple of hundred dollars. But still!"

Sympathetic murmurs from the guests.

"And don't imagine she was taking it home to buy milk and bread for her little sisters and brothers. She turned up that fall in a leather coat with rabbit fur trim. She was just a kid, a high school sophomore. I really never expected her to be so"—Caroline searched for the word—"so grasping," she finished, and Juliet saw in her bafflement the Peace-flashing flower child she had once been.

"Did you turn her in?"

"To the law?" asked Caroline, who had been told only that Murray Landis was a sculptor. "No. Not my style. I just read her the riot act and showed her the door. Although maybe I should have reported it, because the next summer was when she took Jenny Elwell's eye out at a party. That's her main claim to fame around here."

"What?"

"Well, that and marrying Tom Giddy. And that is a claim. Tom could have married just about anybody he wanted. Have you met him?"

"Actually, he just rescued us," Juliet said, explaining.

"Yeah, that's Tom. Volunteer fireman, Boy Scout, good-looking as hell, I think, and, incidentally, a damned fine mechanic. As the owner of a 1986 Saab, I can attest to that."

Regaining her good humor, Caroline grinned her radiant grin. Juliet wondered briefly what the equivalent of a volunteer fireman was in 1813.

"So he married Cindy Lang, of all people. He's a few years older, of course. Probably thought he was saving her from herself."

"And the eye—?" Juliet prompted.

"Oh, right." Caroline raised a forkful of macaroni to her mouth. "That happened because of a fight over a drug buy that went bad," she went on. "From what my niece told me, Cindy had become a bit of an entrepreneur by then. She is ambitious, I'll give her that. She'd given money to Jimmy Giaconelli or Mike Drelles or someone in that crowd—tough boys—to go to Albany and buy a kilo of grass. Don't ask me where she got the capital, stole it from someone, probably. The boy bought the key, but he thought he was entitled to keep half on account of he went out and scored it. I'm sorry to say Brittany knew all this because that's the crowd she was into then, too," Brittany's Aunt Caroline noted.

"So anyway, they're at a party at Jenny Elwell's house—no parents around, that's the Elwells for you—and Cindy's arguing with Mike. Or no, come to think of it, it was Jimmy, because Jenny was Jimmy's girlfriend. So they're arguing, and suddenly, Jenny literally puts herself in the middle of it. She jumps Cindy—everyone there agreed on that aspect of events; Jenny started the fight—and they begin pounding at each other. And the next thing you know, Cindy's managed to get hold of a cake knife. The next second, Jenny Elwell's permanently lost the vision in her left eye."

Caroline speared a slice of cucumber with her fork, then looked up from her plate to ask if she could get either of them anything else.

Wondering where they'd landed, Juliet shook her head. Adolescent murderers, suicides, drug dealers, embezzlers, brawlers—it all sounded far more sinister than Manhattan. Between that and the bats on the fourth floor, she felt rather nervous about going to sleep alone upstairs (if she was going to sleep alone, a question she immediately shoved aside). That was the trouble with living in a doorman building: you got used to the idea of someone watching out for you all night.

Murray was asking if there had been a trial.

"Oh, sure. But none of the kids would admit to the drugs angle. Jenny and Cindy both testified it was jealousy over a boyfriend. And since Jenny started the fight, and since Cindy was a minor, she wound up with just probation."

Juliet tried to figure out how long ago this must have happened. Cindy looked to be twenty-eight or -nine, so maybe a dozen years back? A person could change a lot in a dozen years, she supposed. From the spruce look of their house, Tom made a decent living. But from the moment she had laid eyes on Mrs. Giddy, the lady had jumped to front-runner on Juliet's local murder suspect list. Would "decent" be enough of a living for Cindy Lang?

Hoping to get Caroline talking about Ada again, she opened her mouth to ask if the AdirondActors were any good. Unfortunately, Caroline opened her mouth at the same moment.

"You first," said Juliet politely.

"Oh, I just wanted to hear about your writing career," said the hostess, and the rest of the meal vanished into the maw of this (to Juliet) exceedingly tedious subject. As they all washed dishes and tidied up, Caroline changed her focus to conduct a vigorous interrogation on the subject of Murray's sculpture. The moment the last dish was done, she declared herself bushed, showed them how to bank the fire and turn down the thermostat when they went to bed, and (with one final offer of her room if they wanted it) went upstairs for the night.

There followed a long, strange moment during which Juliet and Murray stood as if stunned in the vast living-dining room, like children whose parents have suddenly, weirdly, incredibly, turned over the house to them.

Then they went to the leather couch. They sat down side by side, Juliet first, Murray a moment later, a few careful inches away. She looked into the fire and, on the edge of her vision, saw that he was doing the same. They sat this way for some minutes, silent.

The fire crackled and spat. Then Juliet became aware that Murray had turned his head and was looking at her. She turned her head and looked at him. His dark face flickered, liquid under the light of the fire, his small, bright eyes glittering. As near as she could read them, he was willing to go either way.

She looked down at her hands, feeling as she did so the pulse of blood in her ears. Her hands lay folded with deceptive calm in her lap. She looked up again at him. She closed her eyes.

A long second passed. She heard the rustle of his clothes, the slight groan of the couch as he leaned over. He kissed her mouth, a slow, solemn kiss. His lips were soft but dry, as if, she thought, he had not kissed anyone in a while. The small part of her consciousness that was not completely absorbed in sensation considered, in turn, the cold, narrow white beds upstairs, the diaphragm she had left safe in its little case in her medicine chest back home, the time of the month, and the fact that she was wearing a black bra with white underpants. Then Murray moved forward, brushing his mouth across her cheek to the side of her neck.

She fell back onto the couch, bringing him with her, slid her hands up under his sweater, and relinquished thought.

chapter TWELVE

Mrs. Caffrey Recalled

At ten minutes before one o'clock the next day, Juliet sat on a wooden bench at the Regency Funeral Home, trying to figure out what to say when her turn at the podium came.

There were forty or so people gathered already in the small sanctuary. The Regency, despite its highfalutin name, was modest, homey rather than stately, and decorated in plain, dignified style. Juliet had expected most of the mourners today to be old, but perhaps Ada had outlived her cohort too thoroughly for that. Many were quite young—AdirondActors, she suspected, and, no doubt, Free Earthers as well. Not surprisingly for Ada, there were more men than women.

The only people she recognized, Tom and Cindy Giddy, had come in soon after Murray and herself. Cindy, dressed in a slim, black pantsuit trimmed with silver zippers and chains, spotted Murray at once and sent a deeply interested glance his way. While her husband stopped to say hello to someone near the back of the sanctuary, she came forward, nodded at Juliet, favored Landis with a husky hello, then slipped into the bench directly across the aisle from them.

A minute later Tom came up and offered a more traditional greeting to the visiting New Yorkers. He was nice enough, Juliet noticed, to refrain from making any jokes about their misadventure yesterday. Then he had been wearing a parka and a hunting cap with the flaps down; today he was dressed in an ill-fitting blue suit, his thinning blond hair brushed straight back from his face. Even so, he had an outdoorsiness that contrasted strangely with his wife's flashy, stylish, sulky look. Despite his smile, he looked uneasy, tugging at his collar and absently pulling his suit jacket down. With something of nostalgia, Juliet remembered the mental image conjured for her by Ada Caffrey's first mention of her "neighbors" in the country: the cheerful, pie-baking, sturdy wife, the beefy, hard-working lunk of a husband, the two of them kindly dropping by now and then to leave casseroles and loads of chopped firewood for the frail old lady next door. The Giddys she had invented for Lord Spafford's estate were all right, she supposed, but she must be sure in the rest of "A Christian Gentleman" to work against these stereotyped notions of "country" and "neighbors." Perhaps she would go back to the innovative Sir Francis Browne and spike him up a bit. After all, the experimental farmers of the time had been a sort of avant-garde.

She tried to return her thoughts to what she would say when called to the podium. It was fortunate that most of her relationship with Ada had developed long distance, through letters. Because of that distance, she found it possible now to think of her almost as a character, and that made it easier to decide what to say. She would talk about how she had come to know Ada, about the dowdy, depressed Mrs. Caffrey she had imagined before they met, then how the real Ada had astonished and entranced her. Her eyes coming to rest absently on Cindy as she worked out the shape of an ending, she happened to catch the dark, sly gaze Mrs. Giddy cut across the aisle to rest, briefly but with unmistakable lust, on Murray. Tom, seated between the two, straightened as he also saw, his jaw tightening visibly. He was, Juliet realized all at once, lovesick.

She turned her own eyes to Murray, feeling a bit love-sodden herself. It ought to be easy to think about Ada now, to mourn her, in this of all places. Instead, she was intensely, delightedly aware of Murray Landis's warmth beside her. Well, Ada would surely have approved of such a distraction. Juliet noticed his hand resting in mute invitation on the polished wood between them. Gratefully, her own hand crept into it. Murray, she was glad to reflect, had not seemed to notice Cindy Giddy at all.

Around them, people in ones and twos continued to arrive as one o'clock came and went, filling the rows of benches, their voices hushed. There was no casket on display. As Juliet understood it, Ada's cremation was to be an unceremonious event—perhaps had already taken place.

Juliet kept scanning the faces for one to match Matthew McLaurin's hesitant, faint voice on the phone. But when at last a dark-suited funeral parlor functionary appeared at the lectern to start things by introducing him, it turned out that McLaurin was someone she had failed even to notice, a tall, bulky, thirtyish man with a broad red face and a silver ring through his lower lip. She had been looking for a bony, weasly misfit. The real Matt wore his plain wool suit as if suits were a kind of garment unknown to him until this morning, as if he had been inserted into it by machine. His thick brown hair was chaotic, longish, jammed back behind the ears. His wide-boned, dark-eyed face looked raw and artless. He set a thin pile of pages on the lectern, then fiddled uncomfortably with the microphone, touching it as if it might crumble or explode in his hands.

"Good afternoon," he finally said into it, then cringed back from the amplified parody of his reedy voice. With a small smile at his own nervousness, he went on, "I'm here today as a friend of Ada Caffrey. Which I hope—which I guess we all are."

His anxious eyes flew over the scattered assembly. Juliet upgraded his shyness from excruciating to cataclysmic. And yet he was the one who drove Ada to Albany for poetry slams. Should a microphone frighten him?

"Ada was a wonderful friend to me," he was saying, reading

from the papers on the lectern. He looked up only now and then; his voice trembled slightly. "It's funny, but I often felt she was the younger of the two of us. And now that she's gone, I feel as if I've lost a contemporary. I don't think Ada would want us to dwell on the manner of her death, so I'm not going to. Instead, because she loved poetry, I'm going to read a poem I wrote for her just a week ago, when I learned she had left her home and her land to Free Earth." He smiled self-consciously. "It's new, so you'll have to forgive me if it isn't, you know, perfect. Anyway, it's called 'Home.' "

The little sheaf of pages rustled as Matt turned to the poem.

" 'Home,' " he said, looking up with another quick smile, then down at the page again.

"Whose house is this? Of blood and bone,
of wood and brick, of turf and stone?
Whose world is this?
Not mine alone.
Nor is this flesh I seem to own.
Nor do I go when it is gone;
Nor will you, while my heart is warm."

There was the awkward silence that often follows a speaker's words in such solemn situations. People shifted in their seats, reminding themselves not to applaud. Juliet, even as she felt tears spring to her eyes, found herself coolly assessing the poem. The curse of the one-time English professor, perhaps never to be outlived. But whatever the formal attributes of "Home," it was certainly earnest and tender, she noted. She would like to read some of the angry poems Ada had spoken of. There was certainly something off about Matt McLaurin. He was shy to the point of furtiveness. He looked—What was it? Hunted. He looked hunted.

Why?

Meantime, he was introducing a person named Chad Blynn,

president of the Gloversville-Espyville Free Earth Society chapter. A tall, wiry man in his early forties, Blynn rose and took the lectern. He wore black Levis and a thick, brown turtleneck sweater. Despite his age, he had the tense, unhappy face of a graduate student. Glasses flashing, he began to speak rapidly of the devastation local industry had wrought on the land and waterways.

"Ada Caffrey knew all this firsthand," he declared, his pale hands grasping the lectern. "As a girl, her family depended on the bounty of the cultivated land. She grew up close to nature. Yet even when she was a girl, in the 1920s, the Cayadutta Creek stank with pollution. Every day the tanneries dumped more waste into it. In 1947, Ada lost the great love of her life, Frederick Asquith, to cancer—cancer Asquith developed working on the finishing line at Craigie Leathers. Many years went by, but Ada Caffrey never forgot."

Juliet looked around. While some of Blynn's listeners nodded righteously, a mulish look had come over others. Even Caroline Walsh had admitted that the causal link between the tanneries and the local cancer rate remained to be proven. No doubt there were many present who would welcome a new heyday for the tanneries if it meant the return of jobs to the town. Juliet wished she knew whether Claudia Lunceford, despite her personal antipathy to her late aunt, was here.

Meanwhile, Blynn was going on about Ada. ("She knew that the earth is forgiving, but she also knew its limits. She knew that those who take from the earth must also learn to give back. And so we are honored, we are humbled by the act of giving represented by the legacy of . . .") From the generality of his remarks, Juliet gathered Blynn had not known Ada well, perhaps not at all. Then, suddenly, Matt was at the podium again, this time asking Ada's friend Juliet Bodine to come up and share her thoughts. Murray squeezed her hand as she left him.

A perverse flicker of annoyance leapt inside Juliet as she walked to the lectern. Forgetting her own reluctance to attempt a eulogy, she began to feel resentful. She wasn't afraid to speak publicly. Did Murray think she was? That squeeze of the hand, as if he were wishing her luck . . . She didn't need luck. She was a poised and seasoned speaker. Even as these thoughts ran through her head, she chastised herself for taking a kind and supportive impulse in bad part. Maybe Suzy was right; maybe she just didn't want to let anyone get close to her.

She took the podium calmly, carefully adjusting the microphone. In relaxed, undramatic tones, she described how she had come to know Ada, how the reality of the woman had overthrown her expectations. Satisfied grunts of recognition and short bursts of laughter greeted her description of Ada at the Plaza, Ada atop the Empire State Building, Ada kissing the startled Ashtray emcee. Only as she finished did she allude to her violent end, speak of her own personal distress that a visit to her city should have been the occasion of Ada's death. By the time she left the lectern, a few people were fighting tears. The Free Earthers, initially slightly aglow in the aftermath of Chad Blynn's remarks, looked appropriately sobered. Juliet noticed Tom Giddy trying to take his wife's hand; but Cindy pulled away, crossing her arms. Matt McLaurin, seated in the front row so that he could come and go from the lectern, bowed his head and closed his anxious eyes.

Juliet had avoided looking at Murray during her talk. But as she finished, she allowed her gaze to meet his. His eyes were, she found, filled with admiration—not soppy, kindly admiration, but respect. She returned to her place next to him feeling pleasantly vindicated.

Not that she could have explained why a person needs to feel vindicated after another person treats her with unnecessary kindness.

Anyway, it was a relief to be forced to quit scrutinizing her own flaws and pay attention to the extremely elderly man currently making his way toward the front of the room. McLaurin had asked whether anyone else wished to speak, and this gentleman had put up his papery hand. Leaning heavily on the back of each bench as he passed, he finally reached the safety of the lectern. He wore a gray pin-striped suit that probably fit him a couple of decades ago but now hung so loosely on his stooped, diminished skeleton that his pant cuffs threatened to trip him. His complexion, however, was still fresh and ruddy, and his expression showed a personality still lively and wry.

"My name is Bert Nilsson," he said, his slow voice quavering slightly. "Over the years, I was Ada Case's friend, Ada Case's lawyer, and Ada Case's lover. That's a statement quite a few men hereabouts could make—except for the lawyer part. And I just want to say for all of us that Ada Case Lensbach Lloyd Caffrey was a lady. And that's all I'm going to say."

And with that, he turned and began the long shuffle back.

Matt, meantime, was left to take the podium amid the laughter Bert Nilsson left behind. Disconcerted, he asked if anyone else cared to speak. When no one did, he noted that refreshments would be served in an adjoining room and so, awkwardly, closed the ceremony.

The Regency's "family parlor," furnished like a large living room, contained a long table on which orange juice and cider were now offered in paper cups, alongside a platter of cheese cubes and crackers. Juliet had expected only a few people would linger, but the room filled almost at once. She made a mental note for "A Christian Gentleman" that one feature of country living was no doubt a scarcity of social gatherings and a consequent tendency to make the most of those there were.

"See if you can find out what the Giddys knew about Ada's manuscript," she whispered to Murray, then bolted away in pursuit of the elusive Matt, who seemed hungry after conducting the service and had gone straight for the cheese. Trapping him in the small space between the serving table and a window, she reached out to shake his hand and at the same time deftly rotated him so that his back was to the room. Behind him, she could see Tom Giddy pour himself a cup of orange juice, then stand absently revolving it in his hands.

"That was a beautiful memorial," Juliet said. "I loved your

poem. You're very gifted. Do you often read at slams?"

Matt's large face mottled as he blushed. "Not very often. I'm working on that. Usually, I just go to listen."

"How is your little girl? Is she here?"

Juliet briefly pretended to look around, noticing as she did so that Murray was talking to Bert Nilsson. The Giddys had begun to form the nucleus of a little knot of people—friends of Tom, to judge from Cindy's bored stare. She hoped Murray would grab them before the chance went by.

"No." Matt shifted uneasily, perhaps feeling cornered. Which he was.

"Is she with her mother?" Juliet suggested brightly. She had noticed he wore no wedding ring, but that meant little.

"No," Matt said again.

Juliet flirted with the idea of asking pointblank who and where the mother was, but something, some hint of fragility in McLaurin, prevented her. Instead, she blundered on, "Wasn't she the one who found the hidden compartment in Ada's bed? She must be very clever."

This time Matt said nothing at all. Was there something wrong with the little girl that her father preferred not to speak of her? Something about the finding of the manuscript that made the topic taboo? (Like, for example, that he knew what it was, followed Ada, and killed her for it?) His job at the insurance agency appeared to be fairly menial. How much did he need money? Was there a messy divorce in the works? Child support? Two households to maintain? Or was there just something plain weird about Matt?

"Does she like poetry? You must have been so excited when she pulled those documents out of the bed—what a moment!"

Matt shook his head. "I never saw them. Gina pulled something out of the bed and gave it to Ada, and that was that."

"You mean, Ada never told you what it was?"

Matt's face darkened, but he only said quietly, "No. But I read about it in the newspaper after she died. I wish Gina had never found the manuscript. Ada would be alive." His voice had dropped to so low a pitch that Juliet could barely hear him. She scrutinized his broad, closed face. "Did you get over there yet?" he asked now. "Did you find her poems?"

"Oh. Yes." Juliet reined in her thoughts and described the orderly pile in Ada's nightstand drawer. This morning she had taken them all to the Copy-Kwik in Gloversville, where she would shortly pick up two sets of duplicates. She had disliked leaving the precious manuscript there even for a few hours; but the pages needed to be hand fed, and she would have been late for the service if she had waited. She had slipped twenty bucks to the teenaged attendant to make sure they didn't get lost.

"I made a set for you. Should I drop it off at your place? You're near Ada, right?"

"Oh, please don't feel you need to bring them to me," Matt said hurriedly. "I can pick them up. Just leave them at the Copy-Kwik."

Juliet said it would be no trouble to drop the poems by—she had to go back to Ada's today anyhow. But the other flatly declined. He did not even say, "It's hard to get to," or, "I won't be home." He was also showing distinct signs of wanting to escape, glancing around him into the room, trying to sidle away from the table against which Juliet had pinned him.

In desperation she blurted out, "How did you find out Ada left her farm to Free Earth? Had she told you in advance?"

Matt's head tilted. "No. As I said on the phone, Mr. Nilsson called me," he said. His tone was mild, but there was something stubborn in it, too, Juliet thought. Angry. Maybe he realized she was grilling him, suspecting him. Whatever it was, he muttered something totally inaudible, then turned his back on her and slipped into the crowd.

Following him with her eyes, Juliet saw that Murray had managed to engage Tom and Cindy in conversation. The Giddys stood side by side, Cindy smoldering up at Landis, her husband watching them, slowly turning the paper cup in his hands. Juliet thought of joining them, then looked around for Chad Blynn—one of the few people here she would have known how to introduce herself to—and discovered he had gone. Indeed, after making a serious raid on the refreshments, many people had left already, while others were drifting toward the door.

Still deliberating whether she would help or hinder Murray by joining him, Juliet found herself set upon by two very elderly ladies she had noticed sitting in the back of the sanctuary. Both carefully coiffed and dressed, they introduced themselves as Mary and Margaret Flood, sisters, lifelong AdirondActors, and (most recently) Ada's fellow witches in the planned production of *Macbeth.*

"We never read Regency romances," Margaret Flood announced, after Mary explained that Ada had tried to share with them her love of Angelica Kestrel-Haven's books. "They're a little unsophisticated for us."

Margaret smiled, as if their lofty disdain for Juliet's life work would naturally ingratiate them to the author. It was a smile Juliet had seen many times. For reasons that escaped her, people often thought she would like them better if they showed they were too intelligent to enjoy her books—as if the whole enterprise were some sort of insider's scam she (and they) practiced upon the brainless masses.

"Try reading one," she suggested. "I'd be curious to hear what you think." She was about to turn away when it occurred to her that the Flood sisters must know a great deal about the locals. Overcoming her pique she added, "I thought Matt McLaurin did a wonderful job today, didn't you?"

The Flood sisters agreed, though both thought more could have been made of Ada's career as a thespian. Juliet politely suppressed the observation that, if they felt so, either one of them could have said something herself.

"I did hope she'd leave some money to the AdirondActors," Mary whined. "We're always so hard up for money."

"Ada mentioned to me that Matt had a daughter," Juliet said, doggedly ignoring her. "Is there a wife, do you know?"

Margaret's eyes lit up and she leaned forward confidentially. The Flood sisters's lives were insured through Gallop Insurance. They had also wondered about this. No, there was no wife—not that they'd ever been able to discover. No wife, no ex-wife, no mother for Gina. Wasn't that strange?

"But—"

"He only moved to town a year or two ago, you see," Mary put in, stage whispering. "No one here knows much about him at all."

"And he won't say anything, either," Margaret took up. "Not where he came from; not even exactly where he lives. Believe me, we've tried."

Juliet believed them. A sudden movement at the corner of her eye told her that Cindy Giddy had torn herself away from Landis and was walking out of the room alone. Fearing to miss the chance of a word with her, Juliet hastily said good-bye to the sisters and followed.

Outside the parlor, Cindy turned down a hall, passed the front entrance to the Regency, and kept going. Finally, she opened a door and went in.

Ah, the ladies' room. Juliet felt a wave of gratitude to fate. She waited outside for twenty or thirty seconds, then entered to find there was only one stall. A wisp of smoke rose from behind its door, and the sharp, spicy smell of burning marijuana was in the air.

Juliet, surprised by Cindy's obvious lack of concern over who might catch her here, opened her purse and began to dig through it for makeup and a comb. She didn't normally wear makeup, but she thought she had a stick of concealer somewhere in there, and maybe even a lipstick. Any pretext would do: When Cindy finally emerged, she would be in no position to ask Juliet what she was doing in the ladies' room.

A full two minutes went by before Cindy flushed the toilet (surely for show?) and sauntered out. She acknowledged Juliet with a dull, "Hello."

"Hello. Let me get these things out of your way," said Juliet, beginning to clear the sink of her odds and ends.

Cindy looked confused, then realized Juliet expected her to want to wash her hands. Or to pretend to want to wash her hands. She shook her head and raised a hand to push open the door.

"Oh, listen, I wanted to ask you about your house being for sale," Juliet blurted out. Anything to keep Cindy from leaving.

"What about it?" Cindy's voice was sharper than Juliet would have expected, especially with the scent of grass still fresh in the air around them.

She smiled a propitiatory smile. "Oh, I just wondered. How much are you asking for it?"

"Why, are you planning to move up here?" Cindy smiled. Juliet thought there was something mocking in her beautiful, sleepy eyes.

"Well, not move here, maybe. But . . . it's a beautiful piece of property. It would make a good investment."

"Oh, sure."

This sounded mildly sarcastic, and Juliet had the distinct idea that Mrs. Giddy was too stoned to say more without laughing outright. For her own part, she was desperate to find a way to bring up the manuscript.

"I guess the area's pretty economically depressed, though," she said. "Unless you find a hidden treasure, like Ada did."

"Ada found a hidden treasure?"

Juliet looked at her carefully. "The manuscript. You know, the reason she came to New York. It was in all the papers."

"Oh, that. Yeah, the manuscript." Cindy's tone was scornful, as if she knew all that stuff about a valuable manuscript was phoney. Now Juliet felt confused.

"Did Ada tell you when she found it?" she asked bluntly.

"Tell me what?"

"What it was?"

"Did she know what it was?"

"No. But I mean—I just wondered if . . . She must have been pretty excited, something like that turning up out of the blue."

"No, she didn't tell me about any treasures," Cindy said. "She just said she was going away and would I watch the cats."

Juliet said, "Oh." She felt stupid, slow. Wasn't there something odd about Cindy's tone, her answers? Or maybe she herself had gotten a little high, just from being in here.

"Anyway, ask Tom about our place, if you're interested," Cindy said, pushing open the door. "Maybe your boyfriend will buy it for you."

"Oh, Murray's not my boyfriend," Juliet corrected her without thinking, as she walked down the hall beside her.

Definitely, she had gotten a little high.

"Isn't he?" The other woman turned to look at her with undisguised interest.

"No, we're old friends. We went to college together."

"Is he rich? What does he do?"

"Well, he's—he's an artist."

"Oh. He must be pretty good at it. He drives a nice car."

By now they had reached the doorway of the parlor, where only a handful of people remained. Murray was talking with Bert Nilsson, Juliet saw. Cindy also saw. She stood gazing at him, as if lost in thought.

"Well, it's not really his—" Juliet had started to correct her, when Tom Giddy suddenly materialized behind them. He, too, had noticed the direction of Cindy's preoccupied gaze.

"We better get going," he said abruptly. "I need to get back down to Harlan's by three."

Cindy pulled away from the hand he tried to put through her arm. But she went with him, sullen but docile. Obscurely relieved, Juliet moseyed up to Landis, who was just saying good-bye to the elderly lawyer.

Juliet also said good-bye, smiling dreamily. She must get over this whiff of dope.

"Did you meet the Luncefords?" she murmured into Landis's ear, forcing herself to come down, sharpen up. If the Luncefords had been here, they were gone now. Only a few very old people remained and a couple of very young ones.

"Bert said they didn't turn up."

"Oh, 'Bert' is it?"

"He's quite a card," Murray said, smiling. "We can still drop by at the Luncefords."

"Can we?"

"Bert says they never go anywhere on Sundays. Sunday is Steve Lunceford's day to have his parents over for a family dinner. No law against ringing someone's doorbell."

"There's a set of Browning I could offer her. It's a nice one, and the bookplates in it are inscribed Charles Jongewaard Case. Probably Ada's grandfather or great-grandfather. No reason Claudia shouldn't want that."

A few minutes later, they left the Regency. On the way to the Copy-Kwik, they traded information gleaned during the refreshment hour. Murray had learned from Bert Nilsson that Ada wrote her current will after meeting Matt and becoming interested in the cause of Free Earth. Her previous will had named a girlhood friend, Emma Luth, as the beneficiary; but Miss Luth had died without issue some four months ago, leaving the bequest moot.

Not that Bert Nilsson thought Ada had much to leave, Murray added, as Juliet eased the Jaguar into a parking spot on Main Street. Once upon a time, when it had been a working orchard, the Case property would have brought a very tidy sum, he had said. But the place had long since gone (literally) to seed; and even if some visionary cared to try to restore it, a small operation like that in these days of corporate agriculture would more likely bankrupt its owner than enrich him. It was just land now; and land values hereabouts were, in general, extremely low. The larger the parcel, the harder it was to sell, and the higher the property taxes. Only working farms were eligible for tax breaks. As for the house, it was so dilapidated that to repair it would probably cost more than to tear it down and rebuild.

Murray interrupted his narrative as they went into the Copy-Kwik. Juliet's heart skipped a beat on finding that the teenager she had carefully bribed was gone. But his replacement located the poems easily, the originals tidily boxed after being duly photocopied and collated. She paid the bill and left the second set for pickup by Matt McLaurin.

"You don't happen to know him?" she hopefully asked the attendant, a pigtailed woman of twenty or so. Somebody around here must know Matt's story.

But the woman shook her head. "Should I?" she asked.

Juliet and Murray agreed to stop for a quick lunch at a coffee shop down the street before going back to Ada's house. There, Juliet tried chatting with the waitress, thinking she might somehow get a conversation going, learn a bit about Ada or Cindy or McLaurin, anything. But the girl was barely sixteen. Everything she knew, it seemed, she had learned from MTV.

Juliet gave up. They ordered, BLTs for both of them. While they waited, Murray wrapped up his summary of Bert Nilsson's information. On the whole, he had been inclined to feel it would have been no favor to Emma Luth to leave her the orchard. People who owned large parcels of land in the area were mostly trying to get rid of it, cash it in for whatever it was worth so they could quit paying taxes and move somewhere they could make a living. Giddy-Up Farm, for example—that was a substantial place. The younger Giddys—Bert had handled Mr. Giddy Sr.'s estate—had put the place on the market as soon as Tom inherited. Though they had also moved in, of course. It was a nicer place than they could afford on Tom's salary. And since there was no likelihood of finding a buyer any time soon, they might as well enjoy it while they owned it.

This being all Murray had learned, Juliet reported the dribs and drabs she had wrested from McLaurin, the Flood sisters, and Cindy.

"Quite the pothead, isn't she?" Landis remarked, as she reached the end of her tale.

"Did you get any better sense of Tom?"

"Doesn't trust his wife. When she left for the ladies' room, he checked his watch."

"People do check their watches. Didn't he say he had to get back to work?"

Landis raised a skeptical eyebrow.

The BLTs arrived, each with a mountain of French fries on the side. Juliet decided to eschew the latter, then ate one, then two, then ten. It had never been entirely clear to her why God invented French fries, since they were so bad for you, yet so delicious. It was a question that, if she had been of a theological bent, she might have pondered with regard to many other eatables as well.

She glanced up from dipping a fry from her dwindling hoard into a puddle of ketchup to find Murray watching her thoughtfully.

"What?"

"Just looking at you," he said. "You okay? You're not upset about last night?"

"Upset?"

"Yeah. You know." He smiled a small smile. "It was kind of . . . sudden."

Juliet put her French fry down. Upset? Sudden? An alarm bell went off inside her. She tried to silence it but failed. Surely these were the kind of words men used who felt they'd made a mistake.

Fear that Murray was about to try to undo last night, back out of it, treat it as a fluke, made her heart begin to pound. Next thing you knew, he'd say "I'll call you" and not call. Come to think of it, last summer he had said he would phone, then disappeared for a month. Of course, they had not been involved then. That was only a matter of inviting her to see the work in his studio. But maybe he didn't think they were involved now. Men could do that, she knew, barge into your life all smart and tender and passionate, sleep with you, then behave as if it never happened. Juliet had learned that the hard way. And her life was all right these days. Not perfect, but fine. She wasn't about to let someone in who was going to play games with her.

"Why?" she asked. She could feel her face become hard, formal. "Are you upset?"

"No," he said uneasily. "I was just checking with you."

Juliet pushed her chair back slightly. "Do you know something about last night that I don't?"

"What should I know?"

"I don't know. Maybe that it will never be repeated? Something like that?"

"How could last night be repeated?"

"You know what I mean."

"No. It was—" Murray leaned forward, his voice dropping even as his Brooklyn accent intensified. "It was the first time, Jule. You can't repeat a thing like that."

"But I mean, that was a peculiar question: Am I upset? Why should I be upset?"

"Take it easy."

"It isn't easy for me. I don't take these things lightly."

Now his voice rose. "You think I do?"

"I don't know. Do you?" asked Juliet, apparently forgetting that Murray had inspired her to create the deliberate chastity of Sir James Clendinning. "Why did you tell me to take it easy?"

"I didn't mean to take *that* easy, I meant—Oh, for crying out loud, Jule, you know what I meant."

"Do I?"

They glared at each other.

"I hope so," Murray finally said.

They finished the meal in silence and said little back in the car. At Ada's, Juliet quietly castigated herself for undue prickliness (the man was innocent until proven guilty, for crying out loud) while she sorted through a few drawers of papers she had only glanced at yesterday. Murray opened the cartons stacked on the disused stairs. They were full of hardcover books, mostly English and American plays and poetry in editions published before World War II. Juliet supposed Ada had little money for buying books after that.

She emptied two of the cartons and refilled one of them with photos, theatrical ephemera, and personal letters to take home to New York. Zsa-Zsa and Marilyn stalked around, rubbing themselves along her legs and the sides of the cartons. Except for a fuller litter box, their lives since yesterday appeared to have been uneventful. Carefully, Juliet lifted the set of Browning and the possible first editions and stacked them into the second emptied carton. The remaining books and papers she would donate to the library in Gloversville.

At length, "Ready?" Murray asked.

At a nod from Juliet, he put on his coat, then hefted the two cartons they were taking and carried them out. Juliet petted the cats good-bye and locked the door. Murray was starting the Jaguar as she arrived. He backed out, then pulled over by the Giddys' mailbox, where Juliet hopped out to leave the key. They had hardly spoken since the contretemps in the coffee shop.

Returning to the car, Juliet said stiffly, "The Luncefords live on Partridge Lane." She opened a local map they had bought at a gas station and directed him. As he drove, she felt herself sink deeper and deeper into self-disgust. How ridiculous to turn Murray's kind, casual question as to whether she was okay into a pretext for discord. Suzy was right. Juliet claimed to long for intimacy, but panicked at its approach.

"It must be the Cape Cod on the corner," Murray said, cruising slowly down a tidy block not far from the Candlewick. His Brooklyn accent was on thick—a distancing mechanism, she thought. "Want me to come with you?"

The Luncefords were fairly wealthy, if this was their neighborhood, Juliet reflected. Certainly no money had come from Mrs. Lunceford's side of the family. Steve Lunceford must have tightened a lot of braces.

"I'll go myself," she said, then slipped out of the car. As Murray popped the trunk, she took out the Browning set, feeling ashamed of the way she had jumped on him, but also incapable of explaining or even apologizing. For one thing, she could not figure out how to explain without referring to the question of whether or not he had another lover, or many lovers—a question she had not yet dared to ask.

The Luncefords' street number was tacked to their front door in handsome brass numerals, and their doorbell sounded two low, elegant notes. Juliet stood in the porch light, dancing in the cold. Half a minute went by, then a whole minute more. The windows were blazing, but Sunday dinner or not, it seemed no one was going to answer. It was dusk; Murray and Juliet would have to leave town soon, especially since he was on duty tomorrow. She had turned away from the door and was going down the steps when she heard a knock on the glass pane alongside the door and turned to see a carefully groomed face peering suspiciously out at her.

After a moment the door opened a few inches, then was stopped by a chain. The guarded face appeared in the crack. "Yes?"

Juliet identified herself. "I'm sorry to barge in like this, but— Are you Claudia Lunceford?"

The door closed, then opened fully. Mrs. Lunceford reluctantly allowed her visitor to advance a few feet into the vestibule, just far enough so she could close the door and keep the cold outside.

Juliet explained her errand. She listened, but heard no happy hum of family conversation from another room. On the other hand, the house was large; the family might be closed into a den in the back. The vestibule was small but thickly carpeted and freshly painted; a convex circular mirror in a gilt frame on one wall reflected the mahogany coatrack across from it. Mrs. Lunceford, Juliet noticed with interest, wore a white silk shirt, a narrow blue wool skirt, sheer stockings, and low heels with her spotless red-and-white-checked apron. Her hair was combed back smoothly from her face into an impressive chignon. She was about fifty, Juliet supposed. In her small frame and large green eyes there was a hint of family resemblance to Ada, but she wore hers with a difference that entirely changed the style of person she was. Mrs. Lunceford was, if Juliet had to classify her, a fussbudget.

"I appreciate your thinking of me with regard to the Browning," she said, in tones that reversed her meaning, "but, as I believe I have already told you, I have no wish to receive anything that belonged to my aunt."

"You must have been so shocked to hear of her sudden death," Juliet said sympathetically, as if this putative shock would account for the other's lack of interest in Ada's belongings. Mrs. Lunceford had neither asked her in nor invited her even to put the books down, but Juliet was determined to stay and talk until she was positively thrown out.

"Nothing Ada Case did could ever shock me," Mrs. Lunceford assured her.

"Still, to be murdered . . ."

"I wouldn't say being murdered was something that Ada did. Presumably, it was done *to* her."

Something in her tone suggested that if Ada had caused herself to be murdered, that would have reflected better taste, more appropriate judgment.

"I understand you had good reason to dislike your aunt. But the Browning belonged to a Charles Jongewaard Case—I imagine that was your great-grandfather?"

"Miss Bodine, if it was in her house, I don't want it. Now, if you'll forgive me, I really must say good night. I have something on the stove."

So saying, Mrs. Lunceford opened the door again and more or less pushed Juliet out into the near dark.

She returned to the street, asked Murray to pop the trunk again, and slid into the car thoughtfully. Murray had "Proud Mary" blasting from the radio.

"Not interested, huh?" he said, referring to the rejected books, as she fastened her seat belt. He turned the radio down.

"No. But I think she'd make a crackerjack murderer," Juliet replied. They pulled away from the curb. "Not with her own hands, of course. She's very small, like Ada. But she would make a dandy Lady Macbeth."

"Was Dr. Lunceford at home?"

"Not that I could tell. But I didn't get far enough inside. She wasn't exactly cordial."

"Welcome to detective work. Want to head home?" They had checked out of the Candlewick this morning (though "checked out" seemed a misnomer for the informal business of handing Caroline Walsh a couple of twenties).

"I guess so." She added halfheartedly, "Do you want me to drive?"

"If you want to."

Juliet remembered the ride up. Landis's driving was on the harrowing side, but she still trusted him more than herself. "Not really."

She consulted her map and advised him on the turns that would take them back to Route 131. A few minutes later, lofted by a sudden puff of courage, "Listen, Murray," she blurted out. "I'm really sorry about that weirdness at lunch."

"Don't be."

"No, I mean it. I just—"

Dear God. What did she "just?" "Just" really liked him? "Just" really wanted it to "work?" If she was honest, what had moved her to push him away at lunch was a fear that last night had been both less important and less welcome to him than to her. Could she say that?

Apparently not.

"It's just, you've been really great," she heard herself say, at the same time as an inner voice screeched, "Shut up, shut up, shut up!" "I really appreciate your coming up here with me."

"No sweat. I enjoyed it."

Congratulations, Juliet. He enjoyed it.

The night was dark and the traffic light. The Jaguar smoothly followed the beam of its steady headlights to the thruway. There, nothing awaited them but the long, dark drive home. Despite sporadic attempts, this was accomplished with none of the engaging conversation they had fallen into so easily on the way up. Around Saugerties, Juliet mentioned her sense that there was something hidden about Matt McLaurin, something creepy. He might have secretly guessed Gina's find was valuable, she suggested, followed Ada to New York, and killed her for it.

But Murray uncooperatively insisted on reading McLaurin as more tense and unhappy than sinister.

Next, Juliet brought up the Giddys. What if Cindy had known about the manuscript? They had only her word for it that Ada hadn't mentioned it. And Cindy had gone for Jenny Elwell's eye with a knife, for God's sake—

"I thought you told me during the missing investigation that Mrs. Caffrey herself said she didn't tell anyone in Espyville about the manuscript."

"Oh. Right," said Juliet, in a small voice.

A few minutes later she hypothesized aloud that Claudia Lunceford might have been so angry at her aunt for failing to leave the family property to her that she had arranged for a hit, choosing New York as the locale perhaps to throw off the police, perhaps because hired assassins were more plentiful there. Or it might be that Dr. Lunceford, self-employed as he was, had taken the day off and gone down to do the job himself.

"All the stories of teenagers run amok Caroline Walsh told us," observed Murray, "you'd think they could find some local talent to carry out a killing."

Juliet tried to imagine Claudia Lunceford arranging a two-part payoff of blood money to some local delinquent. Tried and failed. Dr. Steve?

She supposed an orthodontist must meet a lot of teenagers. But even she had to laugh at the outlandishness of her suppositions. Why not face it? Dennis Daignault had killed Ada Caffrey. And she, Juliet, had brought Ada to him.

The rest of the drive down took place in near silence. Juliet's thoughts drifted uneasily. She felt that she had not only hurt her chances with Murray today, but also that she had actually hurt him. But, as often happened when her emotions became uncomfortable or tender, this recognition only deflected her thoughts toward work.

With all the books she had lugged to Espyville about the commons system and enclosure, she had read nothing over the weekend. Tomorrow, when she sat down at her desk, she would be no more learned about sheep farming than she had been when she stood up from it on Friday. Still, she clung to the hope that something of the country had rubbed off on her to spruce up "A Christian Gentleman."

They crossed the George Washington Bridge and Manhattan sparkled into view—vast, gleaming, packed with life, and (as it always was to Juliet after she had been away) as astonishing and improbable as a flying saucer. Then she remembered the World Trade Center. Momentarily, fear, sadness, and anger swept through her. The body of her city had been mutilated, it seemed to her, as much as if a lover had suffered an amputation. Like everyone else, she had to learn its new shape and how to love it all over again. For her, the new attachment was more fierce and passionate than ever.

Murray insisted on driving her to her building, then taking the car back to the rental agency himself. In front of her awning, with Marco waiting attentively, he went around to the trunk of the car to pull out her suitcase and the cartons of Ada's papers. Juliet hurried to meet him by the trunk, then allowed the doorman to carry her things inside while she followed Murray back to the driver's door. Here he finally turned to face her.

"I'll call you," he said, and she bit her lip. He reached out his arms. She thought he was going to hug her, but a moment later she realized a cab was coming down the street fast behind her, threatening to hit her. So he was just saving her life.

Disappointed, "Thanks," she said. "Thanks for everything."

He looked hard at her. Then he shook his head, as if unable to decide what he saw.

"Murray."

She put her hands behind his neck and kissed him.

He kissed her back. But then he made a fist and lightly knocked it against the side of her hatted head.

"What's in there?" he asked.

Later, alone in bed and unable to sleep, she wondered the same thing. Whatever it was, she decided at last, it was not a comprehensive understanding of agricultural change in nineteenth-century England. With a sigh, she sat up, switched on the light, and reached for the stack of books she had uselessly carried to Espyville and back. There was Burt and Archer's provocatively titled *Enclosure Acts: Sexuality, Property, and Culture in Early Modern England.* Or Warren Ortman Ault's *Open-Field Farming in Medieval England.* Or why not Brian Bailey's *The English Village Green*? In the end, she almost managed to make herself pass over the photocopied pile of Ada's poems in favor of one of these.

But not quite. Which, as it turned out, was rather a good thing as regarded finding Ada's killer.

chapter THIRTEEN

The Sound of One Penny Dropping

Juliet opened the cardboard box provided by Copy-Kwik, hefted out the thick gleanings of Ada Caffrey's mind, sat back against the pillows, and propped the first hundred pages or so against her knees. "The Cider Press" and the next few dozen after it were girlish, amateur affairs—singsong meters and bouncy rhymes used to evoke blooming daisies or autumn leaves. But soon Ada began to develop the voice Juliet had heard at the Ashtray. Soon, too, her subjects grew less pastoral, more erotic. There were witty poems and wrenching poems, sonnets, odes, even haiku, as well as free verse. The language in the better ones was quite down to earth.

Juliet leafed through, setting aside the first batch to delve into a second, then a third. The subjects, she found, reflected the arc of Ada's life, perhaps any life: from discovery of the world, to discovery of her inner world, romance, sex, disenchantment, and back again to the outside world. At one o'clock in the morning Juliet started to yawn and sleep began, finally, to look inviting. But before she closed her eyes, she decided sleepily, she would just take a quick look at Ada's last few poems.

The very last, dated December 2001, was a cinquain called "Morning Birds."

"Mine!" sing
birds while my fine
feathered friend says, "Move, old
crow, we need your place." But I squawk,
"Mine, mine!"

Juliet pushed the covers off her knees, sat straight up and read the poem again. She read it three times, then turned to the previous poem. This, also dated December 2001, was a villanelle, titled "Landmine."

He sips his coffee, turns it in his hand,
Looks out my window, says, "All flesh is grass."
This is my place, this was my father's land.

I listen—seem to listen—but the sand
Runs slowly through my mortal hourglass.
He sips his coffee, turns it in his hand.

"You hold the key to jobs. You understand?"
I bridle at the slur, then let it pass.
This is my place, this was my father's land.

He's not a bad man, but a man unmanned.
He sputters, coaxes, begs, then, like an ass,
He sips his coffee, turns it in his hand,

And brays at me, "It's worth six hundred grand!
"Buy what you like." But I like this, alas.
This is my place, this was my father's land.

At last, "My friend," I say, "here's where we stand.
I make no deals. Now, pay attention, class:

This is my place, this was my father's land."
He sips his coffee, turns it in his hand.

Galvanized, Juliet threw off the covers, scattering poems everywhere. She jumped out of bed. Land, land, land—neglected land, valuable land, the development of land. Land in the English Regency. Land in the foothills of the Adirondacks. With its tumble-down house and untended hundred-odd acres, in a hamlet virtually bristling with FOR SALE signs, the police had accepted it as a given that no one particularly wanted Ada Caffrey's place. Dazzled by the glamour of the Wilson manuscript, they had discounted any other financial motive for killing her.

But the value of land could change, as the enclosure of the English commons proved. What if Ada's farm had special value to someone, great value? Then might it not be worth scheming for, killing for? Juliet thought of what Caroline Walsh had said about her area's vigorous efforts to attract business. Variances, tax abatements, and exemptions, even training for workers, such were the enticements she had mentioned. And Ada's place was just on the edge of the Adirondack Park. Could that combination of circumstances, perhaps, make it uniquely valuable to some business or other? Maybe a resort? Or an industry that capitalized on some resource from the mountains: the plentiful water, possibly, or the fact that development of the land inside the line was tightly restricted? Someone clearly had been leaning on Ada Caffrey to sell, someone who offered a lot of money, who told her the sale would bring jobs to the area, who pointed out to her that she was old.

Juliet dashed down a few quick thoughts in the notebook she kept on her night table. Then she called her father's personal line at the office and left a voice mail message to phone her back the moment he got in. Ted Bodine knew more about office buildings in urban capitals than commercial development in the boondocks; but he was still, by far, Juliet's best source on real estate. If he didn't know someone in Albany or Utica, he would know someone who did.

This done, she got up, peed, then reassembled Ada's carefully numbered pages. She climbed into bed again and methodically checked every one of the 412 poems. She slowed as she got to the last fifty, methodically scrutinizing them for any hint of content concerning the purchase or sale of land. But she found nothing. At four in the morning, she finally set them aside, opened *The English Village Green,* and read herself to sleep.

She was dreaming about seed drills when the ringing of the phone woke her.

"Dad?" she said. Her thoughts flew back into place with unusual clarity as she checked the time. It was just after eight.

"It's me, Jule," said Murray.

"Oh!"

"I guess I woke you. Sorry."

"No, that's okay. How are you?"

"I'm fine. But I thought I'd let you know something that came up here over the weekend regarding the Ada Caffrey case."

"Oh!" Juliet said again. It had already occurred to her that this early morning call might be of the sort that seeks to erase what came before it—for example, a weekend of unexpected sexual passion. On the other hand, it might be the sort of call that seeks to smooth over tensions after same. But it had not occurred to her that Murray might be calling about Ada's murder.

"Look, John Fitzjohn is in the clear." Murray was using his best I'm-just-a-simple-cop-from-Brooklyn voice. "Evidently, he's been having a torrid thing with a fifteen-year-old girl, the daughter of one of his clients. When the blizzard slowed down his office and closed her school, he called her to arrange a get-together at a hotel in your neighborhood. Since he was going to be nearby, he stopped in at Rara Avis.

"Obviously, he was reluctant to reveal all this to Jeff," Murray went on. "To Detective Skelton, I mean. But over the weekend, the girl told her parents. On Sunday they brought her down to the station and allowed her to make a statement. She was with Fitzjohn when he said good-bye to Caffrey; she'd been waiting for him downstairs. So he's pond scum, and he has been charged with rape. But he didn't do the killing."

"Oh," said Juliet, resorting to what seemed to be a staple of her vocabulary today.

"Yeah."

"That leaves Dennis at the top of the likeliest suspects list?" she ventured.

"Dennis and/or you," Murray corrected. "I mean, in Skelton's mind. No offense."

Juliet hesitated. She had meant to trump whatever he had to tell her with her midnight epiphany. But it didn't seem like the moment. "You couldn't—could you have a word with Skelton, Murray?"

" 'Have a word' with him?"

"You know, sort of vouch for me? Explain . . . ?"

"Jeff Skelton is well aware you and I are on a friendly footing," Murray said. "Unfortunately, all that achieved was it precluded my being assigned to the case. It doesn't make him cross you off as a suspect."

"Oh. I see."

Juliet was silent a moment. In her excitement, she had somehow managed to forget that Murray was a policeman a long time before he was her lover. Perhaps she'd better check out some facts before mentioning "Landmine" to him.

"Footing?" she echoed instead. "Is that what you call what we did the other night?"

"I wasn't thinking of that, but yes, we could call that footing. Footing, footsie. Footling."

"Footling," Juliet repeated, then added in a rush, "Do you think we could footle again? I'd like to."

There was a pause, a very long and uncomfortable one for Juliet, before Murray said, "I would enjoy that very much, Juliet."

She smiled.

She rose and dressed feeling—despite her greater legal peril—much more cheerful. Footling apart, if it should happen to turn out that Ada's land figured into the murder, she and Dennis would be demoted to the lowest ranks of the suspect list. At least, she hoped so.

The thought of Dennis gave her a guilty shiver. Apart from deciding he was a murderer (and how guilty she felt now about coming to that conclusion!), she had barely allowed herself to think of him all weekend. She supposed she ought to talk to him, break things off officially. Although "things" had never amounted to much between them after all. By the time of their last meeting, indeed, they seemed to have fizzled to a mutual cinder. Perhaps Dennis had found being viewed as a possible co-conspirator in murder as dampening to sexual ardor as she did. Would it be very cowardly just to skip any breaking off, treat him as if they had never been more than friends?

She decided that she must at least share her suspicions based on "Landmine" with him, and tell him what Murray had reported about Fitzjohn this morning. She e-mailed him but omitted any mention of her romantic adventures that weekend. Instead, leaving the matter unsettled, she diverted herself (as usual) from uncomfortable thoughts with the slightly less uncomfortable thought of work. The weekend's events, and the latter part of this morning's phone call, had suggested to her a rather drastic change for "A Christian Gentleman." Suppose Sir James Clendinning was not the bloodless prig she had taken him for but, on the contrary, so highly charged sexually that he believed only a double-barreled superego, reinforced with weekly lashings of organized religion, could make it safe for him to walk the Regency streets? Why else should he maintain such a fierce insistence on propriety except to check innate torrents of rampant desire?

Looked at this way, Juliet found Sir James instantly more sympathetic. Before going down to eat breakfast, she sat at her desk and allowed herself to glance through the manuscript so far. Indeed, each scene of prudishness made much more sense considered in this light. Cheered, she decided to rewrite these passages so as to make his underlying penchant subtly clear.

But it would not do to be reading *Open-Field Farming in Medieval England* as a preparation, or even *Enclosure Acts: Sexuality, Property, and Culture in Early Modern England.* No, she must find something racier than that to nourish her mind. As she stirred oatmeal a few minutes later, the answer came to her: As soon as she had checked through the last year or so of Ada's poems, in case there were any others touching on land, she would immerse her imagination in the complete, unexpurgated memoirs of Harriette Wilson.

When Ted Bodine finally answered the voice mail his daughter had left for him, the reply came, disappointingly, in the form of a call from his secretary. Mr. Bodine would be busy all day, traveling and in meetings, but he hoped his daughter would meet him and a companion for dinner that night at Le Perigord. An eight o'clock reservation had been made for three.

The nature of the companion, the nature of the restaurant, and the nature of the evening all sprang clearly to life in Juliet's mind immediately. The companion, of course, was the great gal; the restaurant—expensive, formal, and so far east it was nearly in the river—one where "Ted Bodine" was a name to conjure with, a man to truckle to; the evening late and leisurely. For Juliet, who grew up so unhappily on Park Avenue, the Upper East Side of Manhattan was her own private Krypton, the place where the powers she had acquired as a grown-up had no force. Immediately upon crossing the threshold at Le Perigord, she would become a mere mortal.

Still, she meekly agreed to be there and hung up, reminding herself that there were worse things than being treated to a dinner of first-rate French food. She spent the rest of the afternoon eroticizing Jim Clendinning (as she now thought of him), a somewhat labor-intensive task at first, but an interesting one.

And it was not unpleasant, she confirmed that evening, to be ushered into an atmosphere of lively, fragrant pleasure. She had arrived late, despite her best efforts not to exercise this particular form of passive-aggression. Ted was ensconced at a table by the bar in a snug little room in back, already well into his first bourbon-and-water and holding forth to a rapt waiter on the subject of bartenders in Madrid.

She paused for an instant to take him in. He was a blue-eyed, handsome man whose modest height and proportions ought to have condemned him to a life of being described as dapper. However, his zest, his continual animation, enlarged him, somehow, so that people spoke of him as a streak, a riot, a whirlwind, always some kinetic metaphor. His favorite word was "hilarious." "It was hilarious!" he would proclaim, at the end of nearly every story. "We laughed all night!" he'd recall, and a tear would actually form at the corner of his eye, as if of condensed amusement. "Hilarious!"

The gal, a slender (what else?) blonde in a well-cut business suit, sat toying with something red and fizzy in a Martini glass, politely smiling as her date regaled the admiring staff. Though they had never met, she spotted Juliet before Ted did, looking from him to her and back, and indicating, by an intelligent widening of the eyes, that this was probably his daughter—?

Ted cut short his story ("It was hilarious!" he assured the waiter), pushed back his chair and came to hug Juliet. He brought her back to the table and introduced her to Dara Chaffe.

Juliet shook the other woman's hand and smiled. To her own surprise, the smile was more or less genuine. There was something likeable about Dara Chaffe. On closer inspection, her face was not the hard, perky mask most of the gals wore, but pretty and uneven and animated by a soft vulnerability quite unlike her bladelike suit. Juliet guessed she was forty—not too much older than she was herself, but older, at least. When Ted made heavy jokes at Juliet's expense on the subject of how long he had been trying to engineer this meeting, Dara ignored him and adroitly drew his daughter into a conversation about the gradually lengthening days. Juliet wondered why Dara was going out with Ted and guessed she would not be doing so for long.

Dara worked, Juliet soon learned, as a commercial real estate broker. For much of the meal, conversation turned on why she had come to New York (originally, to study music), how she had come to be in business (it beat starving), the state of the Manhattan real estate market, what constituted a Regency romance, whether they were hard to write, French cooking, and other matters that seemed inevitable but entirely beside the point to Juliet in her slightly feverish state of mind.

But after their plates were cleared away and they had ordered dessert (one crème brûlée for Ted and Dara to share, a second for Juliet to regret later on), she was finally able to mention, apropos of Ted's business trip to Pittsburgh that day, that she had been in Espyville over the weekend.

"Oh, that's the strangest thing!" Dara exclaimed at once. "I just met a man who was there on business a few months ago and woke up with a snake in his bed, can you imagine? A copperhead."

"In Espyville? Was he—where was he sleeping?" Juliet asked, envisioning a campsite.

"In a perfectly ordinary motel. A Travelodge or a Comfort Inn or something. He was all right, luckily, but my God! He said it was three feet long."

"Who was this man?" asked Ted roguishly. "What do you mean, you just met him?"

To her credit, Dara did not smile coyly and tap him lightly on the nose with her fan. She looked a bit uncomfortable, in fact, and, choosing to ignore his tone, explained that she had heard the story at a dinner party, where she was seated next to the man in question, whose last name she could no longer remember.

"Do you know why was he in Espyville?" Juliet asked.

"Oh, yes. He works for a company that develops theme parks, amusement parks—like Six Flags, Medieval Times, that kind of thing. They're thinking of starting a whole chain of theme parks located near various environmentally pristine tourist destinations. Like a Prairieland, was one he mentioned, and a Desertland. They'll be for families who don't really want to go camping out in the open, maybe, but who want to get the flavor of a place. They'll have rides for kids based on the natural attractions—like a geyser ride near Old Faithful, for example—and displays of plants and animals native to the place. Like a zoo. And there will be theme restaurants with specialized foods, pretend things like porcupine quills that would really be potato sticks, but also real things—buffalo burgers, venison . . ."

"So why was he in Espyville, do you know?"

"Oh! The flagship park in the chain is supposed to be a place called Wildernessland. His company wanted to open it near the Adirondack Park."

Wildernessland! Immediately, Juliet heard the word echoed in Ada's thrilling voice. She had spoken it, unintelligibly but with majestic scorn, the very first time she visited Juliet. How could she have forgotten?

"And will they?" she asked, on the edge of her plump, well-upholstered seat. Much as she had talked about development in the

Gloversville area, Caroline Walsh had mentioned nothing of this.

"I don't know, I assume so."

"How could a copperhead get into a motel room?" asked Ted. "Disgruntled former employee?"

"Oh, it turned out it was an environmental thing. There was a note signed 'Mother Earth' slipped under the door. Something to the effect of 'Warning: Development Equals Death.' Something like that. The poor guy's still having nightmares."

Juliet murmured sympathetically. So far, she had said nothing to her father of Ada Caffrey's murder. By good luck, the few articles that had mentioned her own connection to the case had appeared in newspapers her father did not read, and her fear that some tabloid fan in his office might have mentioned them to him had apparently not materialized. She was reluctant to let him know more than was necessary. For one thing, if he knew she was a suspect, he would insist on hiring Alan Dershowitz or Johnnie Cochran to represent her. But if anyone could track down the origin and status of the Wilder-nessland project, it was her father. When Dara excused herself to go to the ladies' room, Juliet took a moment out from praising her to ask Ted to follow up.

"If you can find out, I'd especially like to learn whose land they were looking at for the site," she said.

"Why? Have a friend up there who might be interested in sell-ing?" Ted asked.

"Something like that."

"Companies don't much like to talk about that kind of thing ahead of time," he warned her. "They keep their plans a secret till it's a done deal. So I may not be able to get the exact names."

"I have faith in you."

She smiled and, feeling an unexpected surge of affection, pat-ted his arm. After all, he was only a man. Perhaps she would not have made an ideal single parent herself.

chapter FOURTEEN

Juliet Articulates a Theory

It took Ted Bodine only a few hours to come up with the information his daughter had requested. There were not many companies that created theme parks. Nor were there many occasions when his daughter turned to him for help. Precisely which old connections and hidden strings Ted had pulled to find out, Juliet never knew. But at twelve-thirty in the afternoon on the day following the dinner at Le Perigord, his secretary faxed her the information:

After being promised a number of variances, tax incentives, and the like through the good offices of the local economic development corporation, Fairground Enterprises, a division of Noble Corp., had, on December 10 of the previous year, offered to buy a parcel of land—375 acres altogether—consisting of the adjacent properties of two Espyville landowners: Thomas G. Giddy of 2209 County Road 12 and his neighbor, Ada Case Caffrey. The owners had been given eight weeks to consider the offer, which was approximately triple the going price for acreage in the area. Each offer had been contingent on both parties agreeing to sell.

Mrs. Caffrey's answer, returned by means of a handwritten letter dated December 15, had been an unequivocal, "No." Her neighbors were interested, however, and had asked that the offer remain on the table for the full eight weeks. Given its picturesqueness and its proximity to both the state park and the New York State Thruway (as well as its happy distance from a sewage treatment plant that had ruled out a number of otherwise attractive alternative properties), and in light of the generous flexibility of the local government, the proposed parcel represented a particularly advantageous spot. So Fairground had granted the Giddys' request.

As things had turned out, Ada Caffrey died while the offer was still open. The Giddys had notified Fairground of this fact, and they approached her lawyer, who in turn relayed the offer to her legatee. So far, Free Earth, too, had declined to sell. The offer would expire irrevocably on February 1, at the end of this week.

Before her father's fax about the Fairground offer came through, Juliet had been continuing the work of uniting James Clendinning with his new-found libido. Now she handed the changes to Ames and turned her full attention to making the best use of her father's information. Feeling she owed it to him, since it was chiefly his neck dangling on Skelton's hook, she first called Dennis, to tell him the intriguing news. But Dennis cut her off almost as soon as she'd said hello.

"I'd rather talk in person," he said. "Could you have dinner tomorrow? Maybe at the restaurant you took me to for my birthday?"

It took Juliet a moment or two, but she caught on to his intention. He did not wish anyone listening in to know where they would be meeting. He did not wish anyone listening in to hear what she'd called to tell him. He believed, in short, that someone was listening in.

Meekly, she agreed.

"Eight o'clock?" he suggested. "Take the long way."

Juliet hung up feeling uncomfortably cloak-and-dagger, then tried Murray at the station.

"Yo," he bellowed.

"Murray?"

"Oh, Jule." His voice dropped. "I was expecting someone else.

Listen, it's a bit of a fluke that you got me. I gotta run. Caught a homicide yesterday morning, gang thing."

"Well, I don't want to keep you, but—"

"Yeah, I gotta fly. But since we're talking, lemme warn you, I'm probably gonna drop out of sight for the next day or two. Don't take it personal."

Juliet gave up and called Zoe Grossbardt, first at her office, then on her cell phone. She, too, was busy, just on her way in to court for the day.

"I'll be glad to call what's-his-name, Skelton, for you," she said, her voice clipped, "but I can't get to it till later. Maybe tomorrow, depending on how things go."

"I'd rather not wait."

Zoe hesitated briefly. "If you can't wait, call him and tell him yourself," she said. "But say nothing else. Write down exactly what you're going to say, call up, say it, and hang up the phone."

"Yes, ma'am."

It took two hours to get a call back from Skelton, almost time enough to finish the business of converting Sir James to give off a positive erotic charge. Juliet told Skelton it had come to her attention that a potentially lucrative land deal parceling Ada's farm with the Giddy property had been proposed a few weeks before her death. Editing out the fact that she had gone up to Espyville herself, and entirely erasing Landis, she merely asked if he didn't find that suggestive?

Skelton invited her to come down to the station.

"Do I have to? I'm quite busy."

"Certainly not. At this point in time, you're under no compulsion."

Irritated by the phrase "at this point in time," not only for the implication that she might well be compelled at some other "point in time," but also for its ponderous redundancy, Juliet said she was busy and asked if they couldn't just talk on the phone.

"I find the phone is not as effective a means of communication as a face-to-face meeting, Ms. Bodine. Before I take any action on your allegation, I'd like to discuss it with you directly."

"Allegation?" Juliet echoed impatiently, then decided to capitulate. She had gotten quite a bit done on the book today. And if he was going to delay investigating this angle until she'd come to see him, she might as well get it over with now. "Oh, fine. Give me fifteen minutes."

At the precinct house, she found him at his desk, finishing a meatball hero. He must have been out testifying in court or something when she'd called earlier, she thought; instead of his usual khakis and open-collared shirt, he was dressed in a three-piece suit, complete with handkerchief and watch fob. Crowder materialized from some lair beyond the squad room and escorted her into a small, windowed room down the hall, where they sat wordlessly until the other detective arrived.

"Now, you've said you find this offer to buy the victim's land suggestive, Ms. Bodine," he began, once she had filled him in on Fairground's dates and terms. "In your opinion, what does it suggest?"

Juliet opened her mouth, then closed it. In her excitement about distancing Dennis (and herself) from suspicion, she had forgotten she must, of necessity, implicate the Giddys. But there was no cure for it.

"Obviously," she said, "it suggests a motive for Tom or Cindy Giddy to kill Ada Caffrey." She said both their names, but she hoped Skelton would realize Cindy was the likelier suspect by far. "Ada Caffrey refused to sell, the Giddys wanted to sell, they were yoked to her by the way the deal was structured, and now she's dead."

"Have you asked the Giddys about this? How do you know that they wanted to sell?"

"Well, for one thing, there's a 'For Sale' sign on their front lawn," Juliet blurted out. Too late, she realized what she had done.

How foolishly arrogant she was. Not only had she refused to wait till Zoe could take care of all this for her, she had come down to the station in person, not even bothering beforehand to write down the information she wished to give. Such preparation, she had thought, was unnecessary for someone of her mental powers. Swish of the winding cloth as her undead bête noire left its coffin for a walk.

"Is there?" Skelton asked inevitably. "How do you know?"

Juliet could feel her face flush as she tried to reply, with dignity, that as a legatee of the deceased, she had gone up over the weekend to look over her bequest. And also to attend a memorial service for her late friend.

"That was very conscientious of you, Ms. Bodine," said Detective Skelton, "especially since you're so busy."

She glared at him. "I liked Ada Caffrey," she spat out. Then, with an effort of will, she controlled her tone and spoke more calmly. "But that's neither here nor there. The point is, someone wanted to buy Ada's farm. You should talk to that person. And you should talk to anyone who stood to benefit if she had agreed to sell or suffer if she refused. Or suffer if she agreed," she added abruptly, as it occurred to her that, whether they were responsible for the warning snake or not, Matt McLaurin and Free Earth would surely have been deeply opposed to Wildernessland, with its manipulative exploitation of "pristineness."

In a few words, she told the detectives the story of the Fairground envoy and the copperhead.

"Free Earth may have wanted to make sure Ada didn't sell," she finished up. "Or maybe they knew she had left the place to them and did plan to sell it themselves. Do plan to, I mean," she corrected. "Fairground's offer still hasn't lapsed, you know. Free Earth might figure they can do more good with the money from Fairground than

Wildernessland would do evil. Or, who knows, Free Earth could be a scam, one of those cults that takes in devotees and strips them of their worldly goods."

It was a mixed satisfaction to her to see her listeners exchange slightly skeptical but interested glances. They hadn't done so apropos of the Giddys—but the idea that environmentalists might be the villains seemed to appeal to them. She started to stand up, then sat down again.

"Oh, before I go, here are the poems that made me think someone was after her land," she added. From her purse she pulled out copies of Ada's last two poems. "You can keep these."

The detectives sat unmoving. Crowder looked at her, an elegant eyebrow arched like a circumflex accent above one eye.

"For crying out loud, it's a couple of poems. Just take a look at them. Please."

They obliged, frowning over Ada's spiky, slightly shaky script. Juliet doubted either had looked at a poem since high school. It was as if she had handed them a couple of differential equations. After a minute or two, they looked back up at her. Detective Crowder's eyebrow was still raised.

Juliet tried to explicate. "See, they both describe a man, presumably a representative of Fairground, urging the writer, the 'I' voice, to move off her land."

"Mm-huh?"

"And you notice the dates? They were written just a few weeks before she died. This is what was on Ada Caffrey's mind."

Jeff Skelton nodded. "So you see this as some kind of—evidence?"

Juliet strained to disguise her impatience. "Look, a man is in her house, drinking a cup of coffee, talking to her. He's telling her to look ahead, she's not going to live forever. Why not sell the place, make a pile of dough, and bring some jobs into the neighborhood at the same time? But the writer, the speaker, she doesn't feel she's going to die so soon. She tells him, this is my place, I'm not going anywhere. He gets upset, he tries to flatter her, persuade her . . ."

"Mm. And then he—kills her?"

Now her impatience showed. "If he killed her, she wouldn't be able to write the poem," she said. "It's just—oh, never mind."

Juliet had more to say about the poems, especially "Landmine." In fact, now that she was examining them again, there was something familiar about—About what? A memory glimmered in her mind, then fled down some neural pathway where she could not follow. Moments later, a second glimmer: the villanelle. Wasn't there something off about the structure?

But both nagging half-thoughts refused to surface fully. She stood up, shook the detectives' hands, and left the station feeling dirty. Ada Caffrey had liked Matt McLaurin. And she, Juliet, liked Tom Giddy. Still, if there were any chance either had been involved in Ada's death, it was surely right to point the police in their direction.

This dilute sense of righteousness had to suffice her for the next two days, during which she heard nothing from Skelton, Crowder, or Landis. Nor could she put her finger on what was bugging her about "Landmine," despite repeated readings. But she did manage to make considerable headway in the memoirs of Harriette Wilson. Her reading of this lengthy work—the complete edition, a copy of which she had ended up sending Ames over to Dennis's to borrow, ran to nine volumes—might appear to an outsider as a sort of intellectual junket or boondoggle, she realized. But it was (she kept assuring herself) preparing her well to animate her new and improved Sir James, and therefore counted as legitimate research. Already, Clendinning had begun to write rather suggestive, carpe-diem-style verse (secretly, of course) to Selena. If Landis would turn up, Juliet's preparation would be even better.

But Landis, as he had warned her, did not.

By the time Juliet left her apartment to meet Dennis on

Wednesday evening, Catherine Walkingshaw had survived her near-disastrous brush with the bull and been put to bed, where Selena, much to Sir James's admiration and approval, was gently bathing her wounds while urging her to take a restorative spoonful or two of pork jelly. (The very sight of Selena in a bedroom inflamed Sir James's imagination to the extent that he dashed off a sestina.) Juliet set out for Les Routiers, the restaurant where she and Dennis had celebrated his birthday, feeling rather regretful that she had to leave *A New System of Domestic Cookery,* by A Lady, behind.

She walked through the cold by a circuitous route, looking over her shoulder in case anyone was following her and feeling extremely silly. What did she and Dennis have to say that should not be overheard by the police anyhow? Unless he had something in mind she could not anticipate.

But Dennis, it turned out, chiefly wished to commiserate about their mutual plight. Fitzjohn was off the official list of suspects and so, by now, was Michael Hertbrooke. (Even if he had been sufficiently worried about his ancestor's kinks coming out in public, he was known to have been in the wrong part of town all afternoon on the Friday Ada was killed. And unless he happened to keep a hitman on retainer, he had not had time to hire someone to do the job for him.) Nor had Dennis been much cheered by the the discovery that Ada's land might have unexpected worth. Even more disappointing—he was a poet himself, after all—he hardly made more of "Landmine" and "Morning Birds" than Skelton and Crowder had done. He was interested in her observations of Espyville and its environs, and he still hoped the DNA analysis of the hair would clear him. But his nerves were worn, his business suffering. He was noticeably paler than usual. It didn't help, no doubt, that whatever promise his relationship with Juliet had once held had evaporated. Mercifully, though, he showed no more sign of wishing to scrutinize that loss than she did; he took it for granted, apparently, that their likely trajectory had changed from future helpmeets in life to future defendants in a murder trial.

Grateful to be spared any explanation of her own changed feelings, Juliet did what she could to soothe and divert him. The menu was a welcome aid; in fact, Dennis's personality was such that reading it absorbed him happily for many minutes.

"So sad to have to choose," he said, smiling up wistfully after this perusal.

Juliet wondered what prison food would do to a person like Dennis. She hoped life would spare him from having to find out. The rest of the meal passed in desultory discussion of recent movies and the latest political news. At Dennis's suggestion, they took separate cabs home. Their parting kiss—quick, friendly, and inches away from each other's mouths—said everything they had not.

It wasn't until that Friday that Landis resurfaced from his gang hit and invited Juliet to come to dinner. This time, when she arrived at 229 West 107th Street, he pounded down the stairs to the vestibule, flung open the door, yelled "Hi," and dashed back up without kissing her.

"Just started cooking," he explained over his shoulder, as she climbed industriously in his wake. The hallway outside his apartment was full of the fragrance of sautéing garlic, mixed with something briny. "Make yourself at home."

Juliet took off her coat and hat and joined him in the kitchen. A gigantic pot steamed gently on the range, beside it a large saucepan.

"Linguine with clam sauce," Murray explained, relighting the flame and skillfully flipping the softening garlic with a spatula. "Okay?"

"Fabulous," said Juliet.

She eyed the giant pot with awe. She would never have dared to wrangle fresh clams, never. Murray clattered about the kitchen, draining, reserving, chopping, offering wine, explaining what he was doing, giving her small tasks. Juliet tried not to look completely off her turf, but it wasn't easy, especially after he had to show her how to use the salad spinner.

"Sometime I'll have to cook for you," she offered, vigorously pulling at the whipcord. Did the Learning Annex have cooking classes? She couldn't remember.

"Sounds great. What's your specialty?"

"Oh. Well, maybe it's not a specialty but . . . broiled fish?" Juliet answered. "I can do that. With boiled potatoes, maybe? And asparagus. How does that sound?"

He paused to stare at her. "Broiled fish and boiled potatoes is your specialty? Who cooked in your house when you were growing up?"

"A housekeeper," she said in a small voice, then with more spirit, "That's not a character flaw, you know. I was a child, my father was working, and my mother had died."

She saw his face soften. A few moments later, he left his pots for a moment and came to put his arms around her and kiss the top of her head. She melted against him. Then the lid of the clam pot started to rattle.

"No lollygagging," he said briskly, letting go of her. "Let's see that parsley cut up really fine."

She waited until they had eaten to tell him she had seen Skelton. It was so nice to be with Murray, so nice not to think about murder. But as they cleared the plates away, she sighed and gave in to the necessity of bringing up the subject.

"Listen," she began, "that night when we got back to the city, I stayed up late reading some of Ada's poetry—"

"Yeah, I know," he interrupted. "Jeff told me about your visit. He got the police up in Espyville to go and make some inquiries. I talked to him this morning. I'm gonna tell you the results, but you're not gonna like 'em."

He led her into the living room, sat down beside her on one of the small couches, and took her hand.

"Okay, let's start with the easy stuff. Steve and Claudia Lunceford. On Friday the eleventh, the day Ada Caffrey was murdered, Steve Lunceford saw twenty-two patients, the earliest one at eight in the morning, the last at six-thirty. That morning, Claudia shopped for groceries at the Price Chopper, chaired a meeting of the Optimist Club Subcommittee on Substance Abuse at noon, had lunch with Steve at the Union Hall Inn in Johnstown at one o'clock, helped her friend Denise Mink choose wallpaper for her new house at a new store, also in Johnstown, called Cozy Things—I told you Jeff Skelton is thorough—and took a water aerobics class at her health club from 4:00 to 5:00 P.M. In the evening she and Steve had dinner at a covered-dish fund-raiser for a local scholarship fund. Claudia brought pork chops."

"Okay, I get it," Juliet said. "They're not the killers. Who's next?"

"Well, next," Murray stroked her hand as if to calm her, "let's take our friends the Giddys. Now, Tom Giddy works on weekends. Part of Harlan's operation is emergency towing and repairs, so they're open every day. So the week Ada Caffrey was murdered, Tom did have Thursday and Friday off.

"But," Murray paused dramatically, and Juliet could not help feeling he was enjoying her impatience, "he went rabbit hunting. Tom's dad always kept a cabin up in the state park that he used for fishing and hunting trips. Nothing fancy, but now Tom owns it and uses it, and that's where he was. As for Cindy, she stayed in Espyville, mostly at their house, baby-sitting a niece and nephew of his while their folks went to Albany. Tom's sister needed to have some minor surgery done there. So that's them."

"And Skelton believes that?" protested Juliet. She was dismayed to hear herself sound more whiny than forceful. "Did anybody check out whether what they said was true?"

"They're checking, don't worry. But what we hear from up there is, Tom Giddy is a respected man, a bit of a local hero, in fact. Last year, he saved a kid and a golden retriever from a house on fire. He has no violent history. His boss, Ed Harlan, trusts him like a son—in fact, he had intended to hand the business over to him, only money's been tighter than he expected. So the police up there, they just don't see him for a murderer."

"Yeah, but Cindy—" Juliet said.

"Mrs. Giddy has a more checkered past, for sure. But the nephew she was watching is three years old. He doesn't even go to school; he was with her the whole time. So even if she were strong enough to tackle Ada Caffrey, kill her, and stow her body under an SUV, where did she stash the kid while she went to the city?"

Juliet received this in silence. Then she asked, "What about the idea that someone could have hired a teenager up there to make a hit?"

"I mentioned that," he said drily. "They'll keep it in mind."

She felt deflated but tried not to show it. "And Matt McLaurin? Free Earth?"

"Well, now, your primary suspicion of Free Earth is based on the idea that they knew Caffrey had left her property to them and were worried she'd sell it to Fairground first, am I right? But according to Bert Nilsson, Free Earth had no idea they were the legatee. The first thing they did on learning about it was ask him to recommend someone who could look into the financial implications for them, try to figure out if they could afford to pay the property taxes and keep the place up, and so on."

"But even if they didn't know," Juliet said, "if they just knew there was a possibility that a Wildernessland project was going to open, that Ada had been approached—don't you think they would have done everything they could to stop it?"

"How would killing Ada have stopped it? She was against it. And you gotta remember, they didn't know they were going to inherit. Wouldn't her presumable heir, Claudia Lunceford, be more likely to sell? Especially since she didn't live there."

"Still—"

"On your logic, they'd have killed the Giddys, too. Especially the Giddys. It doesn't make sense, Jule."

Sulkily, Juliet looked into her lap. He was right. It made no sense. "By the way," she asked, "is Free Earth legit?"

"Oh, yeah, your secondary Free Earth theory. Well, yes, apparently they are. They do solicit contributions, of course, but it's not one of those things like the Moonies or whatever. You don't give your all and go live with Free Earth. Most of the members are ordinary folks, what we call citizens, with families and bank accounts and jobs. They're a registered nonprofit, small, but with a good track record. They just received a grant from the Rockefeller Family Fund about eight months ago."

Juliet had been leaning against him. Now she withdrew, curling into her corner of the couch. "What about the snake?"

"Actually, that incident is still under investigation. But it appears the snake was probably left by another group, a smaller and much more radical one. They don't have a legitimate operation, nothing public like Free Earth. They're basically terrorists. And it might interest you to know that one of their apparent victims was Matthew McLaurin. Because of a disagreement they had with Free Earth over a plan to revive a defunct resort outside Speculator—they were against it, Free Earth was more tolerant—they left an entire, inhabited wasps' nest in his car one day. He was in the hospital for two weeks. If his daughter had been with him, she would probably have died."

"Oh." She felt like an idiot. No wonder Matt was secretive about his address, his young, vulnerable daughter. People were out to get him, or had been. People willing to put a wasps' nest in his car, who wanted to harm him for his beliefs. No wonder he looked hunted. He had been hunted.

She was ready to concede, but curiosity made her add, "They didn't happen to learn who his little girl's mother is, did they?"

"Matter of fact, they did. Gina's mom was someone McLaurin dated in high school, up near Buffalo. Couple of years later, she gets knocked up, McLaurin marries her. Not that the baby's his. She didn't know who the father was, coulda been a couple of guys. A few years into this idyllic union, the mom ODs on heroin. McLaurin takes the kid to Gloversville to get her away from the mother's mother, who's doing smack herself. Gina has some learning deficits, but she's doing better now. He works with her pretty intensively, I understand."

"Oh, fine," Juliet snapped. "I give up. Everyone up in Espyville is a saint. They're all noble. All they do all day is rescue dogs and small children."

She stood and walked to the window, not because she wanted to look outside, but so that Murray would not be able to see her face. It particularly troubled her that she had been so wrong about McLaurin. She had been too ready to blame his furtive manner on a guilty conscience. Like a schoolyard bully, she had seen his weakness and picked on him. She had lacked compassion.

When she felt she could face Murray with some composure, she turned around to find he had swung his feet up onto the small sofa and closed his eyes. He was snoring lightly. Dismayed, she hesitated a moment. He looked very handsome, even with his mouth fallen slightly open. It wasn't his fault no one in Espyville appeared to be guilty. Quietly, she began to creep toward the kitchen, to clean up.

"I'm awake," Murray said, midsnore, eyes still closed, as she passed the couch. He put up an arm as if to invite her to lie down beside him.

She considered briefly, then obliged. The couch was not big enough for the two of them unless one was on top of the other, and Murray's feet stuck out a good six inches over the far armrest. After a short struggle, they yielded to the laws of physics and went to bed.

chapter FIFTEEN

The Second Penny Drops

Murray was at his desk two days later, filling in a DD-5 follow-up form on the teenaged hit man, when a shadow fell across his typewriter. He looked up to find Jeff Skelton looming over him.

"So?" he asked.

"So a guy who lives year-round a couple of houses away from Tom Giddy's cabin saw smoke coming up from the chimney there late that Thursday night," Skelton announced. "He also noticed Giddy's pickup truck in the driveway around three o'clock the next afternoon. He remembers because he wanted to get him to sign a petition some neighbors were sending to the county about repairing a local road. Tom wasn't there. The letter went out the next day without his signature."

"Where was he?"

"Well, Murray, it's a hunting cabin. Presumably, he was hunting."

"Is that what he says?"

"That's what he's said all along."

"Why did he leave the truck? Do people go hunting on foot up there?"

"I believe the animals find that means of approach less obtrusive than a motor vehicle. If you're going to ask if we got any bunny rabbits to testify to having seen him, the answer is no, not yet. But we'll work on that."

There was a pause. Then, "What about Mrs. G?" Murray asked.

"Ah, Mrs. G." Skelton settled his large frame on the edge of Landis's desk. "Well, that's a funny thing. Mr. G. doesn't seem to trust Mrs. G. very much. Besides saddling her with his sister's kiddies—and that story is corroborated by the sister and brother-in-law, as well as the parents of a couple of the kids' playmates—it turns out Mr. G. routinely keeps a hidden recorder with a date and time stamp installed on their line, to tape her phone conversations while he's out. He told the guys up there he keeps it on because they've been having some obscene calls and he wanted evidence, but there's no record of his complaining about such calls, and he also asked them not to mention the tape machine to his wife. The sergeant I talked to said if Cindy Giddy was his wife, he'd chain her to the bedpost. Whatever, she definitely received or made nine calls between 11:00 A.M. and 11:00 P.M. on the Friday in question. The phone records show it, and her voice is on the tapes. So that's what, 'so.' Your girlfriend got any other theories?"

Landis ignored the reference to his girlfriend. He liked Jeff Skelton, when he didn't hate him.

"What about the land deal?" he asked. "That check out okay?"

"Oh yes, there was definitely an offer made by Fairground." Skelton resettled his butt, squashing some papers Murray had set aside to file. "LaTonya talked to someone in the C of C up there yesterday. Espyville is very eager to have the amusement park, although they were keeping it all extremely hush-hush until it was a done deal. Start talking about a thing like that, you get other localities chiming in with offers of tax advantages and so on, it seems.

"As far as Fairground, they wanted the Caffrey-Giddy parcel, but for them, it wasn't like a must-have. They're already looking into another piece of land someplace in New Jersey. And by the way"—

seated though he was, Skelton fairly danced with triumph as he went on—"the Honorable Matthew Maher has issued a search warrant for Dennis Daignault's apartment."

"On the strength of what?"

"On the strength of he killed Ada Caffrey."

"Fuck you, Skelton. You don't know that."

"Fuck you yourself. Daignault was the last person known to have the manuscript, he has specialized knowledge of its value, he lied about the value, he lied about where he was, he lied about why he contacted Hertbrooke, we got hairs just like his off the body, he looks like the guy the doorman remembered—"

"Guerro? Don't forget, he's gone back and forth on that. He retracted—"

"Yeah, until he knew it was a murder case. And wasn't that interesting? I wonder who changed his mind."

"Listen, if you think Juliet—"

"Keep your pants on. And I mean that both ways," he added. "As I was saying, plus which, an article in the *New York Times* says Rara Avis is a fringe operation—"

"That was a letter to the editor, not an article, you putz."

"—plus the manuscript is hot, and how's he going to unload it? I say he took it and I say he's got it. Crowder's at his place now with a couple of guys."

With an effort, Landis checked his anger. "Well, I hope she finds it," he said.

"I bet you do."

It took Murray a moment to realize what Skelton meant to imply: that if the manuscript didn't turn up at Daignault's, he would apply for a warrant to search Juliet's place, too. Or maybe he already had one. Probably not, though, or he would have kept the whole thing from Landis until it was over. Probably he had tried to get a warrant and Judge Maher had refused.

"Juliet Bodine had nothing to do with killing Ada Caffrey," Landis muttered at length.

Skelton shook his head. "Boy, are you whipped," he said, heaving his considerable bulk up from the desk. "Whipped like Reddi-wip, you're whipped."

"Thanks for the update," Murray said bitterly to Skelton's retreating back. He was fully aware that at this point, Jeff Skelton did not tell him anything he didn't want Juliet to know. In fact, Skelton doubtless wanted Landis to relay all this information, in hopes it would ratchet up the pressure on Bodine.

In spite of which, he did phone her that night to give her the word that the Giddys' alibis had checked out.

"Mmph," said Juliet, after he had given her the details. "I'd like to interview some of those rabbits." Then, her voice suddenly indignant, she added, "Did you know they searched Dennis's apartment today?"

She turned her chair around so she wouldn't have to watch her soup cool. She had just sat down to dinner and wouldn't have picked up the machine if she hadn't heard Murray's voice.

"Yeah, I did."

"His home and his business," she said. "How can they do that?"

"It's called a warrant."

"They didn't find anything. Did you know that?"

"So I gathered." Crowder had come up empty. Now she wanted a warrant for Daignault's safety deposit box.

"Will they search the Giddys' place?"

"Nah. They don't have cause, Jule. The criteria for a search warrant are the same as for an arrest. You've got to have probable cause, not bare suspicion."

Juliet was quiet for a moment. Then she said, "I wouldn't have figured Cindy for the baby-sitter type, would you? Would you leave kids with her?"

"You think that's fishy?"

"Well, maybe 'fishy' is a little strong, but doesn't it seem unlikely?"

"A little. But by the same token, you have to admit Tom Giddy doesn't immediately present the profile of a killer. Let alone a mercenary killer. More like salt of the earth, wouldn't you say?"

Grudgingly, Juliet agreed. "But he did seem kind of sad under all that wholesome, hearty stuff. Kind of—despairing, I thought."

"That's probably the dame. Speaking of which, how often do you talk to that Daignault guy, anyway?"

Juliet, mentally goggling at his use of the word "dame," asked vaguely, "Why? Are you worried it'll look like we're in on the"—she faltered as she reached the word "murder"—"in on some kind of crime together?"

"No, screw crime. I'm worried you're still seeing him. I'm jealous."

"You are? If you're so jealous, why are we talking to each other on the phone when I have enough minestrone here to feed an army?"

"Homemade?"

"Well—homemade by the folks at Zabar's."

"Mmph."

"Murray, you want to come over here for dinner or not?"

"Be there in fifteen."

It was while she was reading in bed later that night, Landis snoring evenly beside her, that Juliet finally realized why Ada Caffrey had been killed and, more or less, by whom.

Too wound up by events both civil and criminal to sleep, at a little past one in the morning, she had turned on her Itty Bitty Booklight and returned to her unedited copy of Harriette Wilson's memoirs. Luckily, neither she nor Landis had to get up early; he wasn't due in to work till four the next day, and as soon as he said he'd come over she had called Ames to tell her to take the day off.

She had finally come to the later volumes, the part of the story where Colonel Rochfort (aka "the Moustache") enters and Harriette falls (again, again!) in love. In Lesley Blanch's abridged rendition of the memoirs, the only one Juliet had read heretofore, Harriette never even mentioned Rochfort. He was discussed only in Blanch's essay and notes. But the last volumes of the complete memoirs dwelt copiously, tediously on Rochfort. And alas, it was soon all too clear to the reader that William Henry Rochfort was terrible news—a rotter and a sponge.

Reading Harriette's account of their first meeting (by night, by chance, "on the Bond Street side of Orchard Street") was like watching a Punch and Judy show. You wanted to yell, "Punch, look out! Judy's behind you with a hammer!"

For much of the first four volumes, Harriette managed to present herself as so lively and clever that Juliet more or less believed her frequent claims to various moral strengths: honesty about herself, fidelity to her beloved older sister, Fanny, a lack of avariciousness that was almost generosity. She was promiscuous—extremely so—but with a sly good humor that reminded Juliet of a Regency Mae West.

But now she itched to reach inside the book and shake her, warn her off Rochfort. Imagine being such a sap at the age of thirty-six! The woman went on ridiculously about his physical beauty, acknowledged that he was "a libertine," but flew to him like a moth to the flame anyhow. This despite the fact that, well past her prime in her field, she herself was hard up for cash by now, while Rochfort was "in confinement, somewhere, for debt." (The baroque rules of Fleet Prison allowed debtors considerable freedom to roam, as Juliet already knew.)

She read on. The story of Harriette's romance with Rochfort was interwoven with endless digressions, some of them obviously intended to frighten various prospective blackmail victims (King George IV seemed to be one) into paying up before she named them outright in a coming installment. But the main thread of the volume was Harriette prattling on about falling in love with Rochfort as if he were Antony and she Cleopatra. Numerous letters between them were reprinted:

"I am not chaste, and never affected to be so: *au reste,* I am virtuous," Harriette wrote him, "in qualities of the heart, and, in perfect honesty."

"It is true I am charmed with your person, your manners, and your *tout ensemble,*" Rochfort wrote back, "and I fancy you, as you term it, strongly; nor is it passion alone that inspires me; but a regard, which, if ripened into love, will, unless returned, prove productive, to me, of fresh calamity." (Rochfort seemed to want to make up in commas what he lacked in pounds sterling.) Within weeks, Harriette was offering to help him with his debts.

"Can I make love, to your tradesmen, or your relations?" she inquired, with characteristic resourcefulness.

Rochfort wrote to her:

Oh! Harriette! life is on the wing,
And years, like rivers, glide away.
To morrow may, misfortunes, bring;
Then, dearest love, enjoy to day!

Harriette wrote back that Rochfort's eyes reminded her of the great, lost love of her youth—Lord Ponsonby, Juliet presumed.

She recalled of her former self:

I was in, truth, a wild but brilliant being!
What matters it now? He left me,
And, ere I had dreamt of doubting,
From the heaven of his love bereft me.

According to Blanch, Harriette did manage somehow to pay enough of what Rochfort owed to get him out of prison. He repaid her by drinking hard, gambling, seeing other women, and demanding to be maintained in luxury. Yet her own passion was such that, in order to have money to keep him, she eventually produced the *Memoirs*. And by doing so, Juliet considered, she entirely forfeited her hitherto convincing claim to a sort of moral—

"Oh!"

She said it out loud, so sharply did the truth strike her. Suddenly, both the submerged thoughts she couldn't get hold of at the police station shimmered, bright, unmistakable, in her head.

She glanced at Landis to see if she had roused him. He was still snoring happily. Under cover of the noise, she crept out of bed to the dresser, where she had left the stack of Ada's poems. Then she went into her office and reread "Landmine."

chapter

SIXTEEN

Juliet Tells a Story

"It's only a day," Juliet pointed out the next morning. "One day. If it doesn't pan out, what have we lost?"

But Landis continued to look skeptical.

"Go back," he said. "Tell me your thinking again."

He padded across the kitchen to pour himself another cup of coffee, then opened the fridge to get the milk. He was wearing the black Levis he had had on last night. Just those. In the morning light, augmented by the otherworldy glare from inside the refrigerator, he looked wonderful. All the same, Juliet—who felt she had shown heroic tact and maturity in not waking him at two in the morning—had to suppress an impulse to throw the newspaper across the room at him.

Instead, with what patience she could muster, she began to explain again.

"Okay, here's what I realized last night. Harriette Wilson was a decent woman—a decent prostitute, let's say—until she met William Rochfort. She slept with men for money, but she didn't tell their secrets. It was her love for Rochfort that changed the balance. For him, to keep him, because he needed money, she became a blackmailer. So, in a similar way, I think Tom Giddy became a murderer to keep Cindy.

"Now, look again at 'Landmine.' "

As Murray reseated himself at the table, she thrust the poem before him.

" 'He sips his coffee, turns it in his hand,' " she read aloud, pointing at the line. "Turning his cup in his hand. Who does that? Think about it, think about the refreshments in the parlor after Ada's memorial. Try to see Tom Giddy in your mind's eye. That's what he kept doing, revolving his cup between sips. It's a habit he has. This is Tom in the poem. And—"

"Excuse me, you noticed Tom Giddy revolves his cup? This is the kind of thing you keep your eye on?"

"It's a mannerism," Juliet bristled. "I'm a novelist. I collect them." Omitting to mention that she had also stolen Tom's name for her novel, she resumed her explanation. "Look here, Ada calls him a 'man unmanned.' She means he's losing Cindy; she said as much to me the first time we met. But he's not a bad man. He's a good man. See the second line? He starts by reminding her she's not immortal—'all flesh is grass'—then tells her to consider how much good she could do before she dies by selling, how many jobs Wildernessland would bring to an area that needs jobs desperately. Finally, he loses patience and snaps at her, 'you'd be rich, for crying out loud, you could have whatever you want.' But all she wants is what she's got. That's their problem.

"And here at the very end is what's so sinister, what I couldn't quite get hold of mentally at first. Look at the last two lines.

"See, 'Landmine' is a villanelle. That's a very specific form. A villanelle consists of six stanzas: five triplets, then a quatrain. They all share only two rhymes, and two of the lines get recycled through the whole poem. The first line of the poem—think of that as the first refrain—gets repeated at the end of the second triplet. The third line of the poem—call that the second refrain—is also repeated, at the end of the third triplet. Then the first refrain appears again, as the end of the fourth triplet. And the fifth triplet ends with the second refrain. They're interleaved, like double-Dutch jump rope.

"But here's the catch: The last stanza, the quatrain, should close with both refrains repeated in the order they came in: the first refrain, then the second refrain. End of poem.

"But in the last stanza of 'Landmine,' the second refrain comes first. The poem should end with the speaker's affirmation that the land belongs to her. The last two lines should read, 'He sips his coffee, turns it in his hand / This is my place, this was my father's land.' But instead, Ada reversed the refrains, ending with her visitor turning his coffee cup and thinking. He hasn't given up. He's meditating his next move. He gets the last word, not her."

Murray took a sip of his own coffee. Then he asked, "And this means—?"

"Well, it's ominous, isn't it? She knew he hadn't finished with her. This could have been a poem about how one person successfully turned back the force of change. Instead, it's a poem about two people who can't see eye to eye."

Murray grunted. "Explain to me how exactly Tom Giddy turned murderer?"

Juliet hesitated. She hadn't yet figured out the answer to this. So far, all she had was what E. M. Forster would call "story," a narrative of events arranged in their time sequence. The king died and then the queen died. Murray was asking for plot, causality: The king died, and then the queen died of grief, as Forster had it. She would have to fill in a few gaps to forge a persuasive chain of motive and action. But what else was imagination for?

"Okay, try this," she began. "From what Caroline Walsh told us, we know Cindy Lang was a girl who liked money, wanted money. Before they got married, Tom Giddy must have looked to her like a ticket to bigger and better things. He was older, well-liked, solid job, prospects of taking over his boss's business, and good-looking to boot. Plus, his folks had property—a large farm, 250 acres. Someday, Tom would inherit.

"But time goes by, money is scarce, and Tom's boss changes his mind. Tom's still a grease monkey. His parents die, he and Cindy inherit, but they can't unload the place. Tom's hair starts to fall out, and Cindy's still stuck in Espyville. She starts catting around, he knows it—everything's going to pieces. But he still worships her, you can see that—you could see that, couldn't you?" she asked.

"Mm."

"And she doesn't have the time of day for him. So how is he going to keep her?"

She leaned forward excitedly. "See, this is where it's so like Harriette Wilson and Rochfort. Only with the sexes reversed. Tom is a decent guy desperately in love with a woman who isn't, a woman with big ideas, expensive tastes, and no qualms about taking what she wants if she can get it. How is he going to keep her? He can't make himself younger, can't become another man. And that's when opportunity knocks. Suddenly, if only Ada will cooperate, Tom can get a lot of money. And as long as he has money to spend, it's a good bet Cindy won't leave him.

"Only Ada won't cooperate. She loves her place and she wants to leave it to Free Earth. She's just rewritten her will to ensure that. With all the fooling around, all the marrying she's done in her life, she still thinks of Frederick Asquith as her great love—and Frederick, she believes, died because of industrial pollution.

"So Tom starts thinking—or maybe Cindy starts him thinking—Did you ever read Dostoyevsky's *The Gambler?*" she broke off.

"Yeah, I did. I like Dostoyevsky."

"Do you?"

Juliet smiled an open smile of pleasure, all thought of murder momentarily forgotten as she learned this delightful fact about her new lover.

"Me, too. Especially—No, we'd better talk about that another time. My point is that in *The Gambler,* the heroine, the sought-after Paulina asks the narrator if he would kill for her. She's teasing him.

She knows he's completely besotted with her, and she enjoys toying with him this way. She's a cat, and Cindy is, too. So it may be that she goaded Tom to kill Ada. Or it may be that Tom just says to himself, 'Ada's an old, old lady. She's down to the dregs of life. So what if I spare her the last few months?' He'll take out the boring part, like abridging a book. His need for Ada to die is greater than her own to live. And he realizes—anybody would realize who grew up in Espyville—that if Claudia Lunceford inherited, she'd dump the farm in a minute. He doesn't even—"

"Wait a minute. Claudia Lunceford was never going to inherit."

"Yeah, but who knew that? Bert Nilsson, and maybe the Luncefords themselves. But who else? Anyone would assume Claudia would inherit—"

"No, just a minute. Ten seconds ago, you said anyone would know if Claudia inherited, she'd dump the farm in a minute. Everyone knew there was bad blood."

"Yeah, but Ada had no other heir, so who else would she leave the place to?" said Juliet. "But okay, for the sake of argument, let's figure Tom just didn't know. Could be anyone. He'd still figure that anyone, whoever it was who inherited, would be glad to sell it off for a small fortune. And, in fact, almost anyone would. All he had to do was get rid of Ada Caffrey. But he had to do it fast, because Fairground's offer to buy wasn't open forever."

Murray sat back, his hands around his mug, and smiled at her.

"What?"

"I was just thinking how pretty you are when you exercise your intellect."

There was a silence, during which Juliet asked herself what was so urgent about all this murder stuff, anyhow. She was still deliberating when Murray spoke again.

"So, go on, what's keeping you?"

"Oh." Juliet shook herself mentally. "So Tom thinks: I'll kill her. He makes up his mind and starts to think about how. A man his size, he and his wife help Ada with errands, they even have the key to her place—technically, there's no problem! But he must not get caught. So he thinks. Poison her? Pretend there was a break-in, some demented teenagers like the ones Caroline told us about? Smother her in her bed; make it look like she died in her sleep?

"But would it look like that? Could a doctor tell it was murder? Tom doesn't know. He's still puzzling out the ways and means—or maybe he and Lady Macbeth are putting their heads together—when Ada announces she's going down to New York City and could they watch her house and feed the cats.

"Drat! At first they're annoyed—or Tom's annoyed. This is a kink in his plans.

"But then he realizes it could be a great advantage. If he kills Ada in Espyville, no matter how, and there's any sort of criminal investigation—well, there he is. He and Cindy. They're the neighbors. They had access. And, eventually, once her legatee agrees to sell to Fairground, it's going to be pretty obvious they had motive.

"But if he kills her in New York City—ah, what a golden opportunity! In New York there are millions of suspects. All he has to do is intercept her there and do away with her." Juliet paused to take a swallow of tea.

"So he goes to his hunting cabin to think about it," Murray filled in.

"No, of course he doesn't go to his hunting cabin to think about it. He goes to his hunting cabin to have a good alibi. And he arranges—or Cindy arranges—the nephew and niece as an alibi for her."

"By persuading his sister to have surgery?" Murray stood up, poured himself some more coffee, and came back to the table.

"That was a lucky break. But they'd have come up with something else if they had to—sent Cindy on a trip someplace."

juration about the fun she ought to have living here. How Ada would enjoy this scene.

"You mind?"

"Long as I don't have to smoke it, it's okay with me," he said. "Look, Jule, I admit I saw Mrs. Giddy leering at me, but I think you're reading a little too much into that. Lots of women like to know if they can get you into their pocket. They're not really interested in having you there."

"Hmm," said Juliet. She took a deep drag of smoke and exhaled a dirty cloud. "Now, how can I put this? Oh, I know. 'Duh!' Jeeze, Murray, I write romances for a living. You don't think I can read a woman when she's looking at a man?"

"Oh," said Murray. "Okay. I bow to your expertise. But go back a bit. How exactly did Tom kill Mrs. Caffrey? How did he know where to find her? How did he get her alone to strangle her? And what did he do with the manuscript?"

"Okay." This was another part Juliet hadn't thought through. Still, she sketched out a quick scenario, the story taking shape as she spoke, just as it did when she plotted a book.

"First of all," she began, "the Giddys knew exactly where Ada was. Because they were looking after her house and cats, they had Suzy's name and number; and Suzy's address is listed. And according to Suzy's phone record, and what she told you during the missing investigation, Ada called them on Wednesday and told them she had an important appointment on Friday afternoon."

She could hear the wakening interest in his voice as he asked, "Who took that call, Cindy or Tom?"

"I don't know. It was evening. Could have been either of them. If he records her phone calls, maybe both.

"But even if he'd had no idea where she was going or when," she went on, "he could have come down to New York and just hung around where he could see Suzy's door. Sooner or later, Ada was bound to come in or out."

" 'Hung around?' " Landis repeated. "In a blizzard? In twenty-degree weather?"

"He's a hunter. It works with ducks, doesn't it?"

"And nobody noticed him? Your doorman didn't notice?"

"Maybe he stood behind a tree," Juliet said impatiently. She put her cigarette out. "There are trees in Riverside Park. And mine is the only doorman building on the block. Tom's an outdoorsman. Don't you think he knows how to keep from being noticed? Maybe he stood at the bus stop awhile, looking like he was going to get on the bus. Maybe he changed his hat now and then. Maybe he stood inside the park. Riverside Drive curves around. You can see Suzy's door from across the street and two whole blocks north. I know, because I've sat on a bench there and seen her come out myself."

"Okay, let's say he hung around. Go on."

"So eventually, he sees her. Maybe he sees her with Suzy on the way up to Rara Avis, and follows. Ada goes in; Suzy goes away. Tom notices the garbage cans lined with fresh bags, starts to come up with a more detailed plan. Thinks, 'That might come in handy,' crosses the street and takes one, then goes back to wait for Ada to come out. She does, with John Fitzjohn. The girlfriend's there, Ada shakes hands, then trips away down the sidewalk back to Suzy's. She's carrying her purse and a paperback book. He doesn't realize it—he doesn't even know it exists, probably—but she has the manuscript with her; she wants to get it home safe.

"He makes his move. Crosses the street, comes up to her—'Oh, what a coincidence!' he says. 'I knew you were in New York, but I never thought I'd actually run into you. But it's funny we should meet. I had an idea about that land deal; I'd like to talk to you.' "

"Hold on—what if he didn't see her come out of the building with Suzy? How would he have found her then?"

"Then he'd just wait, wait for her to come home. Which she would have. Remember what Ernesto said—my doorman, Ernesto

Guerro? He thought he saw a big guy with her? Well, Tom's a big guy. A big blond guy. Blond like the hair under Ada's fingernail."

"Mmph," Landis said. He didn't mention that he had heard Skelton fulminating on the phone about this hair last week. Apparently, someone had mismarked the sample from Daignault, sent it to the wrong lab. It would be at least a week more before the DNA results came back.

"Yeah, mmph. So Ada says, 'Tom! Fancy seeing you here. Come back to where I'm staying, come inside a minute.' She fumbles for the key, mentions the landlady isn't home. They go inside, bang, before she has time to turn around, he's got her in a headlock; he's choking her. He was a wrestling champion, remember. She tries to fight, grabs behind her, gets his hair—but two minutes later, it's over, she's dead. Now all he has to do is get rid of the body."

"Why? Why not leave it at Suzy's?"

"Why?" echoed Juliet, stalling. Why indeed? "Oh! Because if she's found outside, anyone in the city could have done it. If she's inside, it was almost certainly someone she knew. And the whole point of doing it in the city was the nine million suspects."

Murray gave a skeptical grunt.

"Don't forget, he had no way of knowing that car would sit there so long. In Espyville, you don't just park your car and let it sit for four days."

"Mm-huh."

Murray stood up and began to prowl around the living room, examining the contents of shelves and poking absently into various cabinets. They had never spent much time in her living room; in fact, she realized, he might never have been in here till this morning. She did not complain. Watching him move around in a state of undress more suitable to the shower was very interesting.

"Okay, so go back," he said, pulling open the drawer where Juliet kept remote controls for the TV and stereo. "Tom's standing in Suzy's front hall with Ada's body at his feet. And—?"

"Well, he's got the garbage bag. She's a tiny little person. He puts her in, sees the purse, tosses that in, slings the whole thing over his shoulder and leaves."

"Which, luckily, no one notices."

"Lucky he certainly was. But even if they had noticed—who was he? They're going to stop him?"

"Okay. So he goes across the street and down the block, kneels on the sidewalk, and shoves the corpse under a handy SUV. Which no one notices either." Murray was now peering into the cabinet in which her television was hidden. He opened another door and poked through a jumble of old audio cassettes she'd forgotten.

"I don't know how he did that. He would look pretty conspicuous walking around with a garbage bag over his—Oh!"

She stopped. Murray turned to look at her.

"Oh—?"

"Well, people do come over this way—at least they were coming around then—with Christmas trees. There's a big pile of them still by the entrance to the park. Anyone seeing him would probably have thought he had a Christmas tree inside the garbage bag."

"Are you saying that Tom Giddy knew the New York City Parks Department was collecting used Christmas trees near Suzy Eisenman's building?"

"No, I'm saying Tom Giddy was very fortunate. A number of things went his way."

"And the manuscript?"

She shrugged. "That I don't get. Unless she somehow told him about it and he took it . . ."

"And he got home how—?"

"Train? And then however he got from the cabin to the station, he did that again backwards."

"He was damned lucky if all that happened."

"Yeah, but you know, suppose he hadn't been? All he had to do was wait for Ada to come home to Espyville in a day or two and kill her there after all. It wouldn't have been ideal, but it was a reasonable fallback."

Juliet paused. Murray said nothing.

"So what do you think?" she prodded him.

He shrugged. "It's a theory."

He didn't sound very enthusiastic. Juliet decided not to press her luck. "Will you come up there with me?" she asked.

"And play Mata Hari with Cindy Giddy?"

"Yes."

He hesitated, then said, "We'd better make sure to go on a day when Tom's at work."

chapter SEVENTEEN

A Rustic Interlude

It was as they were whizzing toward Coxsackie on the following Wednesday morning that Murray and Juliet both realized, as if in a moment of psychic twindom, how Tom Giddy could have traveled from his hunting cabin to a train or bus.

"Snowmobile!" they cried in unison, inspired by the sight of a gigantic billboard across a frozen pond advising them that Polar Powersports was one mile ahead.

Murray hit the sides of his head with his hands.

"City mice," he said, his voice dripping with disgust.

"Indeed. But—would you mind keeping at least one hand on the wheel?" Juliet interjected, then resumed, "Do you know if they can be used in the dark? It would have been night by the time he got back."

"And he probably had to leave before dawn. Only one thing to do: Let's go shopping at Polar."

The Jaguar sped along. It had been a bit difficult to get Hertz to agree to obtain and hold a red Jaguar for them, as before. But what charm had failed to achieve, a crisp fifty had accomplished, and Juliet felt she could fairly hope Cindy would assume the car was Murray's. She had hardly dared dictate to him what to wear, but he had done well, complementing his usual black Levis with a royal blue turtleneck sweater tight enough that the musculature of his chest and arms showed through. If they hadn't been on a mission, she would have jumped him herself.

DEK, as his Polar Powersports name tag proclaimed him, looked to Juliet to be all of fourteen. But he was knowledgeable about snowmobiles, and more than happy to show Mr. and—um, Mrs. Landis how they worked. Oh, yes, they certainly had headlights. And, sure, you could easily go a hundred miles on a single tank, more. Were they interested in a new or a used one? Because Polar had an awesome special this week on the Polaris Indy 440 Pro X Fan, so if they wanted a test drive—

Juliet was just about to break the news that they were in too much of a hurry when Murray said they'd be delighted.

She looked at him. It was already past ten-thirty, and Tom only worked until five today. She knew because when she had called Cindy to ask for the key again, she pretended to want to ask Tom about helping her pack and haul away Mrs. Caffrey's books when she was done looking at them. She had been sure to mention that her friend Murray would be coming with her today.

But now Murray just winked and gave Dek his driver's license. Dek took it, escorted them outside, loaded them in, rattled through an explanation of the controls that left Juliet totally confused, indicated the test area—a snow-covered field behind the showroom already crisscrossed with numerous tracks—and told them to have fun.

"Why are we doing this?" Juliet was finally able to yell in Murray's ear, as the motor roared and Dek waved good-bye from the doorstep in back of the shop.

"To have fun!" he screamed back.

They lurched forward, moving slowly while Murray got the hang of the machine, then faster, then very fast. Juliet, no speed freak, clung to the passenger handgrips and squeezed her knees against Landis's hips. She had to admit it was thrilling. Deafening, but thrilling. The motor thrummed through their bodies, the wind enveloped them, and even she could sense the lively tractability of the machine. Even through her helmet, Murray's black leather jacket, worn to just the right stage of beat-upness to attract Cindy Giddy, smelled quintessentially masculine. The whole experience was quintessentially masculine—the speed, the noise, the powerful forward thrust. Which did not mean it offered nothing to her; quite the contrary.

Oh, quite the contrary.

Still, the snowmobile, she felt reasonably confident, had not been invented by a woman.

And then it was over. She found her legs were trembling slightly as she obediently trailed her man into the Polar showroom.

Half an hour later, when Cindy Giddy opened her door wearing a red wraparound sweater with a V in front that plunged to her navel, Juliet had to exert considerable self-control not to snort with laughter.

The sweater was trimmed in fake marabou and was complemented by a red vinyl miniskirt, red fishnet tights, and a pair of black boots with stiletto heels. Cindy made no pretense of even seeing Juliet, instead locking eyes with Murray the moment the door swung open. A pronounced smell of dope billowed from the house, and Juliet found herself reflexively checking Cindy's hands to see if a joint still burned between her fingers. There was no joint, but neither was there a wedding ring.

Muttering something about the possible historical value of some of Mrs. Caffrey's *Playbills*, Juliet accepted the key that was distractedly handed to her and turned away—though not too fast to catch a glimpse of Murray gravely nodding a silent promise to Mrs. Giddy that he would make it his business to get back to her soon.

For form's sake, he came with Juliet into the cold, cat-plaintive house next door and stayed a quarter of an hour or so.

Juliet had brought the remaining volumes of Harriette Wilson's memoirs to while away the time. While Murray used the bathroom, she turned on the space heater, then went back out to the front hall to raise the temperature on the thermostat. Hearing tiny paws skitter over the door that blocked the second floor, she herself skittered back to the kitchen, where she made herself a cup of tea. She offered one to Murray when he reappeared. But he declined and instead stood watching her scrub out a mug—Mrs. Caffrey really had been no housekeeper. Then he strolled into the parlor, humming a Bruce Springsteen song she soon identified as "Man's Job."

Following him into the parlor with her steaming tea, she found him idly examining the teddy bears and ancient dolls in the laden hammock. She sat down on the worn purple couch and made herself as cozy as she could. The cats immediately joined her, one of them walking sedately onto a pile of Harriette's photocopied pages, circling, then curling up neatly upon them, while the other nestled on the cushion just behind Juliet's head.

"What are you going to tell her?" she asked, as Murray turned away from the hammock and zipped up his jacket again.

"Tell her?"

"I mean, why are you over there and not here with me?"

"You know, somehow I don't think she's going to scrutinize my reasons very closely," he said. "In fact, I have to admit, I think you were right about Mrs. Giddy's state of mind. She was very—very come-hither, don't you think?"

Juliet surveyed him. He looked awfully good.

"I'm not sure I like using you as a secret weapon after all," she said. "Just don't forget, her hither is my yon. I've got dibs. I'm hitherto."

He bent down and kissed her forehead. "And henceforward," he said, straightening. "And hereunto."

She looked up, liking this better in some ways than anything he had said to her before. It was, as it turned out, her last opportunity to look up at him for a while.

chapter EIGHTEEN

Murray Undercover

It was a funny thing about sex, Murray Landis was thinking. It was kind of like haircuts. Every generation came of age with a certain style, certain ways of thinking about sex—or hair—that seemed okay, seemed normal, and once you'd gotten those ideas in your head, it was almost impossible to shake them.

Not all that long before his own time, there had been good girls and bad girls. Bad girls "did it," of course, and good girls didn't. Even in his own time, there had still been "it," though he and his friends spoke of "making," not "doing" "it." And he still remembered thinking of "it," thinking and thinking and thinking, with a yearning curiosity that colored almost everything else.

But there hadn't been "good" and "bad" girls anymore. Just girls and boys, and (by the time they got out of high school, anyhow) pretty much all of them had "made it." They made it with fervent, romantic innocence, or in a spirit of affectionate adventure. Some were gay and that was cool, the others assured themselves. And that was the culture of sex for Landis, then and forever. So that even now, even after the slacker disdain for dating, the Gen X triumph of bisexuality, the current teenaged habit of "hooking up" almost meaninglessly, often multiply, at parties—for him, sex still meant one man privately pairing off with one woman and "making it" by mutual consent. Just as he still kept his curly hair short and a little untidy, and nothing else looked quite right to him. Buzz cuts, like crew cuts, were permanently alien to his eye, and he would no more have shaved his head than covered it with a powdered wig.

It was Cindy Giddy, of course, whose cropped blonde aureole of hair and apparent readiness to take him to her bed immediately upon his return to her doorstep had set this train of thought in motion. It wasn't that he found either the hair or the readiness unattractive, per se. The cut was not to his taste, but he had to admit it suited her. And the implicit offer of her body was—well, it was intoxicating, really.

Yet it was not at all difficult for him to suggest, drawing her toward her own front door, that they take a drive "first."

Cindy's initial response was a sullen moue. Then she remembered the Jaguar. It wasn't a Miata or a Lotus, but it was expensive and red and shiny and new. Landis could almost see its image materialize in her dilated pupils as she recalled and anticipated it. With a shrug, she picked up a faux leopard-fur coat from a hook by the front door and slipped it on.

Then she turned to face him, sleepy brown eyes full on his.

"Button it," she said.

Landis had seldom felt the urge to laugh so closely conjoined to the wish to slap someone. The words, "Button it yourself," were on the tip of his tongue. But, reflecting that a few moments ago he had as much as declined to acquire carnal knowledge of her—or, at least, chosen to defer it—he curbed his instincts and obliged her.

Dropping to his knees, "My grandmother always taught us to button our clothes from the bottom," he said, bringing the two sides of her hem together. "That way you don't do them crooked."

He began, very slowly, to button, rising as he went. The coat had big round buttons covered in black leather, eight in all. The fifth through the third were particularly interesting. When he got to the top, he drew the collar a little tighter around her neck than was necessary and leaned his face down over hers as if he planned to kiss her.

But he didn't. He buttoned the final button against her thin, pale throat, then told her, "Get in the car."

She turned and went. This was good, because behind her, he had started cracking up. What a piece of work! He didn't envy Tom.

In the car, after he had backed out of the driveway, it seemed natural to ask, "Where's your husband?" He headed away from town on Route 131, toward the Blue Line. As long as they were taking a drive, he wanted to see the mountains.

For a moment he thought she was going to spit. But she said, "At work. Harlan's Garage, in town. He'll be there till five at least. You don't have to worry that he'll come home early. He never comes home early."

"You say that like you wish he would."

She laughed. "Not unless he went to someone else's home."

"Does he do that?"

"You mean cheat on me?"

Landis nodded.

"I wish. No, Tom's true blue," she said, her tone suggesting this was a contemptible quality in a man. Then she added, somewhat less harshly, "He's crazy, but he's true blue."

Even with his eyes on the road, he had adequate peripheral vision to see her shiver slightly as she said this. "Crazy in what sense?"

"Don't worry. Not like he'll come after you with an axe."

"Yeah, but what do you mean?"

"Oh, just . . . nothing." She pulled the faux leopard coat closer around her, folding her arms on her chest.

Landis hesitated, then decided to leave it alone. One thing he could tell about Cindy Giddy, she was perverse—the type to clam up when you pumped her, talk when you told her to be quiet.

The silence lasted some minutes, only the sound of the tires on the smooth, salt-swept pavement filling the car. Landis was startled by how quickly the rolling farmland fell away behind them. Just a few miles from the Giddys' driveway, they were across the Adirondack Park line and into the mountains. Thick, dark firs closed in on them, branches heavy with snow. Soon, beyond a scattering of bungalows, glimpses of gray-blue water began to wink through the trees.

"What lake is that?"

"It's a reservoir, not a lake." He could hear in her voice the dull charm of telling a stranger something you've known since birth and been bored by almost as long. "It's called the Great Sacandaga Lake, but it's man-made. They made it to stop the floods when the snowpack melts in the mountains. There used to be houses and farms there. But they're under water now."

He glanced at her, surprised that so much history should be at her command. Maybe she was smarter than he gave her credit for. She was playing with one of the leather buttons in her lap. He turned west, away from the reservoir onto a small, winding road. He had been planning to pull over somewhere, take a walk with her in the snow—a walk intimate enough to prompt frank conversation, but too cold for sex.

But the farther he went, the less he liked the idea of stopping. What if the car wouldn't start again? He found it impossible not to think about what would happen if you ran out of gas out here or had a breakdown or an accident. He had grown up in the city, after all; for him, not enough people meant possible danger. How often did folks come this way? He hadn't seen a car in miles.

Suddenly, Cindy's left hand was on his right thigh, her palm stroking slowly up and down along the denim. He tightened his leg muscles, willing himself to keep a steady foot on the accelerator. Thank God his gun was strapped around his ankle, not higher up.

When he glanced at her, he found her indolent gaze full on him, her coat open, her right foot propped up on the dashboard. It wasn't a very subtle invitation. But he was only human, and some of the most human parts of him had begun to respond when, by an act of God, a streak of movement in the corner of his eye became a small deer, dashing into the road a hundred feet ahead. It paused there as Murray stomped on the brake. Then it dashed away again. At that same moment, a snowmobile came screaming up behind the car, its motor so loud that Landis expected it to rear-end them at any moment.

But it wasn't on the pavement, of course, he realized a moment later; it was beside them, on a roadside trail masked by a fringe of trees. It shot past them, doing at least sixty, Landis would have guessed.

All the excitement broke the spell of the moment in the car. Cindy hadn't relinquished her claim on his leg, but she did settle into a more sedate position on her side of the stick shift.

"I like snowmobiles," Murray said, hoping that if he raised the subject, she would confirm somehow that she and Tom owned one. "They're noisy, but they're great."

"You like them? I hate them. Tom spends half the winter tooling his up."

Bingo.

"And repairing other people's," she went on.

"Well, at least that must mean work for him," he suggested. "Gainful employment."

Now she did spit, or at least sputtered. "They're toys," she said, scorn rich in her voice. "The men around here play with them like children."

Glancing at her again, he wondered what grown-up activities she would have preferred. He didn't have to wonder very long. In no time, her hand was flickering over his leg again, heading this time for his crotch.

"Tell me about your work," she said. Her fingers moved over him like water, fluid, slow, thorough. "What's it like?"

"My work?" With relief, he saw they were approaching an intersection. Route something. Route anything. What did it matter? He could turn south, back toward civilization.

"Yes. Your friend, what's-her-name, told me you're an artist. Are your paintings in museums?"

Mercifully, she drew back her hand, pulling her knees up onto her seat. Swiveling to face his side of the car, she raised herself slightly and, with her right index finger, slowly drew a line down the side of his cheek.

He laughed before he could stop himself. "No," he said, then recovered and added, "I'm a sculptor. But you don't have to have work in museums to appeal to collectors."

He could feel that she was disappointed—so close to him, she could hardly help letting him feel it. Doubtless she had been hoping to hear he was well represented in gleaming institutions around the world. He could hear the wheels whir inside her head. Okay, no museums. But collectors, that sounded like money. And he had enough freedom to pal around with that writer lady Ada had made such a big deal about. A New York artist, a man with a shiny car. A man whose jaw was about three inches from her mouth, whose hip-bone was now under the palm of her hand.

"Are you married?"

He shook his head.

"Girlfriend?"

"No."

And then she drew away a little. The Bad Thought had hit her. Artist, New York, not married, didn't jump her—

"You do like women, don't you?"

"Oh, yes."

She came forward again, this time putting her mouth to his ear. Her breath was hot. "Do you like me?"

"How could I help it?"

She smiled. He could feel her mouth stretching over his cheekbone.

"Why don't we stop for a drink?" Finally, she sat up straight, turned in her seat, swung her legs down where they belonged. "There's a place called Ruby's a couple of miles from here. You take your next left."

"Okay."

It was only lunchtime, but he wouldn't mind a drink. And some food, if Ruby's served it. The woods, the long drive of the morning, and, most of all, being expertly pawed while at the wheel had left him a little light-headed.

"Keep right," Cindy said, as the road forked.

And suddenly they were back in civilization again, a scattering of businesses strung at ragged intervals on either side of a two-lane road marked 23a. A tumbledown antique shop called Better Days, a mobile home-turned-office to accommodate Joe's Plumbing and Heating, a large-animal vet, a tiny shack offering "live bait" (Landis was rattled enough to misread this as "love bait" at first glance) and ammunition.

On the south side of the road, just across from the glass front of Four Seasons Power Equipment ("New and Used Trucks, Motors, Skis, Engines, Snowmobiles, Pontoons, Outboards, All-Terrain Vehicles, Trade-Ins Welcome") was Ruby's, a dark wooden cabin decorated with a string of dusty Christmas lights. He pulled into the half-full parking lot and shut the car off with a sense of gratitude. Distracted as he had been, it seemed a miracle he hadn't driven the car into that deer or one of the thousands of trees.

Inside was a long bar, a row of four-person booths beside the windows that faced the road and the parking lot, a strong smell of griddle grease in the smoky air, and a chalked list of SPECIALS on a blackboard over the draft-beer taps. From the look of the clientele on the bar stools, Ruby's was more heavily patronized by alcoholic mountaineers than by townsmen seeking a whiff of rural atmosphere. The barmaid serving them—soon revealed to be also the only waitress and the proprietor, Ruby, herself—was a thin, middle-aged redhead with a small, worn face. She looked thoroughly sick of her regulars. Only a few of the booths were occupied, one by a glum family of three, another by two men still wearing hunting caps. Murray paused on the threshold, taking in the scene; Cindy brushed past him and across the room, sliding into a booth.

He hesitated. She had taken the side facing the door—by training, the seat he always preferred. But after her performance in the car, he hardly dared sit beside her. And he certainly didn't want to tell her he was a cop and could she please move so he could watch who came in and went out. She didn't bother hiding her disappointment as he slid in across from her, settling himself on the wooden bench.

He leaned far across the nicked pine table. "I'd like to sit beside you, but I don't want you winding up in hot water with your husband," he murmured into her ear. He opened his jacket but left it on; despite the griddle and the crowd, it was surprisingly chilly here. He was glad Ruby's served lunch, but he couldn't help wondering why the windows of its main room looked out on the road instead of the woods that must be behind it. Maybe for the light. As it was, he was currently being treated to a view of the sleepy parking lot of Four Seasons Power Equipment, where a thick man in green overalls, a dark jacket, and worn boots knelt behind a pickup truck, apparently laboring to detach a neon orange snowmobile from it.

He turned back to Cindy and found her eyeing him discontentedly.

"Someone could see us and tell Tom," he reminded her.

She seemed more irritated than appreciative. "My husband has our phone tapped so he can keep tabs on me," she told him, none too softly. "He deserves any news he gets." That shudder he had seen go through her in the car recurred in her shoulders before she went on, "Why don't you just forget Tom, okay? I'm trying to."

He raised an eyebrow. "He seems like a nice enough guy to me. What'd he do to piss you off?"

He saw her suppress an impulse to answer him. Instead, she leaned forward and said huskily, "Tell me about New York City. What's it like where you live?"

"Tell you in a minute."

Two laminated menus sat in a rack by the window; Landis picked them up and handed one to her. Something Tom had done was certainly bugging her. If Landis could just get her slightly off balance, he thought he would manage to get the rest of the story.

"I'm not hungry," she said, sulky once more.

Murray studied the menu. When Ruby came, he ordered chicken-in-a-basket and a Michelob. Cindy asked for vodka, Stoli, straight up. A few moments later, he felt her foot arrive on his upper leg. Hurriedly, he put his napkin over it. He supposed he was lucky she had removed her boot.

"I bet New York is incredible," she said, leaning forward again and resting her head on her hands. "What part do you live in? SoHo?"

Murray smiled. "Where did you hear about SoHo?" he asked.

"It was in that movie with . . . Richard Gere, I think it was, about—" she began.

But Murray was not destined to learn which movie Cindy had in mind. Something behind him had stopped her speaking, made her pull her foot out of his lap, changed her expression entirely. Landis turned around to find that the man in the dark jacket and green overalls who had been kneeling in the parking lot across the road a few minutes ago was now standing in Ruby's doorway, his eyes trained on Cindy, then on Landis himself.

Tom Giddy was ready for lunch.

chapter

NINETEEN

In the Woods

In the four or five seconds between the moment he recognized Tom Giddy and the moment Tom Giddy flung himself upon him, Landis had just long enough to curse himself for not sitting next to Cindy, not making her switch places with him on whatever pretext. He couldn't even grab his gun out of the ankle holster; the table was so wide and the booth so narrow, when he dived down to get it, all he did was smack his own jaw against the pine. Now Giddy had the upper hand, not only because he started out standing while Landis was sitting down, but also because he had had those few first moments to take stock of the situation. While Landis, fool that he was, had sat on all unawares, wrestling with a foot in his lap and Richard Gere's filmography.

He did not have long, however, to indulge in self-examination. Giddy's large hands grabbed at his neck with a wrestler's practiced efficacy, his powerful thumbs on his opponent's trachea. In seconds, Landis could feel the trapped blood throbbing in his head. As if from very far away, he heard Cindy scream her husband's name, then call shrilly for the police. At the same time, he managed to get his own knee up from under the table and ram it sharply enough into Giddy's chest that the man's grasp briefly loosened. But a second later, he heard rather than felt his own head thud against the hard wooden bench of the booth as Giddy laid him out flat, then jumped on him with both knees.

Meanwhile, Cindy's voice was shrieking. "Tom, let go of him. Nothing happened. Tom! You crazy fucker! Somebody stop him! Tom, let him go!"

Much later, Murray would retain a mental image of the other, liquor-sodden, lunch-sated patrons of Ruby's, evidently frozen in attitudes of wonder. He couldn't see them, of course, but he conjured them up in his mind's eye. If they even spoke—you would think they would yell "Stop," or "Take it outside," or *something,* for Pete's sake—their words didn't penetrate his consciousness. All he could hear was his own blood thwacking through his ears, his own grunts and gasps, and, as at the far end of some lengthy tunnel, Cindy's voice.

He was fighting back, making some headway—but not enough. Giddy was still at his neck, on top of him, still enraged, and at least sixty pounds heavier than he was. Finally, after what seemed a very long time, he felt a new thud. Cindy had leapt onto her husband's back. She was banging at him with her fists, screaming.

"Murderer!" she shrieked. "Murderer! What are you going to do, Tom, kill him, too? You murderer!"

And then, amazingly, blessedly, confoundingly, Giddy was off of him. Landis heard his boots thud across the wooden floor, then the slap of the door against the frame. For himself, he lay panting on the bench, his head pounding, body still too stunned even to register the pain of the blows it had absorbed. When he sat up, his head seemed to lag behind him, like some horrible extraneous burden tied to his neck.

Yet within a minute or two, he had recovered sufficiently to stand up, then follow his attacker out into the cold. Till now he had acted entirely on instinct, self-preservation. And now that he had, somehow, been preserved, he was mad. Not a little mad, furious, enraged. He had heard what Cindy had shouted, that Tom was a murderer, but that had next to nothing to do with the chemicals pumping through him. All he wanted was to pound the man who had pounded him.

He looked first at Ruby's parking lot, then at the road, then finally spotted Tom's green overalls in the lot of Four Seasons Power Equipment. Too angry even to check for traffic, he sprinted across but arrived too late. Giddy had jumped onto the snowmobile he had delivered just a few minutes before and left on the snowy verge of the Four Seasons lot. Even as Landis watched, the engine roared, the machine lurched forward, and Tom took off around the back of the showroom.

At the same time, drawn by the noise, a salesman came out of the shop, confused and indignant.

"What—?"

In a flash, Landis had his shield out.

"NYPD. This is a police emergency. Give me the key to a snowmobile, then go in and call 911. Tell them a police officer needs assistance."

The salesman, fiftyish, red-faced and bristle-haired, hesitated, glanced across the road at Ruby's, saw the dozen people in the lot excitedly nodding and exclaiming at him, then reached into his pocket. Wordlessly, he handed over a key, pointing Landis to the corresponding vehicle, a black Ski-Doo. Thirty seconds later, Landis was steering the Ski-Doo in Tom's wake. By now he knew that what he was doing was stupid, purposeless, almost certainly doomed to fail. But he couldn't stop himself. The man's hands had been on his neck, choking the life from him.

Behind the Four Seasons showroom was a small test-track area, then the woods. At first Landis thought he was too late: Trails grooved with snowmobile tracks branched out in half a dozen directions from the test area, and there was no telling which Giddy had taken, if any. He scanned the landscape. He had lost him.

Then he saw a flash of orange through the trees, maybe two hundred yards away, heading into a thicket of tall evergreens.

He dived after it, following a curving path that led circuitously to the thicket. The wind slapped his unhelmeted head, his gloveless hands. Thankfully, the controls were equipped with handwarmers. It crossed his mind to shoot his gun in the air, see if that would bring Giddy to a halt. But more likely it would drive him farther away.

He got to the thicket to find it smaller than he had expected. Three different paths crossed at its farther edge. No neon orange machine showed in any direction. With reluctance—but there was no other way—he turned off his engine. Success: A droning buzz came to his ears from the east. Giddy had taken a hairpin turn to leave the grove in almost the direction he had come in. Switching on the ignition again, Landis tore after him once more. Not until his momentary stop had he fully realized how cold he was. Despite the protection of the windshield, his face seemed as if it might crystallize and sheer off. In the tall woods, the fallen snow was blinding, the flashing light and shadows dazzling.

He roared forward, asking himself what to do if he did happen to catch up with Giddy. Run his vehicle around in front of the other man's if possible, disable it, get him out of it. But then what? Tom would still outweigh him. And Tom knew where they were. Left alone in this forest, Landis might never find civilization again. Giddy probably knew these woods like the back of his hand. He might circle around for hours, zigzagging off the trails and doubling back before slipping away altogether. By now, Landis knew he had made a very stupid mistake. He had followed Brer Rabbit into the briar patch, and now (he rode on for a minute, then two—no sign of Giddy), now he was lost. He hoped that guy at Four Seasons had alerted the local authorities.

Fury cooling, Landis slowed, stopped, tried to take his bearings. He couldn't even hear the hum of the other man's machine now. Above the frozen, silent forest, the sun was dropping toward the horizon, casting long shadows to the east. That meant. . . . He looked south, searched the woods for the likeliest path back to 23a.

No convenient track led straight in the direction he would have liked, but—

Faintly, then quickly louder, the drone of a snowmobile came to his ears. Landis chose a path almost at random and slowly advanced. Without warning, just around a winding curve, it led to a straightaway, a place where a path stretched ahead straight as an Oklahoma highway. At the other end, heading away from him and out of reach again, was Tom. Seized again with the mindless wish to grab him, Landis squeezed the throttle out. The machine whipped forward, picking up speed so suddenly he was thrown backward. But Giddy, meantime, seemed to be unaccountably—slowing? Could it be? He was still moving forward but . . . however it was happening, Landis was closing in on the other man. Giddy was only forty yards ahead . . . thirty-five . . . thirty . . . twenty-five—

And then Murray got it. Desperate, jealous, believing Landis had come back here with the complicity of his wife, Giddy was planning to turn around and force the other man to collide with him.

Landis let go of the throttle and, frantically, squeezed the brake. He yelled, "Stop, police!" but could hardly even hear himself above the engines. He thought of his gun, but regulations proscribed firing at or from a moving vehicle. Even if a vehicle came at you, you were required to evade it. Frantically, he scanned the sides of the path for a place he could safely veer off. But it was evergreens everywhere, thick as pickets on an endless fence, whizzing past, narrowing as Giddy's orange deathmobile came at him, big as life, bigger, hurtling at him, ten yards away, ten feet. . . .

Ten feet was about where Landis's memory shut off.

chapter

TWENTY

Out of the Woods

As anyone who has ever waited for a patient to wake from a coma knows, "coma" is a sort of umbrella term that covers many states of being. Sadly, "waking" from one is not much like that wonderful, definitive fluttering open of eyelids (usually followed by the surprised, "Goodness! What happened to me?" or "My, I'm hungry!") so dear to screenwriters in a hurry.

A person may respond to pain, follow verbal commands, open his eyes, even speak (though perhaps not intelligibly), and still remain in a coma. A coma is not so much a clear pool from which the victim emerges, stunned and wet but whole, as it is a dismal swamp in which he may struggle for many days, floundering in hidden quicksands and battling savage beasts. Waking, if it comes, is a gradual business, and the degree to which the swamp is finally willing to relinquish its victim may not be clear for weeks, months, or even years.

In the case of Murray Landis, the first sign of recovery was a thumbs-up, feeble but immediately recognizable, performed with his left hand about twenty-six hours after he first lost consciousness. Juliet, who caught the movement from her post in the vinyl armchair in his room at Nathan Littauer Hospital, leapt to her feet, yelled for a nurse, then collapsed on the floor and sobbed. She had been awake thirty-five of the last forty hours and did not even try to control her tears. When the nurse arrived, she was weeping all over Murray. The wife of the patient in the next bed over had to tell the nurse what was going on.

It was another two days before Landis had recovered enough to want to know what had happened to him, and even longer before he was able to retain more than a few bits of information at a time. During this interval, his parents came up from Brooklyn. Juliet hardly knew what to make of Harry Landis, a spare, sharp-eyed, close-mouthed pitbull of a man. But she found it easy to talk to Rose. The two stayed a day at the same Holiday Inn where Juliet was spending her short nights, then went home, reassured that their boy was on the mend.

It was left to Juliet to tell him, on the Sunday morning after his injury, the story that had come out in the hours and days since the crash. She drew the curtains around his bed for privacy, then took his hand.

"It was pretty close to what I thought," she began immodestly. "The manuscript—"

"You mean Michael Hertbrooke did it?"

For a second, she thought he was losing clarity again. Then she got it.

"Very funny. As I was saying, as I thought, the manuscript had nothing to do with the murder, except that it brought Ada to New York. Tom believed he'd be less likely to be suspected if she was killed there. And he was right.

"Of course, we only have Cindy's word for that. She—"

"Tom's not talking?" Landis interrupted.

Juliet hesitated. This was news she had been avoiding telling him, uncertain of the best way to explain or how he might take it. Finally, she blurted out, "No. He died in the crash."

"Oh." He closed his eyes and was silent a long moment. In that time, a little alarmingly, Juliet saw Harry Landis's tight, tough face in the face before her. Then his eyes fluttered open and he was Murray again. "So tell me."

She told him, stopping often to ask if he wanted a rest, or a pillow, or more water. Threatened with prosecution as an accessory, Cindy had given the police what she claimed was all she knew. According to her, Tom had had the (mistaken) idea that more money would make their marriage happier. When the offer for their farm came from Fairground, they had been ready and eager to sell. Besides benefitting them, it would bring jobs into Espyville.

But their neighbor wasn't interested. For a while they tried to persuade her. She was adamant, maddeningly indifferent to their happiness, the good of the town, everything but her own perfect right to die on the land where she'd been born. Finally—and unbeknownst to Cindy, according to herself—Tom made up his mind to kill her. Whoever her heir was would gladly take the Fairground deal, he felt sure.

He accomplished her murder the way he did most things: resourcefully, skillfully, calmly. The trip to Manhattan presented logistical difficulties but offered perfect cover. Cindy never knew he had gone anywhere but his cabin that Thursday and Friday. The business of her alibi with the niece and nephew was just luck, but Tom would doubtless have rigged up something to protect her if that hadn't come along.

Now, because he had finally told her, she knew the missing persons investigation had been a cruel trial for Tom's nerves. Naturally, he'd expected Ada's body to be found Friday night, when the Xterra owner left his parking space. Instead, she didn't turn up for days. He worried the bag she was in had somehow been thrown into a garbage truck, that it would never surface, that her estate, consequently, would stay unsettled till long after the Fairground offer expired. When the body turned up at last, Tom's relief was short-lived. Very soon, they knew the Luncefords weren't the heirs, and that Free

Earth wasn't going to sell. This, Cindy claimed, was when Tom had at last let her know what he had done. Apparently, he hoped she would see the desperate daring of the act as a measure of his love for her. Instead, according to Cindy, she was repelled. He realized she was going to leave him; it was only a matter of time. When he saw her with Murray at Ruby's, when she denounced him publicly as a murderer, he must have panicked, decided to end it all.

Landis heard the story in silence. Juliet looked at him worriedly. It was a lot to take in even if you weren't recovering from a brain injury and a broken arm and a fractured ankle and a dozen more superficial wounds. And he must realize by now that if he hadn't hared off after Tom, Tom would still be alive.

But Landis remembered enough of the scene in the woods to know this probably wasn't true. In a few words, he described Tom's suicidal charge at him.

They were silent awhile. Then, "What about the manuscript?" he finally asked. "That turn up?"

Juliet shook her head no. "That's the weird thing. Your friend Skelton, I think he still believes Dennis maybe has it. It just vanished."

"How do you know what Skelton thinks?"

She was annoyed to feel herself blushing. Why should she blush?

"Oddly enough, he told me himself. He and Crowder came up here the night the crash happened—you were still out cold—"

Tears came to her eyes at the recollection of this period, and she blinked them back. She had started worrying about Murray at around four o'clock on Wednesday, when he and Cindy failed to come back from their drive, and she hadn't completely stopped worrying since. The cab driver she'd called to take her to a motel that night had told her about the snowmobile crash between Tom Giddy and "some guy up from New York City." The next period was still a painful blur.

"Crowder and Skelton sat in on Cindy's interrogation," she went on. "And later, Skelton came over here to wait with me for a while."

"And told you Cindy's story."

"And told me. I guess I'm not a suspect anymore."

Murray said, "Mmph," again, then rested awhile, eyes closed. Juliet thought he had fallen asleep again when he murmured, eyes still shut, "You know, I believe Tom really was going to kill me at Ruby's. Cindy snapped him out of it when she jumped on him and started yelling. In a way, she saved my life. She's not all bad, Cindy."

Juliet felt jealousy leap in her chest, started to make a crack, then closed her mouth. Some day, when he was feeling much, much better, she would like to know just exactly what had happened between him and Cindy Giddy.

But it would keep.

EPILOGUE:

The Purloined Letter

It was one of those rare days in early March when nature seems to have decided to skip the rest of winter, those springy, temperate days almost always followed by weeks of crushing cold, and Juliet and Suzy had decided to take a walk in Riverside Park.

Unusually, it had been more than a month since they had spoken at any length, so they had much to discuss. Suzy had just come back from four weeks in New Mexico, where she was helping to design the prototype for a new magazine called *Inner Space*. As for Juliet, she had managed to finish and hand in "A Christian Gentleman" early, due mainly to a spurt of industry up in Murray's hospital room in Gloversville.

Determined not to abandon him there, but almost out of her mind with boredom while he dozed and drowsed, she had written a record seven chapters in ten days. Now retitled "A Proper Gentleman," the book's first chapter had already gone up on her Web site. Portia Klein, her editor, had declared its conflicted hero, Sir James, Angelica's strangest but also, perhaps, her best.

As for Landis, he could now walk without a crutch, but would be assigned to desk duty for at least a couple of months.

"And mentally? Emotionally?" Suzy asked somewhat anxiously, when Juliet had filled her in thus far. They were strolling north along the promenade, where the bare branches of the trees made a crisp, dark latticework against the cloudless sky. Behind them, at the entrance to the park, a crew of Parks Department employees was, finally, feeding the pile of discarded Christmas trees into a woodchipper.

"He's okay." She raised her voice above the noise of the machine. "He's fine, thank God."

"But—?" Suzy had heard the doubt in her friend's intonation.

"But . . . You know, I wonder if maybe the accident sort of pushed forward some of the 9/11 stuff he never dealt with. He was always suspiciously unfazed by that," Juliet said. "Or maybe it's just inevitable, such a serious accident. Whatever it is, he's talking about maybe leaving the force, traveling, living abroad, I don't know what. It's like he saw his own mortality—"

The woodchipper suddenly stopped, leaving Juliet more or less yelling into the quiet. She dropped her voice.

"Like he saw that life is short," she finished.

Suzy looked at her with narrowed eyes. "Abroad?" she repeated. "And you and he—?"

As always when she least wished it to, blood rushed into Juliet's fair cheeks. She smiled ruefully. "I don't know. I think we maybe went too far too fast. I mean, not the sex. Though we probably would have been wiser to . . . pace that better," she said. "It was more my being there in the hospital with him, the intimacy of it. I met his parents," she added, and felt her cheeks turning even a deeper red. "I think maybe it was all too much for him."

Behind them, the drone of the woodchipper started again, distant enough now to be only a minor nuisance.

"He's pulling away from you?"

"Well, not in a rude way. Not even openly, really." She wrinkled her nose. How nice it was to have Suzy back to talk to. She usually thought of their friendship as being one of those based in large part on proximity; but with time, she saw now, it was deepening into something better. "I just get the feeling he thinks he's supposed to be grateful to me. As if I think he owes me one because I spent a couple of weeks with him in the hospital. Which I don't, quite the opposite. I dragged him up to Espyville. If it wasn't for me, there'd have been no accident. But Murray—"

"You've said all this to him?"

"Oh yes, of course. We've talked about it, or tried. But he still feels uncomfortable. Beholden. And too much closeness, too much beholdenness—if that's a noun—well, those are not feelings a person like Murray Landis likes to feel he should feel. You know?"

Suzy nodded and sighed. They walked along in silence for a while. A Rottweiler let off his leash rocketed past them, chasing a tennis ball.

Finally, "I guess you need to make some space between you," Suzy said.

"Guess so."

After another silence, "You're a little relieved yourself, aren't you?" Suzy asked.

Juliet wanted to deny it, but shrugged. She probably was a little relieved.

"You wouldn't—you aren't seeing Dennis anymore, are you?"

Juliet laughed. "Hardly," she said. "Jeff Skelton still believes he's sitting on the Wilson manuscript, you know. It doesn't make much objective sense, but I think our having shared this little adventure has permanently tainted any friendly feelings Dennis and I might have had for each other. Though I was able to do him a good turn. Ames found a first edition of Joyce's *Ulysses* among the books Ada left me. Dennis is going to sell it for me, and I'll donate the proceeds to Free Earth. They've decided to turn Ada's whole place into a nature preserve, if they can. They're trying to work out something with the state. So it's all ended up quite comfortably for little

Cindy Lang," she added. "I mean, not that she wanted Tom dead; she probably didn't. But her land will border on a protected area, which is always good for its value."

"It's too bad that manuscript got lost," Suzy said, after a longish silence. "It would have been nice for you to have."

To Juliet's surprise, she found herself shuddering slightly at the idea. "I really wouldn't want it," she said. "Too reminiscent of Ada's death, I guess. If it ever turns up, you can have it." She smiled at Suzy. "Get you out of the bed-and-breakfast biz for a while."

"And Wildernessland? What's happened with that, do you know?"

"It's going to be someplace near the Everglades."

They had reached the pair of public gardens near Ninety-first Street. In one of them, a lone volunteer gardener was poking at the hard ground with a trowel. Without discussing it, the friends circled the farther garden and turned their steps back south.

Then, "How's Parker?" Juliet dared to ask.

Suzy shook her head. "Back with Diana, for keeps."

"Oh, sorry. Are you—?"

"Repining? No." She shrugged. "The whole thing was mostly hope and sex, anyway."

"Things mostly are."

They walked on quietly, enjoying the mildness of the day and hardly talking until they were almost back at their own end of the promenade. Then Juliet remembered to say, "Oh, I heard from Matt McLaurin. Ada's poem about Frederick Asquith is going to be published in something called the *Red Rooster Quarterly*. I've never heard of it."

"Me neither. But how nice."

"It is nice," Juliet agreed.

They turned onto the path that climbs out of the park, passing the woodchipper again as they did so.

"It'll be part of an issue called 'Sex and Love and Sex, Sex,

Sex,'" Juliet added, raising her voice. "I think Ada would have liked that. Want to go somewhere and have a drink to celebrate?"

"Sure. Just come in with me a sec, I need to get a warmer jacket."

They crossed Riverside. Juliet trailed Suzy into her apartment and stood leaning idly beside the tall, mesquite-wood bookcase. The row of Angelica Kestrel-Haven paperbacks caught her eye and she gazed at them absently, wondering where Suzy would fit in the next. Then she saw it. The fourth book from the left was *Duke's Delight.* So was the ninth book from the right.

An image flashed in her mind: Ada, surprised by Tom, still angry at Dennis, but most all, determined to safeguard the manuscript. Ada, coming out of the falling snow, purple purse and paperback book in her gloved hands. Ada walking into the foyer, prudently slipping the book onto Suzy's shelf before Tom was even fully in the door.

Juliet pulled one *Duke's Delight* off the shelf and fanned it open. Nothing. She grabbed the second, held it upside down, riffled the pages. A glassine envelope with a familiar rectangle showing through fluttered to the floor.

A NOTE ON THE SOURCES

Harriette Wilson and her memoirs are facts of history, and the only fiction I have knowingly added is the existence of Lord Quiddenham and his purchased pages.

I am deeply indebted to two scholars with regard to Harriette: Kenneth Bourne, author of *The Blackmailing of the Chancellor,* wrote one of the few truly scholarly books about Wilson, and years ago patiently answered many questions about her for me. The same is true of Françoise Albrecht, whose 1978 Ph.D. thesis, "Une Courtisane Au Début du XIXe Siècle: Harriette Wilson," accorded Wilson's life a serious scrutiny that had been denied it until then.

ACKNOWLEDGMENTS

It takes a village to write a book. Among the many people who helped with this one are: Capt. Vincent DiDonato and Police Officer Joseph A. Agosto, both of the NYPD and both extraordinarily patient; James F. Morrison, Brenda Pedrick, and the very generous Mike Teetz, who educated me about Gloversville; and Tim Johns, Paulette Rose, Steve Weissman, David Morrison, and Christian von Faber-Castell, all of whom answered endless questions about rare manuscripts. Will Osborne set me straight about blizzards, Marian Bock inspired and cheer-led, and my wise friends Ann Banks and Irene Marcuse read the manuscript at a crucial moment. Thank you.